T0357773

ZAKIYA N. JAMAL

IF WE WERE A MOVIE

HARPER
An Imprint of HarperCollinsPublishers

For my mom:
We did it!

ONE

I HATE SUMMER.

Not only is it unbearably hot and humid, it's also a complete and utter waste of time. Every single summer I have to figure out something to do so admissions officers won't look at my résumé and think I did absolutely nothing while I was out of school. As if the summer is actually some kind of vacation.

Nope! Especially not *this* summer.

Everyone knows what you do during the summer before your senior year is just as important, if not more so, than what you did during your junior year.

"Rochelle, what on earth are you doing?"

Everyone except my mother, apparently.

I peek one eye open and find my mother staring down at me, the ends of her silk press swaying above my face as I lie on the floor. As per usual, she is perfectly put together. Her light brown skin shines with whatever new body butter she's trying, and she's wearing a matching tank top and yoga pants set that I'm sure she got out of some bargain bin. It's Wednesday so Ma

1

should be in her Manhattan office taking calls and working on a bunch of corporate law things I don't yet understand but someday will. Instead, she's been cutting back on the number of cases she takes on lately and has decided to give herself the day off.

"Not to be dramatic, but I want to die," I say.

She pauses. "Are you speaking in song lyrics again?"

"Wake me up when August ends," I reply.

I close my eyes again, hoping the earth will swallow me whole and wrap me in a cocoon for the rest of the summer. It'll be like the opposite of hibernation, and I could write an extensive research paper on it that would win me the Nobel Prize. And *then* I'd get into a good college.

My mother lets out an exasperated sigh. I don't have to look up to know she's rolling her eyes.

Ma and I don't look that much alike. She's light; I'm dark. She's tall and slim; I'm short and have needed a D-cup bra since I was thirteen. She changes her hairstyle on a regular basis and owns every Fenty product ever made, while I'm committed to my straight black box braids and natural-faced look.

However, I have adopted many of her mannerisms, which include, but are not limited to, rolling my eyes, deep sighing, and snapping my fingers when I remember something. Thus, I can practically feel when she's rolling her eyes at me. But I can't help it that I'm depressed.

It is almost July and I have absolutely nothing productive on my calendar.

What I need is something to stand out to college admissions, specifically to the Wharton School at UPenn. You would think

Ma would understand since she is an alum, but it's as if she's completely forgotten the work ethic and level of determination it takes to get into her alma mater.

Ma nudges my shoulder with her foot until I open my eyes.

"What happened?" she asks.

I let out my own sigh before I confess my latest defeat at the hands of corporate America. "I got another rejection."

Ma moves around me to sit on my bed. "From where?"

I push up from the floor a bit to face her. "The little bakery down the street," I say. "They said I wasn't experienced enough. How hard is it to frost some cupcakes?"

Ma laughs at that, and I glare up at her. She holds up her hands in mock surrender.

"I'm sorry, I'm sorry," she says. "But I imagine the job probably isn't as simple as you think it is. Besides, Mrs. Gregory runs the bakery mostly by herself. I'm sure she wants someone who can stick around and be there full-time, not someone still in high school who, last I checked, preferred her cupcakes plain, with no frosting."

"I like frosting, they just always put too much, which is exactly why she needs my help."

Ma has the audacity to laugh again, and I groan, throwing myself back on the floor.

"This is no laughing matter, Mother," I say. "I need a job. It's the one thing I'm missing for these college apps. I've done the enrichment programs, volunteering, and even summer classes. But I'm seventeen and I've never had a real job. Not unless you count my tutoring gig, which I do not since, like volunteering, everyone does that.

"And you know how Wharton is. They don't just want some typical straight-A student. Academics is just one part. They want leaders, not lazy soon-to-be seniors who can't even get a job at the bakery. How will it look for me to apply to *business* school when I don't even have anything on my résumé—or LinkedIn!"

"Okay, first of all take a deep breath." Ma breathes in through her nose, and then huffs out a long and slow breath through her mouth. She's taken up yoga this past year, and her solution for most things in life these days is to breathe. I think I'm breathing just fine, but I follow her lead, breathing in and out with her.

"Better?" she asks.

I shrug. It still feels like my world is about to end.

"Now, you are way too young to be worried about LinkedIn," Ma says. "Why not focus on that clock app your friends love so much?"

"I'm not trying to be an influencer; I need a real job."

"Hey, don't knock influencers—they make a lot of money, and some of them even turn their brands into full-fledged businesses. I would know, I've worked with some of them! I'd love to be paid to post but, alas, not even my own daughter will follow me."

Now I roll my eyes. "I *was* following you, but you post five times a day. *All I saw* were your posts."

She looks affronted. "And why is that a bad thing?"

"Because I already see you in real life—why do I need to see everything you're doing on Insta too?"

4

Ma pouts, actually pouts, and I can already feel myself giving in. When push comes to shove, I'll do anything for her.

"Fine, pass me my phone, please," I say.

She grins triumphantly as she hands it to me. I quickly follow her and then show her my screen.

"Okay, now that that's done, can we get back to my dilemma, please? What am I going to do?"

"Oh, I have a wonderful idea!"

I'm suspicious but turn to look up at her. "I'm listening."

"Take this summer off to relax and enjoy yourself," Ma says.

"I knew that was a trap."

"It's not a trap, Rochelle," Ma says, serious voice activated. "I'm just worried that my one and only child has forgotten what it even means to be a child."

"I know what it means to be a child, Ma," I say with a groan of frustration. "But Wharton doesn't want average kids. You, of all people, know how hard it is to get in."

"I do," she says. "Which is exactly why I don't want you twisting yourself all up in knots to get into that school. Life is more than just hard work. You know Amira—"

"Ma, please don't start."

Any sense of calm and ease is immediately gone at the mention of Amira Rodriguez.

Way back when my mom moved us from the city to Long Island, she met Luisa, Amira's mom. The two have been the best of friends ever since, and Ma credits Luisa for putting her back together after losing Dad. While I don't doubt this, I barely have any memory of my dad or the start of this glorious

5

friendship. All I know is when Ma met Luisa, I met her daughter, Amira. At five years old, I thought we were going to be friends forever. I was mistaken.

At the end of kindergarten, Luisa, Amira, and the rest of the Rodriguez family moved two towns over into a bigger house. Ma and Luisa tried to keep my and Amira's friendship going, but once Amira and I stopped seeing each other every day in school, our friendship was quickly forgotten. I thought we could maybe become friends again when we were both filtered into North High School in the ninth grade, but I was wrong about that too.

Amira and I are two very different people. I am committed to my studies and making sure I do everything necessary to get into Wharton, just like my parents did. Amira, on the other hand, is a social butterfly. Everyone at our school knows and loves her. She's the president of our class, captain of the dance team, and she runs track and cross-country.

All of that would be fine if she took her studies half as seriously as I do, but she lacks discipline. I realized we could never be friends when we were made to be lab partners in our advanced biology class in ninth grade, and all she wanted to do was make the frog that we were supposed to be dissecting dance. I ended up doing the whole assignment myself.

Over the years, Ma and Luisa have made more than a few attempts to push us together, but eventually I had to make it clear that I need to be friends with people who are just as studious and dedicated to their work as I am. Amira did not take that well. Since then, she's basically made it her mission to do better than me in all our classes, simply out of spite.

I don't mind the competition, but it is slightly infuriating that at the end of our junior year she very happily revealed to me she's now crossed into the top ten of our class. I know there's no way she'll actually beat me for valedictorian; I take way more AP courses than she does, so my average will be comfortably weighted.

Still, I don't appreciate that she is somehow having the time of her life and is still acing her classes. It simply doesn't make sense.

Even though Amira and I have barely spoken over the past few years, Ma has it in her head that Amira is the yin to my yang, and one day we will "get over our differences" and be BFFs like when we were five. No matter how many times I try to tell her there is absolutely no way Amira and I will ever get along, Ma refuses to listen.

"I'm just saying," Ma continues, "she's just as dedicated to school as you, but she still finds time to have fun. You could learn from her."

I'm thankfully saved from this conversation when my phone rings.

It's a random 516 phone number, but I'm willing to answer anyone's call right now.

"Hello?"

"HI, THIS IS GLORY FROM HORIZON CINEMA!"

From the bed, Ma raises her eyebrows. I pull my phone away, placing it on the bed and putting it on speaker, not that it's necessary with the volume at which Glory is already speaking.

"IS THIS ROCHELLE?"

In the background, we can hear a child crying, a phone ringing, and someone clearly trying to get Glory's attention.

"Yes, this is—"

"GREAT, HANG ON A SECOND! DANNY, I'M ON THE PHONE."

Then there's complete silence. I exchange a look with Ma, whose eyebrows have traveled back up her forehead.

"When did you apply for a job at Horizon Cinema?" she whispers.

I rack my brain trying to remember but come up blank. I've been applying to every job in the neighborhood I could think of, but Horizon Cinema isn't walking distance from our house. At least, not a short walk.

Horizon is the only Black-owned movie theater in all of Long Island, making it a favorite around here. A historical relic from when movie theaters were segregated. Located in South Valley Stream, it's close to a number of towns, and right by the border of Queens, so people from the city can easily get there. Plus, it's across the street from the Green Acres Mall, which is always crowded.

I'm not a big movie person. I've only been once or twice to Horizon, but my best friends Kerry and Taylor told me it recently got a makeover and is now one of *the* spots to hang out at. They keep trying to get me to go since they claim the "pickings" of queer girls are better there than the same people we've been going to school with for the past three years. It's been a mission of theirs to get me a girlfriend since freshman year. But I have no interest in dating anyone, especially right before senior year, so I've found excuses not to go every time.

"I didn't apply," I whisper back to Ma. Which begs the question, why on earth is someone from Horizon calling me?

"Hi, Rochelle?"

"Hi, yes, I'm here," I say. I shrug at Ma's quizzical look.

Glory must've escaped from the theater because I realize there's no more background noise.

"Great, sorry about all that," Glory says. "I thought I'd be able to make one call while running concessions but, alas, craziness immediately ensued. However, I have now squared myself away in our back office so we can talk."

"Oh great."

"Anyway," Glory says, dragging the word out an extra few syllables. "I'm desperately in need of a new front-of-house staff person for the summer, and I was told you were desperately in need of a job. Is that still true?"

"Um . . ."

I don't love being called "desperate" by someone I don't even know, but she's not exactly wrong. Ma nudges my shoulder with her foot until I look up at her.

"Say yes," she hisses.

"Yes, yes, I am," I finally say. I push myself up to stand and start pacing the room, taking my phone with me, as Glory continues.

"Perfect, you'll need to come in first thing tomorrow morning for new hire training," she says. "I can get you all set up with W-9 forms and direct deposit then. Tomorrow is just training so don't worry about your clothes, but going forward you'll need to wear khakis and closed-toe shoes whenever you come in, along with a Horizon T-shirt, which I'll get you tomorrow."

"Wait, you're giving me the job? Just like that?"

Ma looks at me like I've lost my mind, and I know I shouldn't look a gift horse in the mouth, but this is wild. I didn't even apply for this job, and now some woman I've never met before is offering it to me? Just because some mystery person told her I need it? I narrow my eyes at Ma as a thought crosses my mind.

"Did you do this?" I whisper-hiss at her.

Before Ma can respond, Glory's speaking again.

"I was told you're a quick learner and, honestly, if I don't have someone in here to start working by Saturday, I'm screwed. The job's yours if you want it."

"I didn't," Ma whispers back. "But who cares if I, or someone else, got you in? This is what you wanted, right? Take it!"

I'm not sure I believe Ma didn't have anything to do with this. It would be just like her to call in a favor with someone to get me a job she doesn't even think I need this summer. She'll do anything for me too.

It doesn't matter though. Ma is right and so is Glory. A job has fallen into my lap, and I'm in no position to turn it down.

"I'll take it," I say to both my mother and Glory.

Ma beams as Glory says, "Perfect! I'll see you tomorrow at eight a.m. sharp. Please do not be late. We have much to do!"

"I'm never late," I say, but my phone is already beeping, signaling that Glory is gone.

Ma claps her hands enthusiastically, and I sit down on the bed beside her.

"Did that just happen?"

"I can drop you off tomorrow on my way to work," she says in answer. Then she wraps her arms around me in a side hug, giving me a squeeze. "While I still think you should spend your summer on the beach, I'm very proud of you. My baby's first job!"

"There's no reason to be proud of me," I say, pulling away. "I didn't even apply."

Ma waves a hand. "That doesn't matter. All that matters is that someone out there thinks so highly of you that you didn't even need to apply. This is what you wanted. Enjoy it!"

I nod, trying to absorb Ma's excitement. This is good, better than good even.

Still, I can't help feeling like it's too good to be true.

TWO

BLACK GIRL MAGIC GROUP CHAT

Me: Sooooo I got a job at Horizon.

Taylor: ???

Kerry: Horizon Cinema???

Me: No, the line at which the Earth's surface and the sky appear to meet.

Taylor: That's a dollar in the sarcasm jar.

Me: I'll pay my dues after I get my first paycheck.

Kerry: Wait wait wait back up. How did this even happen? When did you apply?

Kerry: And why didn't you tell me to apply? That'd be the perfect job for me! I love it there!

Me: So, that's the weird part. I didn't. Someone recommended me.

Taylor: . . . and they just hired you based on that?

Me: Yep

Kerry: That's . . . interesting.

Me: Yep.

Kerry: Do you know who recommended you? 👀

Me: Not a clue 🫠

Kerry: Interesting . . .

Taylor: Okay well the most important thing here is do you get free movie tickets?

Kerry: Oh yes! That would be clutch.

Me: I have no idea. That wasn't mentioned on the call.

Kerry: YOU DIDN'T ASK?!

Me: Movie tickets were not my top priority.

Kerry: We really have to get your priorities in order.

Me: Says the girl who ate cashews for lunch every day all last year just to save up her lunch money to buy a signed Zendaya poster that turned out to be a fake.

Kerry: We don't know that it's fake.

Taylor: It's definitely fake.

Kerry: IT IS NOT!

Taylor: ANYWAYS! Let's go to Joe's to celebrate this momentous occasion.

Me: Oh, SAT word.

Kerry: DO NOT IGNORE ME. MY POSTER ISN'T FAKE!

Taylor: Can you meet us there in 20?

Me: Yep, see y'all soon!

Kerry: I AM NOT GOING ANYWHERE UNTIL WE ALL AGREE MY POSTER IS LEGIT!

Taylor: Fine fine your very fake poster is totally legit. Now get dressed and meet me outside.

Kerry: I hate you.

Taylor: 🖤

Me: 😂

Living on Long Island, a.k.a. suburbia, there are only so many things to do and most of those involve food. There are diners to grab a bite after parties and school functions; terrible chain restaurants with flavorless, probably once-frozen food for celebrations; and pizza restaurants for your regular, everyday hangouts.

From the day our parents started letting us all walk home from school in the sixth grade, Kerry, Taylor, and I declared Joe's Pizzeria as our spot. A ten-minute walk from our junior high school and conveniently located right at the edge of Elmont (my town) and Valley Stream (Kerry and Taylor's town), Joe's became our home away from home.

Joe's is owned by a Black man named, you guessed it, Joe. He's as old as my grandpa, with the wrinkles and fully gray buzzed haircut to prove it. Even though he's getting up there in age, he can still be found in the back every day cooking various different new kinds of pizza that no one asked for, but we occasionally enjoy. Most recently, he made a chili cheese pizza that left much to be desired, but he loves us and always lets us try his experiments for free.

Tucked in a little shopping center with a drugstore that's now been closed for months, the local bank, a convenience store, and a Chinese restaurant, Joe's doesn't always get the most foot traffic, but somehow he's kept the place afloat for over twenty years.

It's small, with only four booths lined up against the windows, and you can smell the burnt cheese as soon as you walk in. The seat cushions are held together with duct tape, and the tables are covered with scratched-in notes from people who were there years before. Joe plays only a mix of old-school R & B, hip-hop, rap, and reggae music, most of which came out before I was born. I imagine the music selection is off-putting to many of the palm-colored people who make up much of the population in the nearby towns, but that's okay. Joe doesn't do it for them. He doesn't even do it for us. He just plays what he wants, and we're here for it.

When I arrive, Joe's at the register. His white apron is covered in splotches of tomato sauce.

"Hi, Joe!"

"Well, hello, Ms. Rochelle," he says. "Fancy seeing you here."

I laugh. He's always so formal. It's always Mr. Someone or Ms. Somebody, never just our names. "I'm always here, Joe," I reply.

I quickly spot Kerry and Taylor already sitting on opposite sides of our favorite booth (the one right by the door) with a half-cheese, half-pepperoni pie between them. I give a quick wave to Joe before crossing the short distance to my friends.

As always, Kerry and Taylor look like the pink and black house meme—i.e., two very different sides of the same coin. They're both "full-figured" as Ma likes to say because she still feels uncomfortable saying "fat," which honestly says more about her than them, but we never have time to unpack all that. Anyway, Kerry and Taylor have always been proud of their bodies, and they've definitely helped me learn how to love my own curves over the years.

They consistently wear their best, no matter where we're going. Even though the only other people in Joe's besides us are an acne-ridden white boy who's just taken Joe's spot at the register and an elderly Asian couple, Kerry has her lavender kinky twists pulled up in a bun, a full face of makeup with matching eye shadow and lipstick, and she's wearing a purple corduroy overall dress with white platform sneakers. On the other side of the table, Taylor, the Black goth queen, is in all black as always. She rocks a buzz cut like Joe, dyed silver, has a septum ring, and is currently rocking her favorite black lipstick and a short-sleeved black dress that falls right above her knee-high combat boots.

Meanwhile, my regular black braids are pulled back in a ponytail, my version of makeup is cherry lip gloss, and all I have on is a random *Steven Universe* graphic tee and denim shorts. But my casualness doesn't matter to Kerry and Taylor. They love me for me, not what I wear.

I slide into the booth next to Kerry and help myself to a slice.

"All right, so how are we celebrating you finally getting the job of your dreams?" Kerry asks as I'm midchew.

The pizza tastes slightly different today, maybe spicier. Joe must be messing with the sauce again.

I give myself time to swallow before answering. "Seeing as how I didn't even apply for this gig, I wouldn't say it's my dream job, but a job's a job and I need it for Wharton. Besides, I thought this *was* the celebration."

"Okay, well, it's *my* dream job," Kerry says. "Well, not my *dream job* dream job, but you know what I mean. This would be perfect for me. I must live vicariously through you. Thus, we must celebrate."

"And hanging out at Joe's as always is *not* a celebration," Taylor adds.

I glare at her. "This was your idea."

Taylor shrugs as if that's a moot point.

"We need to go *out*," Kerry says.

Taylor nods in agreement and I let out a groan. I should've seen this coming. After Amira moved, I stuck mostly to myself in school. I've never been all that outgoing, and I don't mind my solitude. But in second grade, I was put in Mrs. Greene's class and sat at the same table as Kerry, Taylor, and this boy whose name I don't remember. Kerry and Taylor were already BFFs, having been in the same classes since kindergarten, and for some reason they were determined to make their duo a trio. They decided I was their missing piece.

Even though I was quiet and only spoke to them when they spoke to me first, they persisted. Next thing I knew I was being invited, almost commanded, to go to their houses for sleepovers and pool parties, and I've been stuck with them ever since. Recently, they've committed to making me a more sociable person. They've dubbed their plan "Break Rochelle Out of Her Shell."

The rhyming was intentional, thank you for asking.

The closer we get to finishing high school, the more they're always trying to make me do something or go somewhere. But I love my shell. It's comfortable, familiar, and keeps me focused on my goals: to go to Wharton, get my bachelor's in business, my law degree from Harvard or Yale (I'm not picky), and become an international trade law attorney like Ma always wanted to be. She had to pivot her job goals after Dad died, leaving her to raise me on her own. Although she claims she's happy doing corporate law now, she still talks about what it would've been like to travel as a representative for the US and see the world.

And now that's what I'd like to do. One does not simply get a job working for the US Department of Commerce, however, especially if they spend all their time hanging out.

Also, most people annoy me. Kerry and Taylor are simply exceptions to the rule.

"My training is at eight a.m. tomorrow," I say. "I can't go out tonight even if I wanted to."

"It is literally only five right now," Kerry says.

"We can have you back home by nine at the latest," Taylor adds.

"No!" It comes out a bit harsher than I intended, but I've learned with Kerry and Taylor, I must be firm, otherwise they will push and push until I give in. I must be a rock.

"I think you're being contrarian just to be contrarian," Kerry says.

"SAT word," I say automatically.

"Thank you for noticing, Rochelle the Shell." Kerry gives me a smug smile, and I know I've somehow stepped into a trap. "Taylor and I have been studying our flash cards because despite popular belief, we can go out *and* study. Something you should give a try."

Taylor snorts, and I give them both the finger. I change my mind; they *do* annoy me.

"I'll party once I'm at Wharton with a full ride," I say.

"But it's summerrrr!" Kerry whines. She's shifted in the booth now so she's facing me, and from the corner of my eye, I can tell she's got a full-on pouty face. Clearly, she's been spending too much time with my mother. I'm sure she is somehow to blame for this ambush. Everyone is out to get me today.

"You don't even have homework," Kerry continues.

"We have summer reading and packets for both AP physics and AP calc to do," I say.

Kerry waves a hand. "I'm sure you've already started all of

those and will be done by the end of the week."

She's right. There's no way in hell I'm telling her that, but unfortunately my silence is confirmation enough.

"Right, so we're going out tonight," Kerry says. "Shawn is having a party on the beach, and everyone will be there."

I raise an eyebrow at Taylor. "You want to go to Shawn's party?"

Shawn's the most popular guy in our year, mainly because he's one of our top athletes and has the energy of a golden retriever. I once saw Shawn high-five every single person he passed in the hall, including me. Naturally, I immediately washed my hands after because who knows what kind of germs my classmates are carrying around.

He also happens to be one of Amira's BFFs, which is a minus in my book.

Last year, for reasons I still don't quite understand, Shawn asked me to tutor him in pre-calc. My first instinct was to say no, obviously, but then he said his parents would pay me $20 an hour. Shawn's grades improved, which was a given. However, what I didn't expect was Shawn asking me endless questions about Taylor.

While Taylor's more susceptible to being dragged to whatever function Kerry wants to attend, Taylor's still only slightly more sociable than I am. And while I know there are tons of theories about how opposites attract, I didn't think they would ever work out. And as usual, I was correct.

Shawn somehow convinced Taylor to go on one date with him. Afterward, Taylor refused to give us all the juicy details, but she swore that she would never go out with him again. Since then, Shawn has been persona non grata in our friend group. I honestly thought we'd never speak of him again, much less that Taylor would want to go to one of his parties.

"I have no ill will toward him," Taylor says, with a casual shrug. "We simply aren't romantically compatible."

"You sound like a robot," Kerry says.

Taylor just shrugs again, and it's clear that's all she's going to say on the subject.

"Anyways, we're going to Shawn's party and you're coming," Kerry says. She's using her "don't even bother arguing because I have made a decision and we are going to do what I want" voice, but I am unmoved.

I am a rock.

"I'm not going, and you can't make me." I sound like a five-year-old, but I don't care. "Y'all will just have to go and have fun on my behalf."

"That's not how having fun works!" Kerry says.

Taylor nods in agreement, and I'm starting to get sick of this. There was a time when Taylor and Kerry understood my dedication to school more than anyone else. Kerry was focused on her acting, and Taylor was always occupied with her artwork. We were all determined to achieve our dreams, no matter what sacrifices needed to be made. So, why is everyone so concerned about my social life now?

"That's how it works for me," I say. "I'll come to the next party."

"You will not," Kerry whines.

She's right, but at this point she should know how this goes. She invites me out, I say no, she pouts, I say I'll go to the next one. Wash. Rinse. Repeat. It's all very straightforward.

Kerry, however, has decided to go into full drama queen mode. Her aspiration to be the next Black woman to achieve EGOT status truly shows in times like these. She's thrown herself back against the booth with her arms crossed and slides down so far that only her neck and head are still above the table. But I know better than to let her theatrics sway me.

One of the few benefits of summer is not having to see my classmates on a regular basis, so going to the beach to hang out with them is counterintuitive. Plus, if this is Shawn's party, that means Amira will be there, and she's the last person I want to see.

I do want to hang out with Kerry and Taylor though. I always do, even when they are driving me crazy. They're always there for me when I want to stay in and play Codenames or rewatch *Gilmore Girls* for the thousandth time. So, yeah, sometimes I do feel guilty about the fact that, without fail, they've always invited me to go out with them, even though I've turned them down 98.5 percent of the time. And yes, I did the math.

Though there is a small part of me that fears one day they'll realize I'm the boring, wet blanket people like Amira think I am.

Maybe Kerry, Taylor, and my mom have a point. Would *one* party really wreck all my plans? If I could handle taking four AP exams, the SAT, and the ACT all within the same month this year, I should be able to handle one little party.

Just not tonight.

I will not be showing up to my first day of work tomorrow a hot mess. Someday though, I'll enter the party scene. Or at least dip my toe in.

Maybe.

With newfound conviction, I turn to Kerry and poke her until she finally looks me in the eye.

"I'll go to the next one," I say again. "I promise."

Kerry looks at me skeptically. "You swear?"

"Swear."

Then, I hold out my pinkie to her, and a slow grin appears on Kerry's face. She pushes herself up in her seat and wraps her pinkie around mine. We kiss our knuckles, sealing the deal, and Taylor softly claps, approvingly.

All the while, I try to convince myself I didn't just sign a deal with the devil.

THREE

MA LOVES TO SAY, "To be early is to be on time, and to be on time is to be late."

I'm pretty sure she got this motto from *Drumline* but, regardless, it is the mantra she lives by. Which is why we're currently sitting in her car outside of Horizon Cinema, half an hour early for my first day.

Also, Ma said she'd have to drop me off early to make her train.

She's swapped out her athleisure for her more typical corporate attire: a light blue fit-and-flare cotton dress that stops just above her knees and pointy nude-colored heels that are a shade lighter than her almond-colored skin. She's also got a navy-blue blazer hanging up in the back along with her blue medium-size Telfar bag.

Ma turns so she's facing me. "So, how are we feeling? Are we excited?"

Whenever Ma is trying to pry me open to see my emotional insides, she whips out the royal "we" as if to remind me *we're* in this together. I think she picked it up from the family therapist we used to go to when I was little, and she hasn't figured out how to stop doing it. In some ways it's comforting, but mostly it makes me feel like I'm seven and not seventeen.

"Not really," I say, pulling at a string on my khakis. Even though Glory said I didn't have to wear the uniform today, I wanted to show from day one that I was taking this role very seriously, even if it was only a part-time, minimum-wage gig.

Ma shakes my shoulder and grins at me like I just won the lottery or something.

"Well, get excited," she says. "This is a big deal. It's your first real job!"

"Weren't you just telling me yesterday that I should be relaxing this summer?"

Ma waves a hand in the air, dismissively. "That was yesterday. Today is a new day, and after talking to Luisa—"

"You talked to Amira's mom about this?"

My mother, the traitor, simply shrugs. "She happened to call after you left for Joe's, and it came up."

"How did me getting a job 'come up' in conversation?"

"She said, 'How's Rochelle?' And I said, 'She just got a job.'"

I stare my mother down, but she only looks back at me with the same big brown eyes she blessed me with, unmoved.

"Is you having a job supposed to be a secret?" Ma asks, ending our staring contest.

"No, but—"

"Then it's fine if Luisa and Amira know," Ma finishes.

"Besides, Amira was going to find out anyway."

I frown. "I mean, I guess if she comes to the theater, but I'd rather dive headfirst into popcorn before having to serve her anything."

"Okay, first of all, that is incredibly overdramatic, and second, it would take you forever to get all that butter out of your fresh braids," Ma says. She gently tugs on the end of one of the two big cornrows I fashioned my box braids into for today.

"But third"—Ma catches my eye with a look that has me immediately on edge—"that's not what I meant."

I'm almost too scared to ask, but I force the question out anyway. "What *do* you mean?"

Before Ma can say anything else, someone taps on her window and we both jump.

Speak of the devil, Amira Rodriguez is standing right outside the door, bent at the waist, waving at my mom. A few loose curls are falling in her face from the messy bun she has them pulled up in. I haven't seen her since the last day of school, but it's clear Amira has already been to the beach this summer because her normally light brown skin is inching toward Ma's caramel complexion, and the sprinkle of freckles across the bridge of her nose and cheeks is more prominent.

She's swapped out her nose ring for a shiny gold hoop that looks brand-new. I swear she swaps out that ring like people change clothes. Why does she have so many?

Taking all of this in, it's not until Amira stands up straight and moves back a bit that I notice her clothes.

She's wearing a Horizon Cinema T-shirt and khakis.

"No. Freaking. Way," I say.

Ma turns back to me with a hesitant smile. "Happy first day!"

I've always believed it's a waste of energy to hate people, which is why I try to simply not think about Amira at all. Maybe that was the wrong strategy. Because if I had, I would've known that Amira works at Horizon, and I certainly wouldn't be standing here on the curb next to her with absolutely nothing to say.

Actually, I have a lot of things to say.

First, why does she work here, of all places? And why does she smell like a cake fresh out of the oven? She's not a baked good. She is a person. No person should smell like a cupcake! It's unnatural.

Thankfully, before I accidentally let any of these thoughts fly out of my mouth, Amira breaks the silence.

"Congrats on the new gig." She doesn't turn my way when she says it, and I can't figure out from her tone if she's being serious or sarcastic. It's hard to tell with her. With everyone else, Amira is a sweet innocent angel, but with me it's like I'm the gum stuck to the bottom of her shoe.

It's infuriating. Not because I want her to like me or anything. I chose not to be friends, and it's clearly worked out for both of us. It's more that she somehow always makes me out to look like the bad guy whenever I complain about her. She's Little Miss Perfect, and I'm everything not.

"Thanks," I finally say. I may not like Amira, but my default state is to be polite.

"I'm surprised you have time to work," Amira says. "I thought you'd have your head buried in books all summer like you usually do."

And there it is.

It takes everything in me not to turn and glare at her, but I refuse to give her the satisfaction of bothering me. I choose to limit my social engagements. Not all of us crave popularity like some people.

"As you very well know, getting into a good college isn't just about one's academic prowess, but also their commitment to being a well-rounded student."

"You sound like a college brochure," she says with a laugh.

Now I turn to face her only to find her already looking down at me. Amira is taller than I am by a good three or four inches, and while I am a solidly average height of five foot five, being around her always makes me feel miniature. Also, at some point she freed her loose curls from their bun, so now they're fully out, framing her heart-shaped face, and the cake batter scent wafting from her is even stronger now that I'm facing her.

It not only smells good, but is making me hungry, which is ridiculous because I had a ham-and-cheese croissant on the way here.

"You make that sound like a bad thing," I say finally. "Don't tell me you haven't also memorized the brochures for Dartmouth or whatever school it is you're trying to go to."

"UPenn."

I blink. My brain must be malfunctioning or my hearing has actually been damaged from listening to my music way too loud. There's no way she just said what I think she said.

It's bad enough that somehow Amira's class ranking keeps inching closer and closer to mine, but she cannot be applying to the same Ivy as me. No Ivy is going to take two kids from the same high school. Not a public school at least. While I'm confident my spot at the top of our class is solid, and I'm thankfully a legacy kid, I'll begrudgingly admit that Amira is a more "well-rounded student" than I am. If she's actually trying to go to UPenn, she could ruin my chances of getting in.

My throat feels incredibly dry when I force out the words, "Come again?"

"UPenn," she repeats, with a smile. "You know the school in Pennsylvania," she adds. "I hear it's a good one, so that's where I'm applying. The only school I'm applying to actually. I hope I get in. I hear it's hard, but I'm not too worried."

My mouth literally falls open, and I don't know whether I want to scream or shake her. How can she be so flippant about school when I'm here, having to take this job at Horizon simply to add one more thing to my already stellar résumé?

That's when Amira starts cackling, bent over with a full belly laugh.

I feel the heat flush my cheeks, and it's in moments like this that I am thankful I was blessed with dark skin.

"Oh wow, okay—you should see your face," she says, once she comes back up. She's wiping tears from her eyes. "Rochelle, I am fucking with you. I have no interest in going to UPenn. It's like the one Ivy I'm not applying to. Trust me, you don't have to worry about competing."

"Ha ha ha, you're so funny," I say. "Truly hilarious." I don't even know if I'm mad or simply embarrassed for letting her get to me. "How did you even know I'm applying to UPenn anyway?"

Just as the question leaves my lips, I know the answer before she even says it.

"Your mom."

Seriously, my mother can't hold water. I know she and Mrs. Rodriguez are BFFs, but I wish Ma didn't feel the need to talk to her about everything, especially when it comes to me. Moreover, if Amira's mom is running back to Amira to tell her all my business, why doesn't Ma do the same? This should at least be a fair trade.

Before I can say anything else, a red car that looks like it's being held together by glue and tape speeds into the lot. They're coming down a row, right toward us. Just as I'm beginning to think we should move, they slow down a smidge before cutting their wheel and pulling into the last spot in the row.

"That's Glory," Amira says.

I nod, only slightly concerned that our boss apparently drives as if she's in a *Fast & Furious* movie. Maybe her welcome speech will open with her talking about the Family.

Glory practically jumps out of her car, long red locs swinging down past her waist as she runs over to us, her dark brown skin glistening with sweat. She's a short, round woman, coming up to only my chin when she stops in front of us.

"Sorry, sorry, sorry," Glory says. "I meant to get here earlier, but you know what they say about the best-laid plans."

I do not know, but I'm guessing it's the antithesis of Ma's *Drumline* motto. I try to keep a straight face, but I can feel a frown forming despite my best efforts. I've never had a poker face, and I'm struggling not to feel some type of way about Glory's reckless driving and appearance. Her clothes are all wrinkled, and although she is wearing the same Horizon shirt as Amira, she's wearing yoga pants instead of khakis and her "closed-toe shoes" are Crocs.

I know we weren't required to wear the uniform today, but I'm having trouble believing this is the person I'm supposed to report to all summer.

Amira and I watch as Glory, who has both a backpack and a fanny pack for some reason, shifts through her obscenely large key ring until she exclaims, "Aha!" holding a key up in triumph.

"Do you need help?" Amira asks as Glory bends over to lift the gate.

Her tone is the same sickeningly sweet one she uses with our moms and teachers in school. I almost gag.

"Nope, I got it," Glory says, even though she clearly does not.

Amira walks over and helps Glory pull the gate up, and I stand by, feeling useless. I start chewing on my thumbnail, before pulling my hand away so Amira doesn't see me and think I'm sucking my thumb or something. In hindsight, I should've stepped in to help, but now it's too late. Once again, Amira has made herself look good. Now Glory probably thinks I'm rude, instead of a hard worker who will certainly be employee of the month.

Just as Glory and Amira give one final push to get the gate all the way up, two Asian girls who look nearly identical skid to a stop in front of me. I'm sure they've got to be twins. Same long black hair and they're wearing the same T-shirt, except one is red and the other is pink.

"Hi! We're sorry we're late!" they exclaim at the same time.

"Um, no worries," I say, though I have no idea why they're saying this to me.

Thankfully, Glory steps around me and shakes both girls' hands. They look between me and Glory as they all shake hands, and I feel slightly vindicated that they didn't even consider Glory could be the one running Horizon.

"Hi, I'm Glory," she says. "You must be Jennie and Lisa Choi."

The girls focus their attention on Glory as they nod, then Glory turns to me. "And you're Rochelle, right? Apologies for not introducing myself first thing. I'm a bit frazzled this morning."

Somehow, I get the feeling Glory's frazzled a lot of the time, but I keep those thoughts to myself.

"No problem," I say. "And yeah, I am."

"Great, thanks for joining up with us at the last minute," Glory says. "Remind me to get you all your paperwork and everything you need before you leave today."

"Sure, will do."

Glory's already turned back to the door, so I'm not sure if she heard me.

In the short time I was talking to Glory, Amira has already

introduced herself to the twins, and they're eagerly taking turns shaking Amira's hand. Their flushed cheeks let me know they've already fallen for Amira's charms, but that's how it always goes. All Amira has to do is turn her dazzling smile on people and they immediately fall for her. Meanwhile, I have what Ma likes to call a "prickly personality."

Rather than try to test my social skills with these girls, I move to hover by Glory as she opens the front door.

"Here we go." She pulls the door open with a flourish, almost smacking me in the face. I jump out of the way just in time. Glory doesn't even seem to notice. I'm genuinely starting to be concerned for my health and safety in this job.

"Follow me, everyone," she says as she goes inside.

Amira is right on Glory's tail, with the twins following right behind her, but I pause a second to actually look at the place and soak it all in, as Ma would say.

Craning my neck, I can see the vertical "Horizon" sign lit up in neon red, and beneath it is a white board that's backlit with what's currently showing. Some of the movies I recognize, like the latest Disney and Star Wars films, but there are two I've never heard of, and then, for some reason, *Shaft* is up there.

On either side of the doors are the movie posters for each film currently showing. I bypass the franchises and check out the ones I don't know. One is clearly a Japanese anime and the other one looks like an indie film, possibly also international, and it's giving romance vibes. Finally, I move over to check out the old-school poster for *Shaft*. Above it, unlike the others that say "Now Playing," this one says "Monthly Classic."

Interesting.

"Hello, are you planning on coming in?" Amira's holding the front door open, looking at me like I have two heads or something.

"I'm just looking at these posters," I say, walking over. "I didn't think that was a crime."

"Look at them later, we've got work to do."

"Relax, you're not the boss of me."

There's a slight twitch to Amira's lips like she wants to smile, but in a blink it's gone. Then she's gesturing for me to walk in first. A part of me thinks this is a trick, and as soon as I get close enough, she'll close the door in my face. But as much as I dislike Amira, she's never been a bully, so I step through the door and come to a stop in the lobby.

"Whoa," I say.

Amira pulls up beside me and nods. "I know, right?"

From the outside, Horizon looks like every other theater I've seen. The inside though?

It's clear it's been recently renovated, as everything looks shiny and new. To the right are bright red, glossy leather benches. They make an L shape along the walls and windows where the twins are currently situated.

To my left are a variety of video game machines: *Ms. Pac-Man*, *Galaxian*, *Crazy Taxi*, and *Street Fighter*. There's also a coin machine. Straight ahead, Glory is standing by concessions, which is set up at a circular counter with digital menus hanging above and a register directly in the center. Besides the regular candy and popcorn I'm used to, it looks like they also offer beer and wine.

On opposite sides of concessions are the restrooms for men, women, and a separate all-gender handicapped bathroom. The theaters are in the back, with a sign pointing to theaters 1 and 2 on the left and theaters 3, 4, and 5 on the right.

All of this is great, but it's the art that really makes the place stand out. Painted on all the walls is one extended black-and-white mural of Black actors in different films. There's Whoopi Goldberg in *The Color Purple*, Jamie Foxx as Ray Charles in *Ray*, Will Smith from *Men in Black*, Pam Grier as Foxy Brown, Chadwick Boseman as the Black Panther, and on and on it goes, wrapping around the whole place.

I can see why Kerry loves it here. It's all her idols in one place. Black Hollywood brought to life.

Wait a minute. Kerry loves it here. As in, Kerry is here all the time.

"There are still a few I haven't been able to place yet. I'm guessing they're from older movies."

Amira's voice makes something click in my brain, and I turn on her.

"Have you ever seen my friend Kerry here?"

Amira looks startled. "Kerry who?"

"Kerry Williams," I say, like it's obvious. "She's in our year. She's been in every musical and play the school has ever done. How do you not know who she is?"

I'm slightly offended on Kerry's behalf. I may not venture into whatever the scene is at our school, but Kerry is maybe just as well-known as Amira is, if not more so, honestly.

"I know who she is," Amira says, eyes narrowed. "But there

are two Kerrys in our year, something you would know if you had more than two friends."

Before I can respond to that dig, the front doors open behind us and Amira lets out a shriek of excitement, our conversation completely forgotten as she runs right into the arms of one of the newcomers.

Shawn.

It shouldn't surprise me that Amira's BFF also works here and yet, here I am, shocked. Will wonders never cease?

He swings Amira around in a full circle as if they haven't seen each other in years, even though I'm pretty sure they were both at his party last night. The other people who came in with him, a white girl and guy who look like Barbie and Ken come to life, skirt around them and walk right past me to talk to Glory.

Well, hello to you too.

I attempt to move around Amira and Shawn's lovefest, but Shawn puts Amira down right as I'm about to pass.

"Roe Roe," he says, using my unauthorized nickname. He then proceeds to pick me up and twirl me around.

"What? Hey! Put me down," I yelp.

Thankfully, he immediately obeys. I step back, taking in the larger-than-life persona that is Shawn. He is gigantic, both in height and width. His chest is broad, and his muscles are huge. Just looking at him, you know he spends all his free time exercising.

His usually pale skin has already taken on a more golden hue from being out in the sun, and his light brown hair is currently tied up in a top bun. He is also wearing the Horizon Cinema uniform, though the T-shirt looks to be a size too small on him. I get the feeling that it is intentional.

"I'm so glad you're here," he says.

I eye him with suspicion. "Did you know I was going to be here?"

"Yeah," he says with an easy grin. "I told the new boss lady you'd be perfect for this gig, and it took some persuading, but she can't resist me."

Then he winks and that's all the confirmation I need. I cannot believe I have Shawn Grady to thank for this job. Have I stepped into the Twilight Zone?

"Wow, well, thank you," I say. And I mean it. I'd probably still be at home searching for a job if it wasn't for him.

"Oh, no need to thank me," Shawn says. "Honestly, it's really all because of—"

Whatever he was going to say is cut off when a T-shirt hits me right in the chest.

"Oh, sorry, Rochelle. I thought you'd catch it!" Amira says, innocently. She then proceeds to hand Jennie and Lisa their shirts.

It takes everything in me not to chuck my shirt right back at Amira. I hold it out in front of me. It's much bigger than the size I need, but I'm sure Taylor, who dabbles in sewing when she's not painting, can fix it for me somehow.

Looking around the room, it's clear that me, Jennie, and Lisa are the newbies. Shawn and Amira are talking to Barbie and Ken, though Shawn is doing most of the talking. Jennie and Lisa are still off to the side, inspecting their own shirts, probably making their own plans on how to style them. And then there's me in the middle, unsure what to do with myself. In hindsight, I should've considered that having a job meant having coworkers and prepared for that. Instead, I'm just . . . here.

I pull out my phone and am about to text Kerry and Taylor when Glory suddenly reappears.

"Okay, everyone, gather 'round!" Glory says, clapping her hands. We all move toward where she and Amira are standing in front of concessions. Amira's the only one next to Glory instead of facing her like the rest of us, but Glory doesn't seem bothered by this.

Meanwhile, inside my head an alarm is ringing. Something's not right, but I'm not sure if I'm just irked because Amira clearly has well-established relationships with Glory and the returning staff, or if my Spidey senses are in fact tingling, and something is amiss.

"Welcome to the Horizon Cinema family!" Glory says, freeing me from my thoughts.

Wow, maybe she *is* a fan of *Fast & Furious*. Though if Glory subscribed to the *10 Things Before the Opening Bell* newsletter from *Business Insider* like I do, she would know that companies who call their employees "family" are usually the worst ones. No one else seems bothered by Glory's word choice though. I try to fix my face before anyone notices, but of course that's when Amira catches my eye. She's looking at me as if I've descended from another planet, eyebrow raised and lips pursed. I quickly shift my attention back to Glory, who's still speaking.

"Way back in the seventies, Horizon Cinema was founded

by Christian Handler and his wife, Sarah," Glory continues. "The first Black-owned movie theater in the area. Probably all of New York. They absolutely loved movies, but theaters at the time were still mostly segregated despite the laws, and many white theaters didn't play Black films.

"So, they wanted to make a place where Black films, as well as other films that featured the voices of marginalized groups, could shine.

"And thus, Horizon Cinema was born!"

Everyone applauds, and I join in, only slightly delayed. This is obviously the reaction Glory was hoping for, and her face breaks out into a huge grin.

"Unfortunately, a few years ago, the Handlers were ready to retire and wanted to sell this glorious landmark," Glory says. "Enter my uncles, Derek and Eric! They met right here, working at Horizon Cinema as teenagers, and fell in love with movies as well as each other. Just like the Handlers, they were another Black couple who found love through film. For them and me, this is home. I grew up here. So, they bought the theater from the Handlers and renovated it into what you see before you today, a celebration of Black Hollywood and a space for us."

Glory raises up her arms, somewhat dramatically, as if to show off the place. We all clap again, and this time, at least for me, it feels more genuine. It is a pretty cool story.

"Now, it's up to us to make sure the theater continues to be the great place that it's always been, bringing in new customers and caring for our returning ones," Glory continues. "So, are you all up for the challenge?"

There are a few head nods, and Shawn, Jennie, and Lisa all say, "Yeah!" way more enthusiastically than is necessary, but Glory loves it.

"Amazing! Now, before we get started, I have some very exciting news," Glory says. "I'm thrilled to announce that Amira here is our new assistant manager!"

Everyone once again erupts in applause. Everyone except me. I'm frozen as Glory's words reverberate in my head.

Assistant *manager*?

"Amira has been with us for about two years now and has proven she knows Horizon Cinema inside and out. We're so lucky to have her on our team," Glory continues, but I'm barely listening.

I look over to Amira, only to find her looking back at me with a smile that says she knows exactly what I'm thinking.

If she's the assistant manager, that means she *is* the boss of me.

And she will be . . . for the whole summer.

FOUR

GLORY IS ON A MISSION to kill me.

Okay, not really. But she follows up that little revelation with the amazing suggestion to do an icebreaker.

Icebreakers were originally a torture device created by the military, I'm certain.

Glory has us form a circle in the lobby, and I somehow end up sandwiched between one of the twins and Shawn, who is so excited to participate, he's practically vibrating.

"Okay, so the game is simple," Glory begins. She's standing directly across from me, between Amira and the couple whose names I still don't know. Maybe this game might actually be useful.

"Introduce yourself by saying your name, your pronouns, what school you go to, and your favorite movie theater snack. I'll go first," Glory continues. "I'm Glory. They/them." Mentally, I reprimand myself for assuming their pronouns and make the switch in my brain. "I'll be starting grad school in the fall to get my master's in fine arts at Parsons School of Design, and my favorite movie theater snack is a hot dog."

I throw up a little in my mouth. Mystery meat mixed together in a casing and then rotated for hours under a hot lamp. Sounds like a guaranteed trip to the bathroom. Or the ER.

"Let's go clockwise," Glory says, turning to the couple.

"Hi!" The girl's and the boy's hands are still intertwined, but she uses her free one to give an energetic wave. "I'm Brigit, she/her, and this is Danny, he/him." Danny simply nods. "I go to Sacred Heart Academy, and Danny goes to Chaminade."

Even though they're both wearing the same Horizon uniform as the other returning staff, theirs are giving upper-middle-class energy. Brigit's platinum blond hair is slicked back in a tight high ponytail, short bangs falling right above her manicured brows, and she has a silver cross necklace resting comfortably on her T-shirt. She's the only one of us wearing a khaki skirt instead of shorts or pants.

Danny has the same blond hair, but it's gelled down and coiffed. He's also wearing square-shaped sunglasses even though we're indoors. His khaki shorts fall just above his knees, and he's got on Sperrys.

"We're both going to be seniors in the fall," Brigit continues. Her bright blue eyes seem to get brighter with excitement. "And our favorite snack is popcorn."

There's an awkward pause before Shawn realizes Danny will not be speaking today.

"Oh, all right. I'm Shawn of North High fame. He/him. My favorite movie theater snack's gotta be Buncha Crunch."

"Great choice, Shawn!" Glory says. Then their eyes land

on me, and everyone turns.

I pick a spot above Glory's head and, using a trick from my public speaking class last year, I focus all my attention on it before I begin.

"Hi, I'm Rochelle, she/her. I'm also at North High, and I don't have a favorite movie theater snack."

"What do you mean you don't have a favorite?" Glory asks, looking genuinely confused.

I shrug. "I don't really go to the movies that often and when I do, I don't usually buy any snacks."

"Okay, well, what would you get if you were to buy a snack?" Amira butts in. "You can't skip the question."

I frown. A part of me wants to ask, Why not? How helpful is it for everyone to know my favorite snack? But Amira is my boss, and I'm not about to talk back to her in front of everyone else before my first day even begins.

God, I hate this.

I look past Amira at the concessions menu and pick the first thing I see. "Raisinets."

Shawn literally gasps beside me, and Brigit scrunches up her face in disgust.

"Really?" Amira asks. "Don't you hate raisins?"

I do but (a) why does she know that? And (b) who cares? This is just a silly game. "Nope! They're the best. I'd marry a raisin if I could. Even have its babies. Anyways, who's next?"

I turn to my left and face the Choi twin in a red shirt, who's more than ready to dive in.

"Hi, I'm Jennie. I go to South High, and my favorite movie

theater snack is strawberry Pocky sticks. I have to sneak them in though. Theaters don't usually have them."

"Oh, maybe that's something we can add to our concessions," Glory says, sliding out a phone from their back pocket and typing the note. "Lisa, it's your turn!"

Lisa seems slightly startled by her name being called. I know the feeling. But after a gentle nudge from her sister, she speaks. "Hi, I'm Lisa. Also, South High. And chocolate Pocky sticks are superior."

Jennie rolls her eyes in the same way that Kerry and I do when Taylor starts broadcasting her loud and wrong opinions on music.

"Awesome! Last but certainly not least, we have Assistant Manager Amira!"

I hope Glory isn't going to call Amira "Assistant Manager Amira" all summer long. I do not need the constant reminder that Amira has seniority over me here.

"Hi, everyone!" Amira waves with both her hands. "Like Glory said, I'm Amira, your new assistant manager. I attend North with Shawn and Rochelle—"

I look up, surprised to hear my name, but Amira has already moved on.

"—and my favorite snack is also popcorn, but I like to eat mine with Twizzlers."

"Gross." Shawn laughs.

"Thank you!"

Glory claps their hands. "Okay, perfect, that's everyone. Well, mostly. You all are my front-of-house staff. You'll be

taking care of everything from concessions to checking people's tickets before they go into the theaters to cleaning up any
messes in the theaters or bathrooms."

I look over at the bathrooms on either side of the room and
frown. I can wash dishes and wipe down a counter with the
best of them, but bathrooms? I don't even *use* public restrooms
if I can help it, much less clean them. My gag reflex kicks in.
The smells that come from bathrooms always make me nauseous and occasionally sick, especially if I see something gross.
I can't even see vomit on-screen. *Knives Out* and *Pitch Perfect* are
banned films in my house for this reason.

The things that can come from our bodies are truly
disgusting.

I'm debating asking Glory to expand on the "messes" thing,
but I can already imagine how that would come off. I don't want
to seem like a prima donna, so I swallow my question and pray
any bathroom issues will be handled by someone else.

"We're a customer-first team," Glory explains, "and while I
don't believe the customer is always right, I do believe in making
them at least feel like they are."

I spy Lisa and Jennie with perplexed looks on their faces, and
I am happy to see I'm not the only one confused by that. But
none of us are bold enough to ask for clarification.

"Okay, so that about wraps up everything I had to say," Glory
continues. "If you all need me, I'll be in the back finalizing the
schedule, which I hope to have ready for you by the time you're
done with training. Also, Rochelle—"

"Yes?"

"Make sure to stop by before you leave and fill out your paperwork."

"Will do." I salute them for some reason, and Amira barely hides her snicker. I can feel heat warming my cheeks again.

Glory starts to walk away, but Amira stops them.

"Wait, Glory, shouldn't you tell everyone how training will work?"

Glory grimaces. "Oh, right, of course, sorry. I do not know where my head is this morning." They knock on their cranium to emphasize their point. "All right, let's have two groups. First group will be Amira, Lisa, Danny, and Brigit at concessions. Amira, show them how to operate the ordering system, register, and proper food prep. Second group will be Jennie, Rochelle, and Shawn. Shawn, I want you to walk them through greeting folks and using the ticket scanner. There are two scanners under the counter."

Shawn nods with a look of determination on his face that is so serious, you'd think he was going to war or something. I just gave a dorky salute, so I have no room to judge, but I do want to laugh a little.

"Vets, I expect you to show our newbies the ropes, and then the groups can switch."

"Actually, what if we have Brigit and Rochelle switch?" Amira holds up a hand, interrupting Glory.

"Wait, why?" Brigit tilts her head, confused.

I'm glad she asked, so I don't have to.

"Because you and Danny would spend the whole time making out instead of helping Amira teach the newbies how to run concessions." Shawn points at the two of them, chuckling.

"That's not true," Brigit whines.

Danny shrugs and speaks for the first time. "Eh, it kind of is."

Brigit smacks his chest, and Jennie, Lisa, and Shawn all laugh. Amira rolls her eyes, clearly exasperated. It's the first indication that Amira isn't one of us. She's our (assistant) manager.

And now she's training me herself. Great.

"Okay, yes," Glory agrees before pointing at me. "Rochelle, you'll go to concessions; Brigit to the ticket booth." Their phone rings just then. Glory frowns and says, "I have to take this," before crossing the room to the door marked "Employees Only" by the ticket booth.

"All righty, then." Amira scans our little group before her eyes land on me. "Shall we begin?"

FIVE

THE ACTUAL TRAINING DOESN'T TAKE very long, which begs the question, *Why did we have to be here so early?* I consider asking Amira, but my pride demands that I do no such thing.

Amira has us walk around the concessions counter so we can get a "lay of the land." The counter is silver granite all around, except for two glass cases that show various candies and snacks on display. Amira explains that at the start of every shift we'll need to do inventory for everything in the cases, as well as the drink cups and popcorn and hot dog containers. At the end of each shift, we'll do inventory again and cash out the register to make sure everything adds up.

Amira shows us how to get behind the counter, using the flip-up section near the register. She then introduces us to the popcorn machine, and even though there is no popcorn in it today, we can all smell the salt and butter in the air. At the end of each shift, someone will need to clean it out, and Amira points out where all the cleaning supplies can be found under the counter. If needed, a mop and bucket can be found in the employee office. Meanwhile, Danny simply stands around, quiet. Honestly, I'm not sure why he's even here.

Amira takes us through the beverages and when we get to the alcoholic drinks, Danny finally steps in to tell us that as the only eighteen-year-old in our group, only he will be able to serve the beer and wine.

At this point Lisa raises her hand, and Amira nods to her like a teacher in class. "Don't you have to be twenty-one to drink alcohol?"

"Yes, but—"

"You only need to be eighteen to serve," Danny says with a grin.

The fact that he's still wearing sunglasses indoors and the only thing he seems to care about at this job is getting to pour drinks makes me question why there are even legal ages to determine anything in this country. Clearly, age does not indicate maturity.

"Right." Amira keeps things moving along. She shows us the little machine that they use for hot dogs and the mini fridge under the counter where they store them, as well as the buns. Lisa and I listen as Amira shows us the register. For the first couple of weeks, it'll always be a vet handling the money, presumably until they can trust us. We also get to see the credit card machine, which is pretty straightforward. Finally, when Shawn, Jennie, and Brigit come over to swap, Amira pulls our group to the side to show us how to use the ticket scanner.

Lisa, Amira, and I stand by the red benches at the front of

the theater while we wait for the other group to finish their own concessions walk-through. Danny returns to Brigit's side as soon as Amira says we're done.

All in all, I'm confident I can handle this job without a hitch. I say as much under my breath to Lisa, who is nervously picking at her nail polish.

Unfortunately, my volume was not low enough, because Amira turns around.

"You really think you've got everything handled, Coleman?" she challenges.

Ugh, I really don't want to pick a fight, so I try to make my next words less . . . demeaning, even though I meant what I said. Most people at school think I'm a know-it-all and stuck-up or whatever, and I'd rather not get that same reputation here.

"I was just saying I don't think this will be too difficult to manage."

Amira scoffs, crossing her arms. "Right, of course. Because everything comes *so* easy to you."

"Um, no? I work really hard at everything I do, actually."

Unlike some people, I think, but thankfully I don't say it.

"I'm just saying," I continue, "in comparison to school, this should be a piece of cake. I'm sure that's why you like it, right? It's another activity you can do outside of school."

"Did you just call my job an 'activity'?" Her eyebrow lifts with annoyance.

At this point, everyone at concessions is making their way over, either because they're actually done with training or they can sense a fight brewing, which, again, I was trying to avoid.

"Is it not an activity?" My question is genuine, but I can tell by the way Amira's eyes have narrowed that she doesn't see it that way. Seriously, no matter what I do or say, it's always wrong in her eyes.

"I swear I didn't mean that in a derogatory sense." I put my hands up defensively.

"What's going on?" Shawn walks up to us with that concerned puppy-eyes look of his.

Everyone has now formed a sort of circle around me and Amira, with Lisa and Jennie flanking me on my right and left, Shawn on Amira's right, and Brigit and Danny hovering on her other side. Clearly, lines have been drawn between the trainees and vets. I'm not sure if it's simply because we're all new, but it feels nice to have Lisa and Jennie behind me.

"Oh, nothing, just Rochelle being Rochelle." Amira smiles at Shawn.

"What's that supposed to mean?" I ask.

"Nothing, it means nothing," she replies.

It doesn't take my 4.0 GPA to know that she's lying, but Amira has decided she's done talking to me now. And that's fine with me.

"Training is officially over," she announces. "Glory will be sending out the full schedule either today or tomorrow, so please keep an eye out for that. First shift of the summer is this Saturday. Make sure you know if you need to be here or not. Otherwise, I'll see y'all around. You're free to go."

With that, Amira makes for the exit. Shawn gives me a helpless shrug as if to say, "What can you do?" before running after her. Brigit and Danny aren't far behind, and then it's just me, Jennie, and Lisa.

I feel like I want to punch something, and before I can bite it back, I let out a groan of frustration.

"Are you okay?" Lisa steps closer, her eyes filled with worry.

Obviously, I am not okay, but how can I even begin to explain this . . . thing with Amira? It's like we fundamentally, on a cellular level, cannot coexist. She's just so . . .

I let out another groan.

"Yeah, I'm going to go ahead and say no, she is not okay." Jennie grimaces. They're both now eyeing me like a bomb that might explode.

Taking a page out of Ma's playbook, I take a step back from the twins, close my eyes, and take a long inhale through my nose before letting it out through my mouth. I do it again a few times, before I feel more like myself. When I open my eyes, Lisa and Jennie are still looking at me, worried.

"I'm fine, thank you."

"So, I'm guessing you two don't like each other, huh," Jennie says.

The straightforward way she sums up me and Amira makes me bark out a laugh.

"Yep, I guess you could say that."

"So, what happened?" Jennie presses. "Did she dump you or something?"

I choke on my own spit and start coughing. "Excuse me?"

Lisa elbows her sister. "You can't just ask someone if they've been dumped."

"Why not? I've just been dumped too. We can commiserate together. It'll be fun."

"She did not dump me. We didn't date. We would never. Ever!"

The twins share a look before Jennie nods. "I see. So, this is just the start of your love story, then."

"I—what? We're not in love!"

"Please excuse my sister," Lisa says, giving her sister another gentle push. "She's been on a K-drama kick lately and believes everyone is about to fall in love. Yesterday she tried to convince me our mail carrier was the one for me. He's, like, thirty-five."

Jennie rolls her eyes. "I didn't mean right now. In, like, ten years when he'll probably be running some business and be a millionaire. You'll bump into each other on the street, and he'll remember you, *and then* you'll fall in love."

"If he's looking at her as someone he should date now, I don't think he'll make a good love interest in the future," I say, only slightly concerned.

"That is exactly what I said." Lisa shakes her head.

"Neither of you has my eye for these things," Jennie says. Then she looks directly in my eyes, as if to drive her point home. "There is tension here. A true love story in the making. I can feel it."

"I mean, I am stressed like twenty-four/seven, if that's the tension you mean."

"It is not."

"All right, enough sniffing out love stories like some kind of romance bloodhound." Lisa grabs her sister's arm and leads her toward the exit. "It was nice meeting you, Rochelle."

"Likewise," I say.

And then there's just me.

I pull out my phone to text Kerry and Taylor and then remember Kerry's betrayal. There's no way she didn't know Amira worked here, not with how much she allegedly loves this place. I was already planning on meeting up with them, but now it's urgent. She's got some explaining to do.

Once I shoot off a text, asking for a pickup, I head to the office to get my paperwork. I raise my fist ready to knock when I hear Glory on the phone.

"It's not going to come to that," they say. "This summer is going to be good; I can feel it. We'll turn things around."

I'm frozen. It feels awkward to interrupt what sounds like an important conversation, but now I'm just hovering, eavesdropping.

Have they been on the phone this whole time?

"You guys just have to trust me. I can do this." Glory sounds so earnest, almost like they're begging whoever's on the phone to believe them. It makes me feel kind of bad for doubting their capabilities earlier. Though in my defense, they're wearing Crocs. I have nothing against Crocs; they're as comfy as they are ugly. But they are not managerial attire.

"Okay, yeah, no, I get it," they say, sounding defeated. "I love you too. Okay, thanks. Bye."

I wait a second longer at the door, making sure they're truly done, before knocking.

"Come in!"

I pull the door open and step inside. The office looks more like a closet, with only enough room for Glory's desk, a computer that looks like it's from the Stone Age, a filing cabinet, and the mop and bucket Amira mentioned, tucked away in a corner. There's also a single framed photo beside the computer, but it's facing Glory so I can't see what it's of.

"Oh, hi, Rochelle. How was your training?" they ask.

If Glory's upset, they're doing an excellent job at hiding it. Their smile looks genuine as they wait for me to step farther inside.

"It was great." A bold-faced lie, but what am I supposed to say? That they made my mortal enemy their assistant manager? That I'd literally rather have any other job than this, but it's all I have?

"Awesome." Glory pulls open the top drawer of the filing cabinet and grabs a folder that has my name on it. "Do you need a pen?"

"Oh, no, I've got one." I riffle through my tote bag, until I pull out one of my favorites. I awkwardly bend over the desk, filling out the information as quickly as I can.

"All done." I slide the papers over to Glory, who smiles as they look them over.

"Great! Oh, wait, do you have your passport? I'm so sorry I forgot to ask you to bring it."

"No worries." Thankfully, Ma thought to tell me to bring it, and I pull it out of my bag.

"Amazing, thank you!" Then they disappear underneath their desk.

"Um, Glory?"

"I'm here." They raise a hand up to wave. "The scanner's down here."

"Oh, right." Because, of course, it is.

"Just one sec." I can hear the scanner whirring from under the desk. Glory comes back up with my passport, handing it back to me. "You're all set! See you on Saturday!"

"Saturday?"

"Oh, yes, since you're still here, do you want a printout of the schedule? I'm going to email them in a sec, but I know some people prefer hard copies."

"I actually love hard copies, thanks."

"No problem at all." Glory smiles. "I do too. Things just feel more real to me when I can hold them in my hands, you know?"

I nod because I do. Am I bonding with Glory? Weird.

"All right, let me just pop down and get this for you." Glory disappears again under her desk and reemerges a moment later.

"Woo, okay, it just takes a second to warm up." They brush some wayward locs out of their face and turn their attention to the computer, clicking a few times, until finally we hear the telltale signs of something printing. A moment later Glory reaches their hand down and retrieves a piece of paper.

"Here ya go!" They hand it over, and I see it's double-sided. They have a double-sided printer/scanner hiding under their desk. As a member of every office store's rewards program, that is incredibly cool to me.

Perhaps I misjudged Glory a smidge. I apologize to them in my head, as I thank them for my schedule.

"No problem! And thanks again for deciding to join us this summer, Rochelle. Truly, I'm excited to have you here. I've only heard good things about you."

It takes everything in me to resist the urge to ask exactly what things they've heard. I knew Shawn liked me fine enough as his tutor, but the fact that he was able to talk me up well enough to convince Glory to hire me is still too hard to compute.

"I'm excited to be here."

Despite the Amira of it all, I think I might mean it.

SIX

WHEN TAYLOR'S BEAT-UP GRAY HONDA pulls into the parking lot, I can see Kerry waving from the passenger seat. Her hand quickly drops as she notes my "You've got some serious explaining to do" face. Then she bows her head in shame, and that's all the confirmation I need.

"You knew!" I barely have the door closed before I'm thrusting the accusation at her.

Taylor turns in her seat. She's actually barefaced this morning and wearing a thrifted 2005 Warped Tour T-shirt. "You know most people say hello when they get into the car of the person who has so graciously come to give them a ride home, especially since they don't have their own vehicle."

"Hi, Taylor," I say.

"Hello, Rochelle the Shell." She turns back in her seat and drives off.

Kerry is noticeably silent and has slid down farther in her seat as if I can't see her. I lean forward so I can poke my head between the two front seats.

"Back it up and put your seat belt on," Taylor tells me without even looking. Driving always activates her mom-of-the-group mode. I harrumph, but do as I'm told, falling back into the seat behind Kerry's and clicking my seat belt on.

Then, because I am a very mature person, I kick the back of Kerry's seat.

"Hey!" she shouts, finally turning to look at me.

"We don't kick parts of Sadie!" Taylor says. Sadie is, of course, the Honda.

"Sorry, Sadie," I say. "But *someone* needs to answer for their crimes."

Taylor pulls up at a red light and looks between Kerry and me.

"Someone please explain what is going on here."

Kerry, the coward, says nothing.

"Guess who works at Horizon?" I don't wait for Taylor to answer. "Amira Rodriguez. And not only does she work at Horizon, she's also the assistant manager, which means she is basically my boss."

The light turns green, so Taylor's eyes are on the road and not on me when she speaks again. "Okay, so that means you're mad at Kerry because . . ."

Kerry throws up her hands. "Because I knew, okay! I knew! Well, not the manager part, but I knew she worked there."

"And yet you said nothing." I fall back in my seat, arms crossed in fury and betrayal.

"You needed the job!" Kerry turns in her seat so she can look at me.

I ignore her gaze.

"What difference would it have made if I had told you? You said yourself you need it for Wharton, and you were already clearly meh about working there, so why would I make things worse by mentioning the fact that I've seen Amira working there a few times? I didn't want to stress you out unnecessarily, and there was a possibility that she wouldn't even be there today for your training. I didn't want to risk saying something if it wasn't even relevant."

Now I look at her. "So, instead you chose to keep it to yourself, so I'd just have to deal with it? Because that's what happened, Kerry. And, of course, she was the absolute worst today."

"What did she say?" Taylor looks at me via her rearview mirror.

I wave a hand. "The usual. That I was a nerdy hermit know-it-all who spends all her time at the library, or something like that. I don't even go to the library that often. It's too far."

Somehow, we're already pulling up in front of my house. "Shall we continue this discussion inside?" Taylor puts the car in park.

"I don't know if I want to allow a traitor into my home." I shoot a look at Kerry.

She throws her hands up and says, "I'm sorry. I should've just told you. I'll never keep a secret from you ever again, even if I think it's in your best interest, okay?"

I'm quiet for a moment, pursing my lips, considering her promise. "Fine, apology accepted."

"Thank God," Taylor says. She hops out of the car, the door squeaking out an unholy sound as it opens then closes.

I go for my door, but Kerry is still eyeing me.

"Do you really forgive me?" she asks.

There's a hint of worry in her voice that makes whatever was left of my annoyance melt away. With all of her bravado and self-confidence, I sometimes forget that Kerry is not unbreakable. There's nothing she hates more than having anyone be mad at her. Especially her friends.

"Yes, we're fine. But if you know anything else about Horizon or Amira, you'd better come clean."

Kerry winces. "Well, Shawn also works there too, I think. I'm like 99.9 percent sure."

"Change that to one hundred percent." I roll my eyes and open the car door.

Once we're both standing on the patch of grass that lies between the curb and the sidewalk, I continue, "He was there today too."

"Oops, sorry. Again."

We start walking up the path to my front door, where Taylor is already waiting, watching us, clearly impatient.

"It's fine, I actually don't hate him that much," I tell Kerry. "And I'm pretty sure he got me the job at Horizon."

"Who did what?" Taylor asks.

I exchange a quick look with Kerry, who shrugs and looks away, leaving me to deal with Taylor. Though Taylor claimed just yesterday that she has no issue with Shawn, I'm not so sure I actually believe her.

"Shawn works at Horizon and seemed to imply that he got me the job," I explain. "He said he told the boss all about me, and then I got the job, so, you know, one plus one equals two."

"Oh." Taylor's quiet after that.

Kerry and I exchange another look, but it's obvious that's all Taylor will say on the subject, so I step around her and open the door.

When I first became friends with Kerry and Taylor, I was shy to show them my house. It's pretty small with just one floor that consists of the living room when you first walk in, followed by the kitchen right behind it, and a hallway to the left that goes to the bathroom, my room, and Ma's room. That's it. No second floor. No basement.

I remember asking Ma once why we didn't move somewhere else after she got her new, as she put it, "high-paying job," but then she asked me what we would do with a bigger house if it was just the two of us anyway. I couldn't really argue with that.

We all kick off our shoes by the big brown leather couch next to the door, and I grab three of the many throw pillows; tucking them under our heads, we form a circle on the floor, staring up at the popcorn ceiling.

"So, besides Amira, how was your first day?" Taylor asks.

"It wasn't really my first day," I say, for what feels like the hundredth time. "It was only a training day."

"Good movie. Denzel in his prime," she replies.

Kerry cozies up beside me. "But most importantly, did you find out if you get free movie tickets?"

The question comes out soft and hesitant, as if she's not sure

63

if she's allowed to ask me for things yet. Now I feel even more guilty for making such a big deal about the Amira thing. I hate making Kerry feel bad.

I reach out my hand, threading my fingers through hers, and give her hand a little squeeze. Kerry turns slightly toward me, and out of the corner of my eye, I see her lips tilt up in a small smile. She squeezes my hand back but doesn't let go, and her hand remains rested on top of mine on the floor between us.

"No," I finally say. "It slipped my mind, sorry."

Kerry's twists brush my shoulders as she shakes her head.

"No worries. It's still so cool that you work there. Isn't it amazing?" Kerry says.

"Yeah, actually, it is pretty cool." And I mean it. The artwork is stunning, and the history of the place is kind of amazing. While some of my coworkers leave something to be desired, at least Jennie and Lisa were nice. "I was a little worried because my actual boss, Glory, seemed like a bit of a space cadet, but it's possible I was being a little judgy because of their Crocs."

"You? Judging someone before getting to know them? Shocking." Taylor laughs.

"That's a dollar in the sarcasm jar." Kerry holds out her free hand, palm outstretched.

Taylor fishes out a dollar from the back pocket of her jeans and hands it over.

"*Anyway*," I continue. "The point is they seem okay enough. Their uncles apparently own Horizon, which is interesting."

Kerry sits up quickly, breaking our forgiveness hand sandwich, and I am amazed at her core strength. She turns, and then her face is inches above mine, twists tickling my cheeks. "Your boss is related to Derek and Eric?"

"Yes?"

"Oh my God, they're amazing." Kerry squeals way too loudly. I cover my ears until she stops and keeps talking. "I heard they both ended up working on Broadway as actors but moved back here to save Horizon. They used all their Broadway money, which honestly probably wasn't much, to buy it and restore it."

"Hm, Glory did not mention *that* in their story."

Kerry finally sits back, now using her pillow as a seat, and takes my hand in hers again, this time holding it tightly in her lap as her eyes bore into mine. Honestly, I'm slightly frightened by the intensity. "You have to meet them and then introduce me. They could be the stepping stone to my first big break."

Taylor flips over so she's lying on her stomach, facing us. "How can you have a 'first' big break? Shouldn't you only have one of those?"

"Hush. Do not speak on what you don't understand."

"Okay, prima donna."

Kerry is still gripping my hand, so I try to wriggle free, but she won't budge. Her eyes are still fixed on mine, as determined as ever.

"Promise me, Rochelle. You must make them love you so they will in turn love me."

"Kerry, they weren't even there today." I finally pull free. I also sit up, pulling my legs under me.

"You'll be there all summer! You'll see them eventually!"

"You really want me to go to my boss's boss's bosses and

basically slide them your résumé?"

"Nooooo." She drags the word out dramatically. "Just meet them, chitchat, and casually, when the moment is right, tell them you have a friend who's about to be a huge star and you're giving them first dibs on seeing my audition tape."

"Wow." Taylor rolls her eyes.

"Promise me, Rochelle," Kerry repeats. "I will owe you my firstborn child for this."

"I don't want kids."

"My firstborn dog, then."

I mull this over, and then nod. I have always wanted a dog, but Ma is allergic. Allegedly.

"Fine. If, and only if, they make an appearance at the theater, I will do my absolute best to talk you up."

"Shake on it."

Kerry thrusts out her hand and I'm a little nervous to entrust my hand to her again, but I take hers in mine.

When we're finished shaking hands, Taylor turns to me. "Okay, now that that's settled, are we allowed to talk about the elephant in the room?"

"What elephant?"

Taylor quirks an eyebrow. "The elephant that is Amira being the boss of you for the whole summer."

"She's not the boss of me." I pause because that's not entirely true. "She's just . . . my boss. Kind of."

Kerry winces. "Yeah, there is no way this ends well."

"It'll be fine. We'll both just be professional."

Taylor and Kerry exchange a look but say nothing.

66

"What?"

Another look is exchanged.

"What?"

"Remember when you and Amira were partnered up to do an experiment in AP chem and you almost blew up the science lab?"

I don't know why Kerry has to bring up that specific incident. But I bite. ". . . Yes."

"Just like that, this isn't going to end well," Taylor declares, pursing her lips. "I'm calling it now."

Jeez, a little faith from my two best friends would've been nice. At least Kerry adds a good luck and a thumbs-up. I fall back on my pillow and groan.

SEVEN

MY FIRST REAL DAY OF work is chaotic, to say the least.

Me, Amira, Jennie, and Danny are running concessions, and it is nonstop customers all day long. Every time I think things are slowing down, a new group of people come in for the next movie, and we're running around again like headless chickens.

I know I can be a picky eater, but these people? Wow. One person asks for a hot dog with nothing on it and no bun.

"Sooo, he just wants a plain hot dog?" I ask Amira to confirm.

"Yes," she says without even looking up.

"Right." Gross!

Though I'll never say so out loud, I am glad Amira and Danny are around. If Jennie and I had to manage the register and try to put orders together, we'd probably fall to our knees and scream in agony. Maybe Kerry's dramatics are rubbing off on me too much, but my point stands.

I'm barely surviving, and I think Jennie is actually struggling even more than I am. She truly has the worst case of butter fingers I've ever seen. She's dropped three bags of popcorn and two hot dog orders. Statistically, that's very improbable for one person to do in one day, much less during one shift.

Meanwhile, Amira and Danny are pros. Though Danny is still wearing his sunglasses and gives off the vibe that he'd rather be asleep or literally anywhere but here, he knows what he's doing. And Amira is Amira. Every time Jennie and I make a mistake, she's right there behind us to pick up our slack or apologize profusely to a customer. Once someone asked for the manager and I froze, until she was suddenly standing next to me and saying, "You can speak with me."

The way she handles the customers is pretty impressive, but that is also something I'll be keeping to myself. I can't give her that satisfaction.

Things are finally slowing down after the afternoon rush, so Amira tells Jennie and me to take our lunch break, thank God. Even though I'm wearing my most comfortable sneakers, my feet are killing me. There is nowhere to sit behind this counter, and even if there was, we'd never have time to use it. I haven't been this active since my last gym class, which was only a couple of months ago but feels like a different lifetime.

Plus, working with food all day has me starving.

Jennie and I barely finish grabbing food for ourselves before a stampede of angry parents, dragging their crying kids along behind them, come storming out of theater 2.

One mother, presumably the leader of the pack, stops in front of Amira.

Amira stands up straighter and uses her perfect customer-service voice.

"Hi, how can I help you?"

"Are you the one in charge here?" the lady barks.

Amira glances quickly across the room at the employee office before saying, "Yes, what's going on?"

"I brought my daughter here to watch the new Disney movie, so why on God's good green earth are you playing some gritty, violent detective film in there?"

Amira can't even say anything because now the other parents are gathering around, talking over each other. Jennie and I exchange glances. Meanwhile, Danny is off to the side of the counter, talking to a tall, thin white guy with a patchy beard and short, curly hair. I think Danny may even be smiling, which is rare since he usually looks bored.

As Danny says goodbye, I catch the guy's name is Pete. I store this information away, curious to know who this person is that gets a reaction out of the typically unbothered Danny. I thought only Brigit could do that. Now's not the time to ask though.

"Should we get Glory?" I whisper to Danny once his friend is gone.

Danny shrugs in response, any hint of a smile gone. So helpful.

I'm about to go to the office to find Glory when Amira speaks. "Okay! Okay!" She holds up her hands in the universal sign for stop, and surprisingly the parents listen.

Amira turns to Danny. "Can you go find out who's running the projector in theater two and figure out why the wrong movie is showing and get the right one on in there, please?"

Danny is about to take off when Amira grabs his arm. "And make sure whatever theater *Shaft* is supposed to be playing in, it's actually on."

Danny makes a clicking sound with his mouth and flashes finger guns before running off to theater 2. That boy is a riddle wrapped in a mystery.

Amira turns back to the parents. "I am so sorry about this major misstep, and we will get this all sorted out ASAP. In the meantime, please feel free to enjoy our arcade and you can each get a complimentary soda or candy, on me." She looks at me and Jennie. "Can you guys please get them the drink or candy of their choice?"

I look down at the beautiful plate of cheesy nachos I've just crafted that will probably morph into a solid state by the time I get back to it, but what choice do we have? So much for a lunch break. Jennie and I reluctantly nod. The parents, who are still grumpy but at least somewhat satisfied, begin stepping up to the counter to make their requests.

We're just about done with the parents and their kids, when I feel my phone vibrate in my pocket. Based on the way Jennie and Amira both stop in their tracks, I already know this has to be a text in our work group chat.

Yesterday I got added to the Horizon Cinema Summer Team chat by Glory. At first, I was irritated that Glory clearly took our phone numbers from our applications and put us all in a chat without asking our permission, but logically it makes sense for us to all have one place to communicate about any and all work-related issues. The problem is Shawn decided to use that chat as a jumping-off point to make a separate chat, Movies That Feel Like Movies, whatever that means, without Glory, where he could basically text us any of his thoughts and feelings at any point in the day. This morning he let us know he was eating oatmeal with blueberries before coming in.

Obviously, I have that chat muted.

We all pull out our phones to see a text from Glory.

Glory: Emergency in the men's restroom. Whoever's closest and available, please come ASAP.

All three of us look up simultaneously and then over at the men's restroom. Without hesitation, Amira puts a finger on her nose and screams, "Not it!" Jennie is quicker on the uptake than I am, and her finger is already on her nose and she's saying "Not it" too, before I've even registered what just happened.

"No way." I shake my head. "I cannot go in there."

"And yet you must." Amira smiles.

I keep shaking my head. Just the thought of going in there is making me feel nauseous, and I don't even know what's in there yet.

"No, seriously, I cannot go in there," I say again.

Amira tilts her head, eyes narrowed as she inspects me. My arms are now crossed around my stomach, and I close my eyes, trying to think about literally anything else to prevent bile from rising up my throat.

"Why not?"

I hesitate. I could tell her I am prone to throwing up quite easily and would probably make whatever situation is going on in the bathroom even worse, but telling Amira that makes me itch with discomfort. She already knows way too much about me as it is, and I don't want to give her more ammo.

I open my eyes, shake out my limbs, and take a deep breath, in and out. "Never mind."

"Why do you look like you're about to go to war?" Amira asks.

She and Jennie are both looking at me like I've grown another head, but I don't care. I feel better. Kind of. So, it's working.

"Because I am." I pull my T-shirt over my nose, holding it there, and march out from under the counter toward the men's restroom without looking back.

Even with my shirt over my face, I can smell it as soon as I open the door.

"Oh my God," I gasp, then gag.

Stepping in a bit farther, I see Glory standing in front of the urinals. Inching toward them from the stalls is water filled with God only knows what.

I'm definitely going to be sick. I back up to the door, pulling it open to stick my head out, and take a deep breath of clean air before covering my face again with my shirt. When I go back in, I only go far enough so that Glory can see me and wave until I get their attention.

"Oh, hi. I've already called the plumber to figure out what's going on in the first stall, but the second seems like some kid stuffed it with paper towels and God knows what else. We need to clean this mess up."

"We?" I honestly don't know how I can be expected to clean when I'll need at least one hand to hold my shirt up over my nose.

"Yes, remember how I said cleaning was part of the job?"

"I do, but—"

"Right, so head to the office and get the mop, bucket, gloves, and some soap, please?" The bags under Glory's eyes look deeper, and their voice is soft but stern. This situation's definitely drained them of their energy, and I want to help, not be another problem. So I accept that this is just going to be something I have to endure.

"And also, the Caution sign. The last thing we need is anyone coming in here."

I barely catch the end of what they're saying as I happily escape and go back to the food counter. For once, I'm glad to see Danny has returned. Perhaps I don't have to do this after all. I run up to him like he's a life preserver and I'm drowning. "Danny, Glory told me to tell you to get the mop and bucket from the office and help them in the bathroom."

"No, she did not." Amira steps up beside Danny, her arms crossed. This close, I can smell her perfume again. It's still the sweet cake-like smell from training day but different.

God, she smells so good. In comparison to the bathroom, I mean.

"Why would Glory tell you to specifically get Danny to do this job?" she presses.

"Because it's in the men's bathroom." I must've taken too long a pause because Amira's not buying it.

"If they specifically wanted a guy to do it, they would've said that when they texted."

"True," Danny agrees. Of course, now he speaks.

"Just go get the mop and bucket so this mess can be cleaned up quickly. You're wasting time. Do your job." It's the first time I've heard Amira's voice get so serious, and honestly it throws me off-balance. This is not the laidback, carefree Amira I've come to somewhat know against my will; this is an Amira who means business.

I'm not entirely sure what to make of this, so I look to Jennie for help, but she's chowing down on a hot dog, and even that is making me nauseous. Bye-bye, appetite.

I glare at Amira before doing as I'm told.

I see the mop, bucket, and soap as soon as I walk in, but it takes me about five minutes to locate the Caution sign, sandwiched between the wall and the desk. It's a struggle to get everything back to the bathroom, and I have to pretend like I don't feel Amira, Danny, and Jennie watching me walk past concessions. By the time I get back to the bathroom, I open the door to find Shawn has replaced Glory.

"What are you doing here? Where's Glory?" I put down the Caution sign just outside the bathroom door and then push the mop, bucket, and soap past the threshold while I stay on the other side, covering my nose and mouth with my shirt again.

"The plumber called so Glory went to go talk to him, and Amira sent me over as soon as I clocked in."

"Wow, well, welcome to the chaos."

Shawn laughs. "Thank you. Amira told me about the mix-up

in theater two. Thankfully, that's fixed now, but Glory looks one incident away from completely losing their shit."

"Ugh, please do not say shit with all of this in here."

Shawn laughs again. "Sorry."

He grabs the bucket and goes to the sink to fill it up. "Well, at least one of the stalls was an easy fix with the plunger," he says, once the bucket is filled. "And the second stall's issue isn't with the pipes."

I remember Glory mentioning the toilet being purposefully clogged, so I just nod, only paying attention to half of what he's saying. The mantra *don't throw up, don't throw up, don't throw up* is on repeat in my head.

Shawn looks over at me and grins. I imagine I look atrocious right now with my Horizon shirt half covering my face and sweat beading down my forehead.

"I can handle this myself if you want to head back to concessions," he says.

"Really?" I'm so surprised, I let go of my shirt for a split second, but it's enough to take in the smells. I gag a little, but Shawn looks completely unbothered.

"How are you breathing right now?" I ask.

Shawn shrugs. "Honestly, I think the locker room at school smells about the same."

"That is the most distressing thing I've ever heard."

"Just go." He waves me away. "I've got this."

He does not have to tell me twice.

"Thank you, I owe you one." I'm almost halfway out the door when his next words stop me.

"Get me another date with Taylor, and we can call it even."

"You still have a crush on her?"

"'Crush' is a strong word. But yeah."

I'm honestly shocked. I study him, looking for any telltale signs that he's joking, but he looks completely genuine as he leans on the mop, his cheeks slightly redder than they were a moment ago.

"I can't make any promises," I warn. "But I'll talk to her."

"That's all I ask." He flashes me a smile that reminds me once again why everyone loves him.

I leave him with the shitty bathroom situation and make my way back to my own shitty situation with Amira at concessions.

EIGHT

AFTER MA PICKS ME UP and takes me home, I don't remember much except eating some food and crashing into my bed. Apparently I didn't even shower or get out of my clothes, because when I wake up the next morning, I'm still wearing my Horizon uniform.

My limbs are screaming at me, and while I know that the best course of action is not to move for the rest of my life, I resist their cries and grab my phone.

I blink at the screen trying to make sense of it. It's already after ten in the morning. I've always been a morning person, much to my mother's chagrin. Even when I don't have school, the latest I'll get up is eight a.m. I, Rochelle Marie Coleman, do not sleep in. Except apparently, this morning I do.

I'm struggling to push myself upright when there's a knock at my door.

"Come in."

Ma pushes my door open and stands in my doorway. Her silk press is gone, and her natural hair is now in cornrows.

She's wearing her best yoga gear, which includes a yoga mat tucked under her arm. Based on the sweat stains on her clothes, I'm assuming she's coming back from a class and not going to one.

"Oh, good! You're up," she says. "I was beginning to worry. You never sleep this late."

"I know," I groan. "Why didn't you wake me?"

Ma shrugs. "Looked like you needed the rest. You do realize you're still wearing the same clothes from yesterday, don't you?"

"Yeah, I was too tired to take them off."

"Well, make sure to wash your sheets. And your clothes. It's smelling like popcorn and hot dog water in here. Did they only give you the one shirt?"

I nod, barely able to move. I have been ended by a job I didn't even want. I should probably have Kerry write my eulogy now. How will I survive a whole summer of this?

"That's going to be a lot of laundry." I look over and she's frowning now.

Realistically, since I'll be working at least five shifts a week, the odds of me actually washing the shirt before every shift may be slim, but I know better than to say that. Ma puts cleanliness right next to godliness, and while I love things to be organized, I also don't mind an organized mess from time to time. Ma does not agree.

"Did you have a yoga class this morning?" I ask, even though the answer is obvious.

She nods. "Sunrise yoga. I was opposed to it at first since personally I believe nothing should happen before the sun is up, but Luisa convinced me it'd be fun, and she was unfortunately right."

I should've known if Ma was doing anything at the crack of dawn, it would be with Luisa. Over the years Luisa has convinced my mother to step out of her comfort zone to try dancing, scuba diving, karate, and they even skydived once, though my mother swears she will absolutely never do that again.

"Amira came too," Ma adds. "I would've invited you, but you were still sleeping when I left, and I didn't want to wake you."

"Amira was there?"

"Yep." Ma steps into my room and then promptly sits on my bed, sweat and all. I pull my legs up and out of the way.

"Ew, Ma! Why?"

"You have to clean these sheets anyway." She lets her yoga mat fall to the floor and pulls up one of her legs underneath her, letting the other hang off the side of the bed.

"So, Amira said you had a good first day."

It takes everything in me not to roll my eyes. Of course, not only was Amira somehow able to get up and do yoga this morning, but she also reported back to our moms about my career progress. Perfect.

"It was fine." I shrug. "I told you that yesterday when you picked me up."

"Yes, but you didn't really give me any details." She has that look on her face that lets me know she won't be dropping this.

"There's not much to say. I worked concessions all day, doing all the food and candy stuff. It was fine."

"Well, Amira said you did great."

I scoff. "She did not."

Ma pins me with a hard look. "She did."

I break eye contact first, turning my head down as I turn my phone over in my hands.

"Rochelle, I do not pry into the goings-on between you and Amira." Ma's voice is gentle. "I never have. Luisa and I decided a long time ago that whatever issues you girls have are none of our business, which is why we stopped trying to push you two together.

"However, from where I'm standing, that girl has been nothing but nice to you, so what is it that I'm missing?"

I can't very well tell Ma that I once told Amira I didn't think we could be friends because she "lacked drive and focus." Ma wouldn't understand. She already thinks my obsession with going to Wharton is "misplaced" and claims she'll be happy with whatever college I decide to go to. I've never believed her. I've seen the picture of me, Ma, and my dad all in Wharton tees at the school. She's told me about how she and my dad would talk about showing me around one day and pointing out the spot where they first met and fell in love.

Wharton is where I belong, and so that's where I'm going to go, no matter what it takes to get there. And that means *not* being friends with someone like Amira, who would only be a distraction.

I'm smart enough to know I can't say all that though. So instead, I just shrug. "It's complicated."

Ma gives me another look that makes it clear that is not enough of an explanation for her, so I sigh.

"She just—" I close my eyes and heave out a breath. "We just don't click. We're too different. That's all."

"Different how? You're both young, intelligent Black women. What more do you need?"

"Technically, Amira is Cuban and Puerto Rican," I counter. "And you know that is not enough to base a friendship on."

"First, she's Afro-Cuban and Afro–Puerto Rican, which means she's Black, and I know you know that, so don't play with me." Ma's tone is firm and unyielding, so I know I've gone a step too far and I can feel the guilt bubbling up inside me.

"Sorry," I mumble.

It's not my best apology, but Ma accepts it with a nod, pushing on.

"Second, I think that's plenty to build a friendship on. All you need is one thing. You know how Luisa and I became friends."

"Yes." She's only told me this story a hundred times. "It was right after we moved here. You were in the grocery store with me, and you just started crying. Everyone else ignored you, but then this really nice lady named Luisa approached you, asked if you were okay, and then took us home and brought you groceries the next day. You've been friends ever since."

I recite the story with the diction of a teacher reading the Declaration of Independence, and Ma gives me a look like she's not amused, but I can't help it. I love that Ma has a friend in Luisa. Ma was young when she had me. She was literally pregnant when she and my dad graduated from Wharton, and rather than pursue her dreams of going to law school, she instead got married to my dad and raised me while he got a job at a consulting firm in Manhattan.

Most of Ma's friends from that time could barely understand her life as a wife and mom, and then when she became a widow, they understood her life even less. We have family, but most of them are scattered across the US, and Ma's an only child, so she was pretty much on her own until Luisa came along. It was Luisa who helped Ma study for the LSATs, get into law school, and finally get her degree. All while keeping a roof over our heads.

Their bond is unbreakable, and I love that for them, truly. But Amira and I are not them, and we never will be.

"I have Kerry and Taylor. They are the fierce Black girl-friends I need," I say.

Ma pushes herself up so she's standing in front of me and puts her hands on my shoulders. "You can never have too many friends, Rochelle," she says. "Moreover, whether you like it or not, you will be spending a lot of time with Amira this summer. Don't you think it would make both your lives easier if you at least tried to find some common ground with her?"

My first thought is to say no. I like this cold war between us. It drives me. Occasionally, it is exhausting, especially when it seems like no one else seems as bothered by Amira as I am. Even though Kerry and Taylor have never really complained, I've learned to tamp down my Amira rants, writing most of them in my journal when the need arises so I don't annoy them.

Okay, maybe there's a sliver of a possibility that Ma has a point.

"I'll think about it." I hope this satisfies her, and I think it does, because she has the audacity to hug me, sweat and all.

"That's all I ask."

"Ugh, Ma, no, you smell."

"I'm not the one who didn't shower after working all day yesterday," she singsongs into my hair, pulling me up so I'm standing with her. Ma hugs me tighter, turning me around in a circle, until I finally hug her back. She drops her arms and gives me a wicked grin. "You're welcome."

"I absolutely did not say thank you." I pull my shirt up and take a whiff of it and then full-body shiver. Whether it's Ma's fault or my own, I do smell.

"I'll save you some hot water."

"Thanks," I grumble as she leaves.

I fall back on my bed and start counting the glow-in-the-dark stars that have been on my ceiling for as long as I can remember. They don't even glow anymore, but I can never seem to find the energy or heart to take them down. Instead, I find myself counting them over and over again while I think or de-stress after doing hours of homework. For whatever reason, looking at the stars almost always helps.

Right now, though, I can't stop thinking about what Ma said and what I'm going to do when I see Amira at our next shift.

NINE

I ONLY GET A TWO-DAY reprieve from Horizon before it's time to return for my next shift. The days off are almost enough rest for the soreness in my muscles to have gone away. That is, as long as I don't move too much. Who knew working at a movie theater would be such a workout?

Ma drops me off at the theater again, and this time Amira is already there, standing in front of the doors when we pull up. Instead of wearing her work shirt, she has a spaghetti strap tank tucked into her khaki pants, her thick curls are pulled up into space buns, and she's got a tote bag that has clearly seen better days hanging from her shoulder. She looks nice if you're into glistening brown skin and rosy cheeks, I suppose.

Amira waves to my mom as I get out and Ma waves back. She's heading into work early today because she needs to prep for a big meeting with a client. Her train into Manhattan leaves in about fifteen minutes, so there's no time for chitchat. Still, that doesn't stop her from giving me a pointed look and saying, "Have a good day!" before she pulls off.

As soon as Ma's car exits the lot, Amira's smile falls as she looks me over from the top of my head down to my scuffed-up sneakers. I can't help but feel like I always come up short, both literally and figuratively, and I hate that she makes me feel that way. I cross my arms over my chest, a defiant shield against her, but it does nothing to block the sweet bakery scent the wind blows my way. I wonder if she bathes in vanilla or something.

Wait, no, I don't need thoughts of her bathing. No thank you.

I want to say something, anything, to try to clear the already tense atmosphere between us, but nothing comes to mind. Even though I currently have about fifty unread messages from the Movies That Feel Like Movies chat, I haven't actually spoken to Amira or anyone from work since Saturday. In hindsight, I probably should've at least glanced at the messages before coming in today but, alas, it's too late now.

"How are you feeling?" she asks.

I realize a second too late that Amira is speaking to me, and now she's looking at me impatiently.

"Oh, I'm good. How are you?"

Amira rolls her eyes. "I mean how is your body feeling after working your first full shift on Saturday?"

"Oh, right." Her question surprises me, and a part of me wonders why she cares. But in an effort to keep the peace or whatever it was Ma asked me to do, I proceed as if this is a genuine question.

"I'm okay. I was a little sore, but I'm good now."

A little is the understatement of the century, but she doesn't need to know that.

"Good." Amira turns away from me to open the door. "We have a lot of work to do today, so you don't want to start off in bad shape. Glory's already inside."

Ah, the real reason for the question. Glad to know Amira isn't going soft—she simply wants to make sure I'm still useful. Honestly, I kind of respect it.

I follow her in and see Brigit, Jennie, and Lisa are already sitting on the red benches. The twins are chitchatting about something, and Brigit is texting like her life depends on it. They're all in uniform, but each one has their hair up in space buns. Theirs look a bit smaller than Amira's, presumably because their hair isn't as thick. Why do they all have the same hairstyle today?

"*Space Jam* started playing this week." Amira stands beside me. "*Space Jam*. Space buns."

"I got it, thanks." The irritation is clear in my voice, but I can't hide it. The hair thing is whatever, but I somehow missed that the monthly classic had switched over now that it's July. I hate not knowing things.

Amira's eyes drift up to the top of my head again like she did earlier, and I realize now she's examining my go-to high ponytail.

"I'm assuming you didn't check the group chat," she says.

"You didn't put it in the official one."

"Technically, I think both chats are official work chats," Amira says. "And also, this was Jennie and Lisa's idea, not mine."

At the sound of their names, the twins look up and smile at us until they see my hair.

"Where are your buns?" Lisa sounds genuinely distressed as she and Jennie walk over. Jennie, however, snorts out a laugh.

"I think her buns are where everyone's buns are."

Lisa smacks her sister's arm. "Grow up."

"I didn't know we were doing space buns," I whine. I feel my face getting hot. On Saturday, at least Jennie, Lisa, and I were the newbies together. Today, I'm the odd one out.

"I put it in the chat!" Lisa holds up her phone.

"Rochelle doesn't check the chat," Amira chimes in, oh so helpfully.

I glare at her. This seriously can't be how my shift starts. "I check the work chat, but I assumed the one Shawn made wasn't for work-related content, so I didn't need to read it regularly," I try explaining.

"'Work-related content'?"

This comes from Brigit, who has now looked up from her phone long enough to join the conversation.

"Rochelle only pays attention to things that have to do with school and work," Amira explains. "Anything else she finds superfluous."

"SAT word," I say under my breath, out of habit. Amira hears me and grins proudly.

"Okay, well, we can fix this," Lisa says.

I'm about to protest that my hair doesn't need fixing, when Glory appears from the office, their locs also up in two messy buns.

"You've got to be kidding me! They're not even in the chat," I say, exasperated.

"What chat?" Glory asks, when they reach our little group.

Everyone looks at me, and I know I've fucked up. No one wants to know there's a separate chat that doesn't include them, even if it is your boss.

"The chat me and the girls have without the boys." Amira comes up beside me, looping her arm through mine as if we're the closest friends. Her touch startles me. "Isn't that right, Rochelle?"

I quickly nod, and Amira turns her most charming smile full force on Glory.

"We were just about to pull Rochelle into the bathroom and help her get her braids up into buns. Be back in a sec."

Before I can argue, Amira is pulling me away to the bathroom, with Brigit, Jennie, and Lisa on our heels. Once we're all inside, I pull my arm free from Amira.

"I don't have an extra scrunchie," I say, exasperated by the whole ordeal.

"I do," Brigit, Jennie, Lisa, and Amira all say in unison, holding out their wrists.

Next thing I know I'm being guided over to the mirror above the sinks, and though I've just met most of these girls less than a week ago, I let them transform my ponytail into two surprisingly neat space buns on the top of my head. I have to figure out how to return all these scrunchies to their proper owners later, but for now no one seems to care about that. We look at ourselves in the mirror.

"Wow, these look really cute." I hate to admit it, but they deserve the credit. "Thank you."

"Don't sound so surprised." Amira gives me a gentle nudge. The brief contact of her shoulder against mine is . . . not entirely unpleasant.

Lisa's and Brigit's "You're welcome" thankfully stops me from dwelling on that thought. Meanwhile, Jennie just shrugs.

"Let's go take a picture with Glory before our shift starts." Lisa pulls her phone out.

"Glory hates pictures," Amira says. "But they'll take one of us."

"It's so sad." Brigit's eyes are shiny like she may actually shed tears. "Everyone should want their photo taken."

For fear of Brigit trying to give me a pep talk, I refrain from saying I am also camera shy. It'll be much easier to take the photo than convince them I don't need to be in it.

Amira throws on her Horizon tee over her tank top. "Shall we? They'll probably come looking for us soon if we don't head back out there."

We all gather our things and find Glory waiting for us by concessions. Just as Amira said, when Lisa suggests we all take a photo, Glory politely declines, volunteering to take a photo of the group of us outside in front of the *Space Jam* poster. Amira gives us an "I told you so" look behind their back as we file outside. It feels conspiratorial, like we're all in on this secret together or something. And at some point, as we're taking pictures, posing in various different ways until Glory is satisfied, I realize I'm having an okay time.

My smile in the photos becomes genuine, and when Lisa takes her phone back from Glory and shows us the pics, we don't look half-bad.

After our photo shoot, the morning goes by in a blur. It's a Tuesday, which means most people are at work, but kids and teens are out of school, so there's still a pretty solid stream of traffic. Thankfully, it's nothing like Saturday. Today it's just me, Amira, Jennie, and Lisa handling concessions, and Brigit is scanning people's tickets. Shawn appeared right before the first showing to help Glory make sure every theater is playing the movie it's supposed to.

"Did Glory ever find out what happened with the projector?" I ask Amira while wiping down the counter. Some kid was too impatient to wait for his mom to hand him his drink, and his attempt to grab it off the counter ended with him knocking it over instead.

Amira looks surprised. Probably since I've asked her a question not dripping in sarcasm, and I'm slightly surprised myself.

"Unfortunately, no," she replies.

She glances around as if to make sure no one's listening, but the only people paying attention are me and Lisa, who's stepped closer to listen in. Jennie disappeared to the bathroom five minutes ago, and Lisa thinks she's watching one of her dramas in there.

"Jerry didn't know how the movies could've gotten switched," Amira continues. "He put in the right movie and even stayed in the projection room through most of the trailers before he went to make sure the next movie in theater one was set up correctly."

Jerry's the projection guy for Horizon. Saturday was the first time I'd seen him, and I could tell he spent most of his time in dark theaters. He kind of looks like Shaggy from *Scooby-Doo*, all tall and lanky, but his skin is so pale he's almost translucent. He also wears square-rimmed glasses, and his dark brown hair is long and greasy. He looks to be around Glory's age, if not older. When we met, he ended up telling me, Amira, Danny, and Jennie more about movie projectors than I ever cared to know.

He's not here all the time, since we usually can get the movies rolling by ourselves, but he pops in every now and then to help out if things get too busy.

"Weird." Lisa leans against a counter, popping a piece of gum in her mouth. "So, do you think someone went in and switched them?"

"It's possible, but it's not like a regular person would even know how to get into the projection room," Amira says. "I mean unless it was—"

Amira cuts herself off, and Lisa and I exchange a look as Amira shakes her head.

"Never mind," she says quickly, almost too quickly. I eye her but I'm not entirely sure what I'm looking for and Amira presses on. "I don't know why someone would want to do something like that."

"Maybe it was a prank," I offer. "Everybody's out of school and bored."

"True."

Now, I'm surprised by Amira agreeing with me, and of course she clocks it.

"Yes, you can be right occasionally. Don't act all surprised."

The corner of her mouth lifts in a small smile, revealing one of her dimples. Did I know she had dimples? I can't remember. Why am I still looking at her face? I turn away, dropping the dishrag I was using in the small bucket of soapy water we keep under the counter for emergencies like this.

"Lisa, can you go find your sister?" Amira orders. "Unless she is having some kind of emergency in there, she should've been back by now."

Lisa solemnly nods and ducks out under the counter, leaving me and Amira alone. For the first time today, I wish we had a customer so at least I'd have something to do instead of standing here awkwardly. But no one walks through the front doors or comes out of the theaters to buy something. So I'm on my own.

I pull out my phone, deciding now's a good time to catch up on the group chat. I've barely begun scrolling when Lisa runs back out of the bathroom.

"It's Shark Week!"

Amira and I exchange confused glances. Finally, I speak up.

"You mean that thing they do on the Discovery Channel?"

"No," Lisa hissed, leaning over the counter. "I mean it's Shark Week for Jennie!"

Amira and I must still look confused, because Lisa huffs out an exasperated sigh and then leans over the counter, motioning us closer. "She got her period," she whispers. "And there are no supplies in there."

"Ohhh," Amira and I say. This is truly an embarrassing showing for us, two of the smartest people in our year. Allegedly.

"Can I go run over to the mall and grab her something to change into and some pads?" Lisa is frantic now.

Amira looks around the empty lobby and then nods. "Just hurry back, please."

"For sure." Lisa looks relieved. "Can you pass me my bag, please?"

I reach down and grab her drawstring backpack. It's barely in her grasp before she's taking off.

"Shark Week? I don't think I've ever heard it called that before," Amira says.

I turn to Amira, and I can see the barely contained laugh all over her face.

"It's not funny. We've all been there, and you know it," I say, but there's a laugh creeping up my throat.

"I just don't know why she had to say it like that." She lets loose a giggle, and it's an annoyingly cute sound.

"Me either."

And then we're both laughing, bent over at the waist, tears in our eyes. By the time we come up for air, Amira's face is blotchy and red, and my stomach hurts. As our laughter dies down, we stand there looking at each other, not sure what to do next. We just had a laughing fit. Together. Kind of like friends do.

Except we're not friends.

Because I don't like her.

Right?

But then I think about what Ma said. How our lives would be easier if we just squash whatever issues we have with each other and work together this summer. We don't have to be friends, but we can be amicable at least. Amicable coworkers.

Amira finally breaks the silence. "I think I'll go check on Jennie."

"Oh, okay."

Amira waits a second, as if she's waiting for me to say more, but any words I attempt to form feel caught in my throat. She's lifting the flip-up section on the counter when I finally get the courage.

"I'm sorry about what I said during training," I say.

Amira stops and turns to look at me. When the silence stretches on, she raises one of her perfectly manicured brows. "Is that all?"

Of course, she's not going to make this easy for me. A bubble of irritation threatens to pop inside me, but I push it down. "I'm sorry that I said that I didn't think this job would be too hard—"

"I think what you said was it wouldn't be 'too difficult to *manage.*'"

God, she's so annoying.

"Right, and I can see now that it is not a simple job and so I'm sorry. And I don't want to fight with you anymore. At least not at work." I jut out my hand then, waiting for her to shake it, but Amira just looks down at it and then back at me. "You're supposed to shake it."

"Yeah, no, I got that. I'm just thinking."

"About what?"

"If I want to shake it."

I swallow a groan of frustration and instead plaster the best smile I can to my face.

"I am offering an olive branch." I extend my hand out a bit farther. "Calling a truce, if you will. We don't have to be friends. Just amicable coworkers."

"Oh, yes, of course, because you'd never want to be friends with me."

That throws me off. Is she referencing what I said in ninth grade? That was so long ago, and she can barely tolerate me now anyway, so why would she want to be friends? "You don't need me as a friend. You've got plenty of those. I'm just saying for the time we're at Horizon, we can be cool. Cool?"

Amira squints at me, still considering my offer. Finally, she slides her hand into mine, her thumb and fingers wrapping around the outside of my palm. I look down at our hands, almost the same size, hers about two shades lighter than mine, marred by tiny scars along her knuckles. Her skin is ridiculously soft and warm despite the AC being on full blast in here.

"Fine. We're cool," she says as we shake hands. She lets go and walks away without another word.

TEN

WORKING AT HORIZON MORPHS INTO a weekly montage, the routine like a film reel on a loop. God, I must be spending too much time at the theater if I'm making movie metaphors.

I'm paired with Amira during almost every shift, usually running concessions, though sometimes we're sent off to scan people's tickets or clean out the theaters. Thankfully, there's been nothing as disgusting as that bathroom debacle.

Our agreement to be at least cordial seems to work. Of course, we still have our moments, like when we got into an argument about how to pronounce caramel (for the record, it's "care-ah-mel," otherwise why would that second "a" be there in the middle?). But the good, or at least nonconfrontational, moments have begun to outweigh the bad. So much so that when I come in one Sunday and Glory sends me to the employee office to roll the quarters from the game machines with Amira, I don't even flinch.

Being alone with Amira for so long, I thought we'd either

work in silence or butt heads like we do whenever we're paired up in class. Instead, Amira plays music on her phone, and we somehow end up in a discussion about how Black female rappers all face the same issues, but in different ways. It was actually one of the most stimulating talks I've had in a while . . . and we didn't argue for once.

Shawn has also been interesting to work with. It's different than when I tutored him and had to explain differential equations. He's much less irksome when he's the one showing me how to do things. That is, when he's not asking me if I've talked to Taylor for him yet. He *has* reminded me that I still owe him for the bathroom mess. Other than that, he's honestly pretty fun to be around. His endless energy is infectious, and he's even made me laugh once or twice with his ridiculousness. I even almost said yes to Shawn's invite when he asked me to head out to Long Beach with him and Amira for the Fourth of July, but I had already made plans with Kerry and Taylor to have a Jordan Peele movie marathon that night. Kerry told me I could not continue working at Horizon without seeing the "classics," even if I had to watch them through my fingers.

I did not sleep well that night.

Jennie and Lisa are also cool. Though Jennie is determined to get me to watch a K-drama by the end of the summer. I'm not sure I can commit to something that has sixteen movie-length episodes, but she keeps swearing the episodes fly by.

And then there's Brigit and Danny. They're fine. They rarely interact with anyone who isn't each other. Amira and Glory seem to keep them apart for shifts, but there are only so many of us working here, so they have to overlap every now and again. I once caught them making out in one of the theaters they were supposed to be cleaning. While I'm a firm believer in minding my business, at-work fraternization is highly inappropriate. Still, I opted to tell Amira instead of Glory. Except Amira proceeded to go in there, drag Danny out, and make him update the movie times on the marquee.

It was all very dramatic. And funny.

Working at Horizon isn't as awful as I thought it would be. Still, I'm always happy for a day off.

But today my friends have betrayed me by making their own plans without me.

"What do you mean you're busy?" I'm sitting cross-legged on my bed, FaceTiming with Kerry and Taylor. It turns out they're currently in Central Park even though it is only ten in the morning.

"The Linda Lindas just finished performing, and they said they're going to be doing a signing and photos somewhere nearby afterward, so we're waiting for them to drop the info," Kerry explains. "We definitely told you about this."

"You definitely did not," I protest.

"We did." Taylor puts her face close to the camera, so all I can see is her eyes and nose. "You just forgot."

I frown. I am many things, but forgetful is not one of them. And yet as I rack my brain for any memory that could corroborate their story, I find nothing.

"Don't worry about it. You've been busy with work." Kerry pushes Taylor out of the way.

"Yeah, I guess."

"Did you want to come?" Kerry asks. "You don't like the Linda Lindas, and this *Good Morning America* concert thing started at the crack of dawn, so we figured you wouldn't be into it."

I'm not into it. Truly, it sounds like my worst nightmare. I can see swarms of people still milling around them. But I haven't had the chance to properly hang out with Kerry and Taylor that much outside of Jordan Peele night. We've all been busy doing our own things, and I miss them.

It feels silly to say all that though. They didn't purposely exclude me, even if it kind of feels like they did.

"It's fine." I give them a small smile. "I just wanted to hang out with you guys."

"We can catch up later," Kerry assures me.

"Once the signing is done," Taylor adds. "We don't have any more plans after that."

"Right, sure. Just let me know when you're back."

"We will!" Kerry gives me a thumbs-up before Taylor interrupts, pointing at her cell.

"They just posted. We gotta go."

"Oh my God, okay, bye, Roe," Kerry says, and the call has already ended before I can say bye back.

I toss my phone on my bed and lie down beside it, unsure what to do with myself. I've already finished all my summer work. I could do some more SAT prep, but they're all just the same questions asked in different ways. Scrolling through the Wharton website and application requirements again is an option, but I'm sure there's nothing there that I don't already know.

Next to me, my phone lights up and vibrates.

Amira: What are you doing?

I squint at my screen, reading and rereading the text, but it's still not making sense in my head. For a moment, panic surges through me. Did I have work today and I just forgot? Maybe Kerry and Taylor were right, and I am becoming forgetful. Otherwise, why is Amira texting me?

Amira: This isn't work-related.

Jeez, how does she do that? We're not even in the same room, and she's reading my mind. Terrifying.

Amira: Shawn's working today and most of my other friends are either away or at their own jobs. As my amicable coworker, are we allowed to hang out outside of work? I swear I won't tell anyone and ruin your street cred.

A snort of laughter escapes me before I can stop it. I stare at Amira's texts, thinking. We've been friendlier at work together, but this would be different. I would be *choosing* to fraternize with the enemy. On my day off, no less.

Amira: Stop overthinking and say yes so I can come get you. I'm already getting in my car.

It's massively unfair that she knows me this well.

Me: Okay, I'm in.

Malls are not my ministry.

I've never understood why going to the mall was considered a reasonable activity. There are so many people, so many different scents and smells wafting around, and you end up trying on a bunch of clothes that either don't fit or are too expensive to buy, and by the time it's over, you leave feeling sorry for yourself. It is an immense waste of time if you ask me.

And yet, somehow, I've let Amira drag me all the way to the Roosevelt Field mall. It's arguably the bigger and better mall on Long Island, but a much farther drive than if we had just gone to Green Acres. But Amira thought Green Acres was much too close to work to be a suitable excursion for our day off.

I genuinely can't even remember the last time I was over here. Whatever people who haven't grown up on Long Island think Long Island is, that's basically what I feel like when I go to Roosevelt Field. Almost everyone is white except for the people who work there, and the shops range from so cheap you'll have holes in that T-shirt before you leave the mall parking lot to uber-expensive designer brands.

With our measly paychecks, we could maybe get one or two

outfits from one of the bargain stores and grab some lunch, but that's about it. I'm already regretting being here, but as we walk into the mall, Amira's face lights up with excitement.

She's dressed down today, which surprises me. I figured since we didn't have to wear our uniforms, she'd wear one of the flowery dresses or skirts she typically wears at school whenever she's not wearing the dance team uniform or Shawn's jersey for a game. Today we're actually kind of matching. We both have on denim shorts (hers slightly shorter than mine), white T-shirts (hers plain, mine with little green alien heads all over it), and the same sneakers we wear to work (Nike high-tops for her, my comfy Adidas for me).

She is wearing matte red lipstick though, and as always there's a sugary-sweet scent wafting off her.

"Okay, so where do you want to go first?" Amira looks at me as we stand near a directory.

I'm surprised by the question. This wasn't my idea, and I'm really just along for the ride.

"Wherever you want to go." I shrug. "I'm probably not going to get anything."

"You don't have to buy anything. That's what window-shopping is."

The concept of window-shopping has never made sense to me. I don't want to try on things I can't take home with me. That's just setting myself up for disappointment.

I'm about to say as much when Amira's phone lights up in her hand with a call.

"Oh, hang on, it's my mom." She steps a few feet away, but I can still hear when she says, "Hi, Mamí. ¿Qué tal?"

That's about all I can understand as she continues the conversation in rapid-fire Spanish. I stare, surprised. It's not that I didn't know Amira could speak Spanish. I've been around her family at least a few times over the years, thanks to our moms.

However, I guess I haven't heard her use it in a while. Amira sounds different when she's speaking Spanish. I don't know how to explain it, but it's like she's livelier, softer. The words roll off her tongue, and she's more animated as she laughs at something her mom says on the phone.

When Amira hangs up, she finds me still staring and raises her perfectly shaped eyebrows. "What?"

"I forgot you speak Spanish."

"You . . . forgot?"

I don't know how to follow that up.

"Well, it's my first language, so yeah," Amira says. "Mom's Cuban, Dad's Puerto Rican. I speak Spanish. That's not weird."

She says it defensively, and I'm reminded of the stupid comment I made when Ma said Amira was Black. Does Amira actually think I have some issue with her being Latine? Guilt floods me again as I try to find the words to make it clear that that's not even close to how I feel.

"I didn't say it was weird. It's . . ."

Different. Interesting. Impressive.

"Cool," I say finally. "It's cool."

"Thanks."

Amira's looking at me as if the aliens on my shirt have taken control of my brain, and maybe they have, because since when do I get tongue-tied around Amira? It's *Amira*. Get ahold of yourself, Coleman.

"All right, well, what if we go to Claire's?" she asks.

I blink. "Huh?"

"Claire's," Amira says again. "The jewelry store. Please tell me you've been to Claire's before."

"Of course, I've been to Claire's."

"Great, let's go." She starts walking, expecting me to follow. I'm realizing she does this a lot. It's like she knows no matter what, people will listen and do as she says. She's not wrong, but a part of me resents the fact that I'm now one of those people too, trailing behind her like she's the Earth and I'm the moon caught in her orbit.

And yet I still follow her.

Claire's is on the complete opposite side of the mall and one flight up. When we get there, the place is surprisingly empty, with only the cashier at the register. They must use their store discount, because they've got piercings in each eyebrow, a nose piercing, and multiple hoops and studs in both of their ears.

"Hi," Amira says as we walk in.

The cashier gives us a small wave, before resuming playing on their cell phone. Clearly, they want to be here even less than I do.

Amira wanders over to the rotating stand of earrings, and I follow. On top is a little purple sign that says "Buy 2, get the third one FREE!" I don't think I've ever gone inside a Claire's that wasn't having a sale.

I glance around the store, taking everything in. I'm pretty sure the last time I was here was when Taylor decided she wanted her septum pierced. Thankfully, this place only does lobe piercings. Claire's is cute, but I would not trust them to actually pierce any part of my body. Taylor's moms ended up taking her to an actual piercer to get it done for her sixteenth birthday last year.

As I scan the place, my eyes catch on a wall of necklaces in the back. I walk over to inspect them closer. I'm not a big jewelry person. I only wear earrings for special occasions. My ears are pierced mainly because my mom did it when I was a baby, as most Black and brown mothers do. Besides that, I have one cross necklace my grandmother gave me ages ago and a mood ring Kerry got me when we were in the seventh grade. I'm sure if it ever did work, it certainly doesn't now.

Along the wall, there's one necklace that catches my eye. It's a gold chain with a butterfly pendant made of a bluish-green stone that shimmers in the light. I lift it off to take a closer look. It's cute, and less than $10, which makes me worry it'll turn my skin green. But for the price, it's a risk I'm willing to take.

"Want to try it on?"

I nearly jump out of my skin at the sound of Amira's voice in my ear. "Holy shit! I forgot you were here." I turn around and she's right behind me. My breath hitches as she grins at me.

"I don't think I've ever heard you curse before," she says.

"I don't do it often." My heart is still racing, and I have to take slow, even breaths to finally calm it down. I must still be on edge from seeing all those Jordan Peele movies.

"So, do you want to try it on?" Amira points at the necklace. I glance past her at the cashier, who's still on her phone.

"Is that allowed?" I ask.

The necklace is hooked around the placard that was holding it up on the shelf. While the cashier isn't paying us any attention, I don't know how I feel trying it on without paying. But Amira says, "Of course."

She speaks with such confidence that, regardless of whether or not it's true, I let her turn me around and brush my braids over my left shoulder. Reaching around me, she takes the necklace from my hand and unclasps it.

"Hold this. Thank you!" Amira hands me the now empty placard.

I just nod. My throat feels dry, and I don't trust it enough to let words out. I can feel every inch of Amira standing behind me, her vanilla scent enveloping me. She's just tall enough that if she wanted to, she could rest her chin on the crook of my shoulder.

Instead, she pulls either side of the gold chain around my neck, the pendant rising higher up my chest until it stops right below my throat.

"Is this good?" she asks.

Amira's breath is right by my ear, and I shiver, just a little. I pray she doesn't notice. I don't know why I'm being like this right now. Clearly, I am losing my mind, or maybe I'm just hormonal. Whatever these . . . feelings are, I'd like them to stop now. Please and thank you.

"Rochelle?" she says.

"It's good," I croak out. "Just clasp it." I sound desperate, but I don't care. I need whatever this is to be done.

Amira does as she's told, and the pendant falls gently on top of my shirt. She steps back and I move forward, keeping my back to her as I widen the distance between us.

"There's a mirror over there if you want to go take a look." Her voice lacks the confidence that was there only a moment before.

I'm sure I'm just radiating awkwardness. Without another word, I walk over to the mirror and barely glance up at my reflection.

"It looks great on you." Amira stands beside me now, but I can't look at her. It feels too weird. I wish she would stop being nice and say something snippy so we could go back to our regularly scheduled program.

"Are you going to get it?" she asks.

Finally, I make myself look at her. She's gazing at me with a soft smile, and I wonder if she can tell that my head is spinning or if I look like just regular ole Rochelle to her. I try to at least pretend that all is normal—if not to convince her, then to convince myself.

"Yeah, sure, why not?"

Amira laughs. "That's the spirit."

She loops her arm through mine like she did that day she dragged me into the bathroom to fix my hair and leads me to the register to buy my necklace. I didn't even notice Amira grab three pairs of earrings to buy as well. Once we're done, we stand outside of Claire's plotting our next move.

"Food court?" Amira fiddles with the small plastic bag.

My stomach answers before I can, rumbling like I haven't eaten all day instead of just a few hours ago.

"Wow." Amira raises a brow.

"Shut up."

Amira laughs as she leads me and my stomach to where it wants to be.

ELEVEN

"SHAWN WANTS TO GO ON a date with you."

It's been almost three weeks since Shawn asked me to get him another date with Taylor, and while I've successfully dodged all his follow-ups and pestering, I know I can't hold him off for much longer. Hence the reason I convinced Taylor to take me to work today. It didn't take much convincing considering that it's an afternoon shift and Ma is at work. Plus, the buses here are very unreliable.

I may have also promised Taylor a $20 donation to her "Get the Fuck Out of Dodge" fund for college when I get my next paycheck.

The car ride was supposed to be my big opportunity to finally and very carefully present the idea that she should give Shawn another chance, but now with Taylor's car, Sadie, parked in front of Horizon and Taylor waiting for me to leave, my time has officially run out and I've panicked.

"Come again?" she asks.

I sigh, hating that I have to repeat myself. This is already hard enough. "Shawn wants to go on a date with you. Again."

Taylor is in full goth mode today. Black eyes, black lipstick, black spiked septum ring, and a black choker around her neck. So, when she faces me, her look is quite fierce. But inside her dark exterior is a big softy, and she cannot scare me.

"I think he really likes you." I shrug, trying to make the case for him. "And you've never said why it didn't work out the first time. Maybe it's worth giving him another chance."

"Why do you care that he wants to go on a date with me? You don't even like Shawn."

"I don't dislike Shawn though." I throw my hands up. "And that's saying a lot!"

Taylor squints at me suspiciously.

"Is this why you wanted a ride today?"

Ugh, she's way too perceptive for her own good.

"Perhaps." I look toward the entrance of the theater. "I just wanted to tell you he's interested. In case you might be interested too. If you're not, you can pretend I said nothing, but I thought you should know."

I open my door and hop out, then wait a few seconds. Taylor, thankfully, hops out too and looks at me over the roof of Sadie.

"Is he inside right now?"

"Yep."

Taylor taps her sharpened black nails on the car, quiet. I try to read her face, but I think her makeup is preventing me from seeing what she's thinking.

"You could just go talk to him," I say. "Talking to him doesn't mean you're going to go on a date with him."

"I don't like this new you," Taylor says all grumpily. "You're being too reasonable."

"What new me?" I point to myself dramatically, the spirit of Kerry taking over. "I haven't changed."

Taylor gives me a once-over. I'm not sure what she sees, but her perusal makes me squirm.

She closes her car door and comes around to meet me.

"You have. And it's fine. Just don't become Kerry," she warns, pointing a finger at me. "I love her, but I cannot take two bubbly people trying to throw positivity at me all the time. It's unnatural."

I laugh. "I promise. Now, shall we?"

We barely make it through Horizon's doors before Shawn appears right in front of us, all wide-eyed. I get the feeling he didn't believe I would deliver on my promise.

"Taylor!" Shawn is so loud, a number of people turn to see what's happening. It's not that busy this afternoon, thankfully. Red creeps up on his cheeks, and he tries again. "Taylor." He drops his voice a few octaves lower. "Hi. Hello. Welcome."

"Hi." Taylor does not smile or give any indication that she is happy to see him, but it is enough.

Shawn's face breaks into a megawatt grin. "How are you? You look great." Gone is the confident superstar athlete, and in his place stands a boy who is down bad.

"Thanks," she says. "And I'm fine."

"That's good. Great."

I decide my job here is done and remove myself from this very enthralling conversation. I go into the office and clock in with Glory, before making my way to concessions, where Amira and the twins are already hard at work handling people's orders.

This is the first time I've seen Amira since the mall, but she's currently too busy helping someone put their credit card into the machine to even look at me, which is fine. Expected even. Just because we hung out once outside of work that doesn't mean our working relationship needs to change in any way. We're just work buddies. Once this summer is over, we may not even be that, depending on if I stick around at Horizon when school starts back up again.

Except the idea of not working at Horizon anymore causes this odd pain in my chest that I do not like. Oh dear. Have I gotten attached?

I push these thoughts out of my mind and make my way behind the concessions counter. I put my bag away and look at the twins, who are pulling together different orders. "Need help?"

"Please," Jennie begs as she holds two large bags of popcorn that threaten to topple at any moment.

An hour or so flies by as the four of us work in tandem, getting people their food and drinks during the afternoon rush. We barely have a moment to talk with all that's going on. But every so often, my arm will brush Amira's, or I'll get hit with a scent of baked goods, and I'm reminded that she's there.

Eventually, things slow down as the movies start playing and everyone gets situated in their theaters.

"Am I alive?" Jennie flops over on the counter. "I feel alive, but I think I'm dead."

"We're alive," Lisa reassures her, patting her sister's back. "But barely."

"You two can go take a break if you want." Amira also looks drained from the rush. "Rochelle and I can handle things for a bit."

Jennie and Lisa exchange a doubtful look.

"Are you sure?" Lisa eyes me when she asks the question, and I get it. Amira and I haven't gotten into a disagreement in a while, but it wasn't too long ago when we'd never be left alone together voluntarily.

"We'll be fine," I say, waving them off with my hand.

They both still hesitate, and Amira rolls her eyes.

"If y'all don't go somewhere in the next five seconds, I'm going to rescind my offer."

That gets them running. With impressive speed they escape out the doors of Horizon.

"You know, now I'm slightly worried they will never come back." Amira laughs.

"Honestly, that's a very fair concern."

We crack up again, until the laughter eventually leaves us, and all we're left with is the quiet hum of all the machines at concessions and the faint sounds of action and laughter from the theaters. We sit in that silence for a bit, and it's nice. Comfortable.

Of course, Amira proceeds to ruin it.

"You're not wearing the necklace."

Her eyes are trained down at the collar of my shirt, where my neck is in fact bare.

"Why would I be wearing the necklace?" I ask. "We're at work."

"Jewelry isn't prohibited," Amira says, then points at her nose ring, which is a sparkly purple hoop. "See."

"I do see," I say, sarcastically. "But wearing a necklace to work feels kind of excessive. Who am I trying to impress?"

Amira makes a face like she's annoyed, though I don't see why she would be.

"Who said anything about impressing anyone? You should just wear it because it looks nice on you."

As my brain tries to decipher if Amira just gave me a compliment, she adds, "Not everything you do needs to be tied to impressing people or achieving some kind of goal."

I open and close my mouth, looking for a way to respond to that, when I hear the front doors open again.

An older Black lady, who couldn't possibly be more than five feet tall, waddles in. She's wearing a church hat, even though it isn't Sunday. Black square-rimmed glasses cover half of her face but, most importantly, she is carrying a rather large Tupperware container filled with what looks like spaghetti.

"Are you seeing this too, or am I hallucinating?" Amira glances at the woman and back at me. It's enough to make her earlier comment take a step back in my mind.

"Old lady in a church hat with a bowl of spaghetti?" I ask.

"Okay, good, so she's either real or we're both losing it. Do you want to take this or should I?" she asks.

I look at Amira, slightly alarmed. I haven't had to really deal with a customer like this before. Usually, she or Glory step in to handle them. "Me? What am I supposed to do?"

"Stop her, obviously." Amira motions her hand toward the woman. "She can't go into the theater with that."

"Shouldn't the person who's scanning tickets be the one to stop her?"

Amira groans. "It's Danny! You know he's not going to do anything."

Of course, when we both look over to Danny, he's not even standing by the roped-off area to the theaters.

"Seriously, if Glory doesn't fire him, I will." Amira crosses her arms.

"Wait, can you actually do that?"

"Rochelle! Just go stop her!"

"Right, okay."

She sounds exasperated, so I quickly make my way from the counter to the woman. Thankfully, she's moving so slowly, she's only just now walking past the concessions counter when I finally jump into action.

"Ma'am!" I call out to her. "Ma'am!" But she either doesn't hear me or doesn't care to.

I quickly move around her so I'm blocking her path. This finally gets her attention, and she looks up at me.

"Excuse me, dear—" She's got a bit of a southern twang to her voice.

I sigh. I'm going to have to tell somebody's sweet southern grandma that they can't take their spaghetti into the theater. When they write my biography, this will be the scene they use to portray me as a cutthroat monster.

"Um, I'm sorry, ma'am, but you can't go into the theater with that," I say.

"Go in with what, dear?" She blinks up at me and sounds genuinely confused by what I've said.

"The, um, spaghetti." I point down at her hands. "You can't bring outside food into the theater."

"Nonsense, dear, I do it all the time." She waves a hand as if I'm nothing more than a pesky housefly and starts to move around me. I don't want to bodycheck an old woman, so I step aside but follow close behind her as she approaches the rope.

"Ma'am, I'm sorry but I'm really going to have to ask you to get rid of that spaghetti before you go inside." I try to make my voice sterner, tougher, like a teacher or something. "And also, I'll need to see your ticket."

The woman stops again and looks at me. "Dear, I am not going to throw away perfectly good pasta. That would be wasteful, and I'm not made of money, you know."

"Okay, but you can't bring it inside."

"Well, then what do you suppose we do, because I will not be throwing it away." She puts her free hand on her hip.

I look from the lady to Amira, who's moved around the circular counter, so she has the perfect viewing spot for this whole debacle. She is clearly delighted by my predicament, and I know I won't be getting any help from her.

I take a deep and calming breath and offer a solution. "What if I hold on to the spaghetti for you? While you watch your movie. That way you're not bringing it into the theater, and I don't have to throw it out."

The woman considers this for a moment, and since she's quiet, I add, "You'll get it right back *after* your movie. I promise."

It seems to be enough because she says, "Fine, that'll be just fine," and thrusts out the bowl to me. I clumsily take it in my hands.

"Now can you lift this rope for me, dear," she says. "I'm already quite late for my movie."

"Uh, yes, ma'am."

I'm feeling like I really aced my first big test at Horizon as I walk back to Amira. It isn't until I set down the bowl full of pasta that she tells me, "You forgot to check her ticket."

Damn it.

That night, Taylor and I are summoned to Kerry's house for a sleepover, and since Taylor was running errands nearby, she picks me up after my shift. I pester her with questions about Shawn, who mysteriously disappeared after she arrived, but she gives me nothing.

"If I answer your questions now, I'll have to do this all over again when we get there. So, stop asking." She grips the steering wheel with tense fingers as she turns down Kerry's street.

"I suppose that's fair." Then I text Shawn and ask him if he and Taylor made plans to go out again, to which he replies with a GIF of the Kool-Aid Man saying, "OH YEAH!" For now, that's enough information to satisfy me.

Kerry is sitting on her porch steps waiting for us when we arrive at her house. I've always loved going to Kerry's house. It literally looks like that house every kid draws, with the triangle roof, square bottom, round-shaped door, and two front windows. It even has a chimney for a real fireplace, not an electric one.

"Finally, the cavalry has arrived," Kerry says, as we get out of the car. She pulls us both into a group hug. "You will not believe what happened."

I'm pretty sure a lot has happened today, none of which had to do with Kerry though.

"Tell us," Taylor presses.

"We were playing charades and I lost!" Kerry throws her head back and wails, her body shaking as if she's overcome by tears, but her eyes are totally dry. She's still working on crying on demand.

It must be family game night in the Williams house. Family game night can occur any day at any time whenever someone wants to and has enough will to gather the five members that make up Kerry's family. There's Kerry, of course; her younger brother, Kingston; her older brother, Kareem; and her parents, Kaycee and Kevin. Yes, the K names were intentional. It's kind of corny but also cute.

Behind Kerry, the door opens, and her mom steps out and peeks around her. Mrs. Williams looks exactly how I imagine Kerry will look in twenty years. They have the same light brown skin, round cheeks, full lips, hips, and curves.

"Oh, hello, girls," she says. "Why don't you come in? She may carry on like this for quite a while."

"Mooom," Kerry whines, turning her despair on her mother, who is completely unmoved.

"Kerry, you're also welcome to come inside if you're done with your tantrum."

"But, Mom, how could I lose? I'm an actress!" she declares.

"Perhaps you simply need to practice. Now come inside."

Taylor and I follow Mrs. Williams into the foyer, and it doesn't take long for Kerry to give in and follow suit.

The whole house smells sugary sweet like someone's been baking all day. It's familiar in a way I'm not comfortable with, but I snuff out any thoughts of Amira before they can grow legs. By the time the spaghetti crisis was averted, it felt weird to circle back on what she said about me and the necklace, so I let it drop. Though I kept thinking about it all day.

We make our way to the kitchen, where Mrs. Williams has cookies sitting out on a cooling tray, the true source of the smell.

"Mmm, sugar cookies," I say, making my way toward them.

"Feel free to take as much as you want," Mrs. Williams says. "This is the second batch. These animals already went through the first one."

The animals in question come running into the kitchen. Mr. Williams and his sons look like those Russian dolls where you open one and then find an identical one in a smaller size. If Kerry is her mother's twin, all her dad's genes went to her brothers.

"Hello, ladies," Mr. Williams says.

Taylor and I say hi, but he skirts past us to his wife, planting a kiss on her lips.

"Ugh," all three Williams children say.

"That was a chaste one," Mr. Williams says, indignant. "Be

happy I didn't use tongue."

"Please no," Kareem says.

"Haven't I been through enough today?" Kerry adds.

Kingston stuffs his mouth full of cookies.

We all laugh, and then a pang hits my chest. This happens sometimes when I visit Kerry. I don't think about my dad often. There's not much to think about when someone dies before they can even leave you with any memories, but when I see Kerry's parents together, or sometimes even Taylor's moms, I wonder what it would've been like if my dad was still here with me and Ma.

I don't talk about him to Ma too much, mostly because I don't know what to say. She misses him in a way I can never understand, and it feels wrong to open up the wounds of loss in her just so I can learn more about him. The one thing I do know is that he met Ma at Wharton, their dream school. They fell in love instantly during freshman orientation, worked together to reach their dreams, then graduated and had me.

A few years later, Dad was in the wrong place at the wrong time, and he was gone. Just like that. And Ma's life was completely changed.

"I'm tapping out of game night," Kerry announces, and her voice snaps me out of my thoughts. "We'll be in my room if you need us."

She stuffs a cookie-filled paper towel in my hand, then guides me and Taylor out of the kitchen and up the stairs to her room.

The house is two floors, plus an attic that makes up the

pointy triangle on the top of their house, which is where Kerry's room is. It took some convincing for her parents to let her move up here and make the space her own, but now it looks like it's always been hers.

Her pink-and-white bed is in the middle of the room, on top of a floral rug. She has two bright beanbags in each corner of the small room, placed there specifically for me and Taylor. The room's two slanted walls are covered with different posters and photos of the actors Kerry is inspired by, including her namesake Kerry Washington, plus motivational quotes about acting and art.

"Do you guys want pizza?" Kerry asks. She's plopped down on the edge of her bed, while we've made ourselves comfortable in our beanbags.

"Yes, please," I say. "I never really eat while I'm at work."

"You don't get free food?" Kerry raises a brow.

"It's not really anything I want to eat."

"Shawn and I kissed," Taylor blurts out. Her sudden revelation derails our food talk immediately.

Kerry and I both turn to Taylor, and she looks just as startled by what she's said as we do.

"Come again?" Kerry inches her way closer, eyes wide.

"I took Rochelle to Horizon for work, and she said he wanted to try to take me on a date again. I said yes, and then we kissed." Taylor doesn't meet our eyes. She looks just as nervous as Shawn did earlier. I don't think I've ever seen her like this. "It was a really quick kiss," she continues. "Just like a peck on the lips. But I got some of my lipstick on him. And he liked it."

"Did you like it?" I pry.

"Yeah, I did." Taylor isn't grinning exactly, but the corners of her lips are tugged up in a slight smile, and it's enough to make us all giddy.

"Well, I'll be damned." Kerry smiles. "Congratulations on snagging the most eligible bachelor in all of North High. You deserve it."

"Thank you."

"Okay, but now can you tell us what happened the first time?" Kerry sits up on her bed, crossing her legs and holding a pillow tight to her body. "I thought you didn't like him anymore."

"I didn't." Taylor looks down again, shrugging her shoulders. "Or I don't know. I didn't want to. When he took me out before, he barely spoke a word to me the whole night. I kept asking him questions, and he'd only give me one-word answers. It was like he didn't want to be there at all."

I cringe. Maybe I should've asked more questions before I agreed to help Shawn.

"No, no, it's okay." Taylor looks at me.

Obviously, I have no poker face.

"He tried to explain to me before that he was really nervous, but it's Shawn, you know? He's always so chatty and nice to everyone, so I thought something was wrong with me. Like I broke him or something."

"Oh, Tay Tay," Kerry gushes, to Taylor's absolute disapproval.

"Do not call me that."

"Right, sorry, please go on."

I let out a small laugh at their ridiculousness. It's been a while since we've all hung out like this, thanks to work, and I've missed it so much.

"But he said that wasn't it at all. That he just likes me so much, he didn't know how to be himself around me." Another small smile creeps onto Taylor's lips. "So, he wants to try again. To do it right this time."

"And you said yes?" I ask, even though I already know the answer.

Taylor nods. "I said yes."

Kerry squeals, kicking her legs up in the air and throwing her pillow off the bed.

"Ah, this is so exciting," she says, then she starts to sing. "'Summer lovin', happened so fast.'"

"Please, God, no." Taylor grabs the pillow Kerry just threw and holds it around her head to block the singing out.

Kerry ignores her, launching herself off the bed and onto Taylor as she keeps singing.

"'Met this boy, cute as can beeee!'" She grabs Taylor around the shoulders, holding her tight.

"Get off me," Taylor groans.

I take in the messy mix of pink and black as Taylor attempts to push away Kerry and her singing, but Kerry refuses to budge. A warm feeling of fondness for my weird but totally perfect friends sweeps over me, and for the first time it dawns on me that a year from now, we'll be preparing to leave each other. I'll be in Philly, Kerry might be in LA or in DC at Howard if her parents convince her to get a college degree before chasing her acting dreams, and Taylor will be up in Rhode Island at RISD. No matter what happens, we won't ever be together like this again, so close we can just pop over for a sleepover.

"Rochelle . . ."

Kerry's voice has me blinking up, and I find Kerry and Taylor eyeing me.

"What?" I ask.

"You're being quiet," Taylor says.

"Too quiet," Kerry confirms.

"I'm just . . . thinking," I say.

"About?" Taylor asks.

I sigh, unsure if I can even put these feelings into words. It's like I'm suddenly nostalgic for something that's currently happening, which is ridiculous.

"Rochelle?" Taylor presses.

I shake my head, ridding myself of the sudden melancholy trying to pull me down.

"I was just thinking about how if you're dating Shawn, you'll probably end up being prom queen," I say with a laugh that sounds forced to my own ears. But Taylor and Kerry are so distracted by what I've said, they don't seem to notice.

"Prom queen?" Taylor repeats, aghast. "Over my dead body."

"No, she's right," Kerry says, almost sagely. "You'll be the queen to his obvious prom king. Shawn winning the crown is like a canon event."

"I rebuke this," Taylor says.

"You can't rebuke a canon event," Kerry says. "That's not how it works."

"Miles Morales would disagree," Taylor shoots back.

Their conversation quickly dissolves into a heated debate about fate versus free will in the Marvel universe, and I let them have at it, sliding down into my beanbag and simply taking it all in.

TWELVE

MY NEXT SHIFT AT HORIZON is a disaster.

It all starts with the popcorn machine.

I'm handling tickets today, so it takes a moment for me to realize the commotion happening at concessions isn't the regular "You messed up my order" kind of nonsense. Nope. When I finally look over, I see popcorn everywhere, the door to the machine hanging open as more spills out.

"Excuse me!" A young white woman is waving her phone in my face, ticket screen up.

"Right, sorry." I turn my attention back to the line in front of me and keep scanning tickets, though I cannot ignore the extra-strong smell of butter that seems to be permeating the air today.

People who were at concessions begin to give up on food altogether and head right over to me as the crew struggles to get a handle on the popcorn machine. I scan them in, trying to keep the line moving while also watching the mess at concessions.

"Unplug it!" Amira yells. She's using bag after bag to try to clean up the popcorn.

"I'm trying to, but everything over here is slippery," Shawn yells back. He holds up an empty plastic canister of the oil we use for the "butter" pump next to the popcorn. "This is all over the floor. Someone must've knocked it over."

Even from here I can see them both whip their heads around to look at Danny, who's grabbing pieces of popcorn and popping them into his mouth, completely unaware of their glares. The commotion earns a few headshakes and whispers from the guests in line, and I try to maintain a cheery expression.

"Use your shirt!" Amira orders as more popcorn falls to the tiled floor.

"Hello?" A voice drags my attention back to the line. The guy in front of me is tall and looks incredibly familiar. It isn't until I scan his ticket that I realize I've seen him before and that it's Danny's friend Pete. It kind of weirds me out that I'm beginning to recognize the regulars.

"Oh, hey, your Danny's friend, right?" I ask him as I scan his ticket.

"Um, yeah."

"Cool, I—"

The guy—Pete—pushes past me and speed walks to his theater without another word. Rude. Danny isn't the best worker, but I figured he was simply lazy, not a bad guy. But if this is the company he keeps, maybe I was mistaken.

I shake it off since there's still a line and keep working.

When the last person in line has their ticket scanned in, I run over to concessions to try to help. "What's going on?"

"It won't stop making popcorn." Amira's curls, which crafted a pretty halo around her head earlier, have now deflated, sticking to her forehead with what I imagine is stress sweat. It's not her best look. Behind her, Shawn's shirt is covered in oil from his attempt to clean up.

I walk around, duck under the counter, and join in on the madness. I almost slip as I make my way to Shawn, but he grabs my elbow, keeping me upright.

"Thanks," I say. He just nods, focusing his attention back on the mess at hand.

The extension cord we use to plug everything in, including the popcorn machine, is surrounded by the large puddle of spilled oil that already looks like it's starting to congeal on the floor. Gross.

"I can barely get a firm grasp on it, before my feet start sliding in this stuff," Shawn says, exasperated.

"Doesn't this thing have an off switch?" I ask, looking at the machine.

"We tried that," Amira says. "I flipped it off, then back on, then off again. It won't stop."

I look around the mess and follow the line of the extension cord to where it's plugged into an outlet on the carpet just outside the concessions booth, safely away from the oil spill.

"Just unplug the extension cord," I suggest.

"But that'll turn *everything* off." Amira sounds defeated, and it becomes clear that they've already thought of that too. "The register, the credit card machine, the fridge, and the hot dogs. We'll have nothing."

I'm quickly running out of ideas. "Where is Glory?"

"Theater one's projection booth is not working, and unfortunately Jerry is currently at Six Flags, so they're trying to see if they can get another projection guy to come in and look at it," Amira explains. Her eyes look glassy, and she quickly blinks and looks away. I don't think I've ever seen Amira this upset before, and I don't like it.

Or rather, I don't like how it makes me feel. I have the sudden urge to fix this for her, so I won't have to see her cry.

"Okay, I give up." Shawn pushes up from the floor and almost topples right into me, distracting me from Amira's unshed tears. "Sorry, Roe Roe, I didn't see you there."

I don't even bother trying to correct him on my name. Despite my protests, Shawn has become committed to the nickname, and there's no stopping him now.

"All right, so what are we going to do? Won't it just . . . run out of popcorn? Eventually?" I'm still determined to find a solution, even though it seems like they've tried everything at this point.

"I have no idea." Amira sighs. "There shouldn't have even been that much in there to begin with." She grabs a few napkins to wipe her face. "Who filled it?"

The three of us all turn to look at Danny, who's still eating popcorn off the counter as it continues to spill out. When he feels the weight of our stares, he finally stops and looks at us. "What?"

"Did you overfill the popcorn machine?" Amira walks toward him.

"What? No! I only used one bag of kernels like always." He

stands up straighter and wipes his mouth off.

"Then why is so much still popping out?" Amira asks.

"How should I know?" Danny shrugs. "You've been here all day with me—you didn't add more?"

"No," Amira says before turning to Shawn. "Did you?"

"Nope, I'd remember that," he replies.

"All right, well it doesn't matter who added it, what matters is we need to make it stop," I cut in. "I know we'll lose power to the entire stand, but I think we're just going to have to unplug everything."

"But—"

I cut Amira off. "We're losing customers because of this mess anyway. At least if we unplug it, we can clean it up, and empty out whatever kernels are still in there, so it doesn't start going all haywire again when we plug everything back in.

"Besides, all the movies are playing right now, so no one's trying to buy anything right this instant."

When I finish speaking, Amira, Shawn, and Danny are staring at me. I'm not sure if they're looking at me like that because that may be the most I've ever said in one go here at Horizon, or because they're shocked that I'm taking control of the situation.

Either way, I feel good. Confident. Like I'm back in my element, because I know what needs to be done, and I'm going to do it.

Amira snaps out of it first, clapping her hands together. "All right, let's do as Rochelle says. Unplug it."

Shawn wastes no time, taking the extension cord plug out

from the outlet on the floor. All of our shoulders slide down in relief as the popcorn machine stops its whirring and popping. We still have a big mess to clean up, but at least it won't be getting any messier now.

"For now, plug the fridge into the outlet so we don't have to worry about anything going bad," Amira directs.

"You got it boss." Shawn gives her a salute and moves around us to the fridge to find the right cord and gets to work.

"I'll go grab the cleaning supplies from the office." Amira then points at me. "Rochelle, you should go back by the rope in case anyone comes and needs their tickets scanned or tries to run right in without a ticket or something. Anything could happen today."

"Are you sure? I can help you guys clean this up," I say.

"No, it's time Danny earned his wages. Right, Danny?"

"Huh?" Danny says.

He's still grabbing popcorn, eating as he goes. I think this is his version of cleaning.

"Exactly." Amira shakes her head. "I'll be right back. Please watch these two while I'm gone."

"Sure." I watch her as she goes into the office to grab the cleaning supplies, and I wonder if I should go with her. I don't think I've ever really seen Amira this stressed, especially not at Horizon. She's always been cool, calm, and collected, knowing exactly what to do and not afraid to tell us all how to do it, which I usually find annoying.

Today, for at least a moment, she froze, and somehow that was ten times worse.

"Why don't you go help her with the mop and stuff?"

Shawn is standing beside me also looking at the office door, which has now closed behind Amira.

"She told me to watch y'all."

"I don't need watching. And I can handle Danny. He's a goofball, but he works hard when he wants to."

"It's so interesting to hear *you* of all people call him a goofball."

"Hey, I'm not saying I am not a goofball, but I am better at my job." There's that signature Shawn smile again.

"You both know I can hear you, right?" Danny says from behind us.

We ignore him.

"Just go." Shawn gently grabs my shoulders and guides me over to the flip-up section of the counter. There's a knowing glint in his eyes that I don't appreciate. I don't know what he thinks he knows, but I go without further protest.

When I open the office door, Amira is frantically moving things around. "What are you looking for?"

She glances up, pushing some curls from her face. "I told you to stay with the boys."

"I didn't listen. You know, I still don't love you being the boss of me. It's unnatural." I expect to get at least a smile out of this, but Amira doesn't even look my way. Okay, so that didn't work.

"I can help you find whatever you're looking for," I offer. "This office is not that big, but still."

"The soap. It's usually in the bucket, but now it's not."

"Maybe Glory moved it. Do you want me to ask them?"

"No, don't bother them, they're already having a tough day." Amira lets out a deep, heavy sigh, and I eye her carefully.

"Are you okay?" I ask.

"Of course not! I'm stressed because the popcorn machine just lost it, and I didn't know how to fix it! And I should know how to fix it."

I step back, surprised. I don't think I've ever heard Amira yell before. Sure, we've argued and had our spats over the years, but she's never really had an outburst like this. At least, not in front of me.

"Sorry." Amira's voice is low. She hangs her head, and I know she's feeling embarrassed. "That was a lot."

I shrug. "I've had my fair share of meltdowns before. It's nothing I can't handle."

Amira snorts at that. "Oh, I know about your meltdowns. Remember when you got a ninety-nine on that art project, and Ms. Bloom said it was because there was 'no such thing as perfection' when it came to art."

"Which was ridiculous," I say. "I stayed up for hours working on that stupid papier-mâché mask, and Taylor painted it for me, so I know it was, in fact, perfection."

"Wow, I can't believe you confessed to cheating." Amira clutches a hand to her chest dramatically, and I roll my eyes.

"I did not cheat; I outsourced the final step of my project to someone who actually has skills. And I helped her with the English essay that week. It was an even exchange."

"Sure, sure, whatever you say, cheater."

I'm about to level back a retort when I realize she's smiling. She's teasing me. Again.

"You're so annoying, do you know that?" I ask.

"Not as annoying as you."

Somehow, she makes it sound like a compliment, and for reasons I can't explain, I feel the corners of my mouth twitch up in an attempt at a smile. I quickly press my lips together to shut that down, unwilling to give her the satisfaction.

Silence falls between us, and I'm not sure what else there is to say, but it feels awkward not to say something. Amira beats me to the punch though.

"Rochelle, I—"

Whatever she was going to say is cut off when the door bursts open behind us.

Glory stands in the doorway, face red and tears sliding down their face, and all the worry I had for Amira transfers over to Glory.

"Are you okay?" I ask.

"I'm fine." Glory hiccups. They come farther in, plop themselves down in one of the chairs, and promptly bring their forehead down to the desk.

"I don't think you are fine." The words slip out before I can catch them, and Amira elbows me.

Glory's head pops up, and more tears are sliding down their face.

"Glory, what happened?" Amira walks over to them, holding their hand.

"Today has been a disaster. Everything is going wrong! Sales are going down and nothing I'm doing is working," they say.

Amira looks at me, the stress from earlier creeping back onto her face.

"Don't worry, Glory." I consider patting their back in reassurance but decide that may be too weird since I barely know them. "I'm sure things will get better soon."

"We don't have time though!"

Glory leans back in the chair and throws their head back, locs falling over their shoulders.

"What do you mean?" Amira stands up straight.

"My uncles are only giving me the summer to turn the place around. Otherwise, they're closing Horizon."

"What?!" Amira and I exclaim at the same time.

Glory straightens their head, sitting upright as they look at us.

"I shouldn't be telling you both this, but my uncles have put everything into reviving Horizon," Glory explains. "All the money they made on Broadway, all their savings, everything. At first, I think they really believed in it, you know? It was the start of their love story, and they wanted to keep it under Black ownership for the community. It's a landmark. But now it's just become too stressful, especially since they were finally able to adopt their baby girl this year. They're worried about her future too, you know? And I get it, but I don't want to lose Horizon. I can't lose Horizon."

Glory's words wash over me, and it takes a second for all of it to sink in. Horizon is in serious financial trouble. Edge of bankruptcy trouble, it sounds like. And we've only got maybe a couple months left to turn it around.

I think about my time here, working with Amira, Jennie, Lisa, Shawn, and even Brigit and Danny. It's been way more fun than I ever thought it would be. And I like the people who come here. Mostly kids and families, or the elderly in the mornings and afternoons. I've even gotten to know some of the regulars who are just like Kerry, absolute film lovers. Plus, the art on the walls and the overall history of the place. It's a real tribute to Black Hollywood. It's incredible. A clear example of the love and care that's been put into the theater.

Horizon isn't any regular ole place to watch movies. It's a place worthy of preservation for the community. A reminder that someone made something just for us, when others wanted to keep people like us out. It's home for a lot of people. Maybe it could even be that for me.

If we can save it, that is.

"You're not going to lose Horizon."

The words come out of my mouth with more confidence than I truly feel, but I want to believe it's true. I need to believe it's true, for myself and for Glory.

Glory takes my hand, giving it a little squeeze.

"Thanks, Rochelle. I hope not, but it's not looking good, and all these issues that keep popping up aren't helping. It's so weird. All of these bad things just started happening this summer."

"Maybe there's something we can do to help," Amira says. "A fundraiser or something. To bring more people in."

"Yeah, exactly. We just have to think of something big. We can do this." I give Glory's hand a squeeze back.

"I appreciate the enthusiasm. But right now, I just need a moment to think. Do you mind giving me the room for a bit?"

"Right, yeah, of course, Glory. No problem." Amira takes my hand, surprising me, but I barely have time to register the feeling, as she lets go of me as soon as we're out of the office.

"Okay, so what are we going to do?" She's looking at me as if I have the answers, and I stare right back at her.

"I have no idea; you've worked here longer than me," I remind her.

"Well, you're allegedly smarter."

"Is it allegedly if my GPA is actually higher than yours?"

"By like one point."

"More like two."

"What's happening here?" Shawn asks.

I hadn't even noticed Shawn and Danny staring at us, or that we'd reached concessions already.

"Horizon might be closing," Amira says, her voice low.

"What do you mean, closing?"

Amira shushes Shawn.

"Lower your voice," she hisses.

"Horizon can't close," Danny says. "It's Horizon." For all of his slacking off, I know that this place also means a lot to him.

"It might unless we do something about it." Amira crosses her arms, thinking.

"All right, well, what's the game plan, then?" Shawn asks.

Amira, Shawn, and Danny stare at me as if they're waiting for some sort of grand reveal. "Why are you all looking at me?"

"Because you're the one who has some kind of extensive plan

of attack for everything you do." Amira's not wrong, but still. "If anyone could figure out what's going on with Horizon and how we can fix it, it's you."

"I second that motion." Shawn comes over to stand right behind me, like he's my bodyguard or something.

"Sure, I believe it," Danny agrees.

I sigh, but inside I'm kind of relishing this. I *do* always have a plan, and besides wanting to keep Horizon around because we need this place as much as it needs us, saving a local business could make for a really good college essay.

I pull out my phone and start typing.

"Before we do anything else," I say, "let's rally the troops."

THIRTEEN

MOVIES THAT FEEL LIKE MOVIES

Kerry Williams and Taylor Brown were added to the conversation.

Me: Testing

Taylor: What is this?

Shawn: Hello my love 🐶

Taylor Brown has left the conversation.

Kerry: LOL

Brigit: Who is that?

Me: My friend Kerry. I have gathered us all here to discuss a major issue.

Danny: Horizon's closing.

Amira: Jesus Danny don't lead with that.

Jennie: WHAT???

Lisa: WHAT?

Kerry: whattttt

Brigit: Sweetie, what are you talking about?

Shawn: Ugh can we not with the sweetie?

Amira: . . . you literally just called someone love.

Me: Can everyone focus? We have a real problem on our hands. Horizon isn't closing, but it might if we don't do something to stop it.

Brigit: Who said Horizon's closing?

Amira: Glory. They're in the office, right now, crying because of everything.

Lisa: Aw poor Glory! 😔

Me: Yes, it's very tragic but the point is we can stop Horizon from closing. We just need to figure out how to bring in more money and stop all these issues that have been cropping up.

Kerry: What issues?

Amira: You haven't told her?

Me: It didn't seem relevant.

Amira: You do realize you don't have to top line the things happening in your life, right? You can just open up to people without qualifying if something is important.

Shawn: Deep

Me: Anyways . . .

Me: There's been an intentionally clogged toilet, movies showing on the wrong screens, and the popcorn machine went rogue today. There was also a lady with spaghetti but that feels unrelated.

Amira: It's been weird. I've worked here for almost two years now and we've never had this many insane mishaps in a row.

Shawn: Word

Brigit: Agreed

Danny: True

Lisa: You guys think this isn't a coincidence?

Me: Probability would dictate that, no, it isn't.

Shawn: Please do not bring math into this.

Kerry: Who would sabotage Horizon though? It's the best!

Jennie: Do we have enemies? 👀

Shawn: Well, Pete probably doesn't love us.

Danny: Speak for yourself.

Lisa: Who's Pete?

Me: Danny's friend.

Danny: How do you know that?

Me: I saw him talking to you at the theater. And he was here today. I scanned his ticket.

Danny: Pete wouldn't do this. He used to work at Horizon. He loves it as much as we do.

Amira: That's debatable but I also don't think Pete would spend his time at Horizon messing with us when he could be doing literally anything else. He wasn't exactly into doing much when he was around.

Jennie: Ah that explains how he and Danny are friends.

Shawn: Damn Jennie.

Me: Anyway, if it's not Pete we need to find out who is doing it.

Danny: It's not Pete.

Brigit: And how do we do that?

Me: I'm not sure yet, but for now everyone keep their eyes peeled for anyone who looks even remotely suspicious. Kerry, can you come in and maybe pretend to be a customer and keep your eye on people?

Kerry: Oh yes it would be my honor!

Jennie: Can you drop a pic? Just so we know who you are when you come in, I mean.

Kerry: Sure!

Kerry: headshot.jpg

Jennie: Wow, you're really pretty, if you don't mind my saying.

Kerry: I don't mind at all 😊

Amira: Enough with the flirting!

Me: Yeah, are we all good on the plan?

Lisa: Is this really the plan? It feels like we should be doing more.

Amira: It's good enough for now. We need to get back to work. Keep your eyes peeled and if you see something, say something.

Me: Please tell me you did not just quote the police.

Amira: I'm reclaiming the phrase! It's fine. Get to work!

Shawn: Oh, how I love when she gets bossy.

Amira: I'm not bossy. I'm the boss. 😊

Me: Here she goes again . . . 😳

With a plan in motion to find Horizon's saboteur, Amira and I take it upon ourselves to find a way to bring in more money.

Unfortunately, neither of us have developed entrepreneurial skills and we are struggling.

My handy-dandy notebook that has a list titled "How to Save Horizon" is blank so far. The only other words on the page are our names.

Currently, we're the only ones at concessions. The place is quiet as the last movies of the night are playing, so Amira sent Jennie home.

"Okay." Amira stands up straight and claps her hands. Her curls are tied up in a messy bun today, and her nose ring is a purple and gold flower. I wonder if she knows purple is my favorite color. Not that she would pick her nose ring based on me, obviously. She just seems to have multiple purple nose rings.

I wish I didn't know that.

"What if we host events here?" she asks. "We can rent out movie theater space to people so they can have birthday parties and stuff."

I stand up straighter too, considering. "But why would someone want to have their birthday party in a movie theater?"

Amira waves a hand. "That was just one example. But I mean companies could do stuff here. The screens can act as projectors, and they could have like huge conferences or something. I feel like I've seen AMC and other theaters offer stuff like that."

I nod and write down "Rent out theaters for events" on the list.

"We'll need to figure out pricing, and how often we can rent out space for events without disrupting the movies too much," I say. "It'll be a balancing act, but if we price it right, this could be a good start at least. Though I wonder how many events we'd need to do to—"

I lose all sense of speech when Amira's hand covers mine. I look down at our hands, the pen now lying flat underneath my palm. I hadn't even noticed I was tapping the pen, leaving a bunch of miscellaneous dots all over the page.

"Oh, oops, sorry."

"You don't have to apologize," Amira says, with a smirk. "It's your paper you ruined."

Her hand is still on mine, warm and soft. It's a bit uncomfortable because my pen is still stuck between my finger and thumb, but I can't seem to tell her to move. Instead, I'm distracted by Amira's golden-brown eyes, which are locked in on mine, and the smirk on her face that falters into a more serious look I can't decipher.

And then she's tilting forward, her head lowering, and suddenly I understand.

Amira's going to kiss me.

In the movie theater.

During work hours.

Is she unwell?

There's time to pull away and put a stop to this madness, but I don't move. Call it curiosity or a certified brain malfunction, but I let her come to me. I keep waiting for her to close her eyes. That's what you're supposed to do when you kiss someone, right? I'm pretty sure. My kissing experience is limited to Kerry once pecking me on the lips to see if she felt anything, after she'd kissed Marcus Little, her crush for our entire freshman year. I consented to this nonsense only because Taylor, who'd just gotten her braces tightened, wanted no one near her mouth, and Kerry was beginning to suspect she was ace.

For the record, neither of us felt the "spark." But I digress.

Now, though, I feel . . . something. Not a spark necessarily, but a sense that this is about to change everything, which of course it will. I'm pretty sure kissing wasn't part of the amicable coworker's agreement.

Time seems to slow and I'm thinking maybe I should close my eyes first so Amira can understand that I am not opposed, even if I probably should be. The very first and most important rule of my get-into-Wharton plan is no distractions. This current predicament being a clear reminder.

And yet.

Amira moves closer, which means her toes are now bumping

against mine. Then she raises her free hand up to my face, leaning in even closer, and as I'm about to let my eyes close, I feel her thumb brush up under my eye and she's pulling away again.

"You've got an eyelash," she says, holding out the eyelash to me. "Make a wish."

It takes me a full five seconds to recalibrate my brain and do as she says, blowing on her thumb. I don't even make a wish because my brain synapses are still struggling to catch up.

Amira pulls back even farther, taking away her other hand, as she moves to the register as if nothing even happened, and I want to throttle her.

I cannot believe I truly thought Amira Rodriguez was going to kiss me and, worse, I was going to let it happen. What is wrong with me?

"Let's shut this place down," she says. "No one else is coming tonight, and the last showing is halfway through."

"Okay" is what I say, but inside I'm screaming, "Are you for real?"

I follow Amira's lead, counting the inventory and wiping down the counters, all the while berating myself for being so stupid. Of course, Amira wasn't trying to kiss me. Maybe we're growing on each other as coworkers and, dare I say, even friends, but romantically?

We're both queer. I know that. It's something our moms bonded over when we came out (Amira was first, of course). But in all the time we've known each other, I've never even considered Amira that way. I know some people like a challenge when they date, and I imagine maybe Shawn feels that way with Taylor, but I've never been that person.

I work so hard for everything else in my life, I don't want to work hard for love, and this thing that I thought was maybe happening with Amira would not only be hard but would also be complicated. Our mothers would lose their minds if we dated, and of course the relationship would only last until we went to college, so then they'd have to deal with us being exes.

It's simply too much.

"Rochelle?"

My head snaps up, Amira's voice breaking me out of my spiral. She's at the register zipping up the cash bag and looking at me with a slight frown of concern.

"Are you okay?"

No, I lost my mind earlier, and I'm still trying to find it.

"Yeah, of course," I say.

"Really? You've been scrubbing at the same spot for a while now," she says, amusement slipping into her voice. "I think it's clean."

I look down at the dishrag in my hand as if I've never seen it before. I don't even remember picking it up. I must've been operating on autopilot.

"Right," I say. "Good call."

Amira's brows rise. "Good call? Are you *sure* you're all right? That almost sounded like a compliment."

"Not a compliment," I say, pushing the words out on a sigh. "Just stating the facts. I can acknowledge when you're right."

Amira has focused her attention back on the register, but I can still see the corner of her mouth curve up in a tiny smile.

Clearly, she loves praise as much as I do. I continue to watch her as she closes the cash drawer with a soft click. Just by the way she's holding the bag, I can tell it's nowhere near full. Rationally, I know most of our sales don't come through cash and instead will be on the credit card machine, but still. It's enough to make my anxieties about Horizon closing seep back in, and I'm happy to have something to refocus on.

"How much did we make tonight?"

Amira shrugs. "Not enough, I don't think, but Glory handles the actual financials. I just do inventory like everyone else."

I nod. Even if we had been packed, the problem seems bigger than one amazing night of sales. Much, much bigger.

"I'm going to hand this off to Glory," Amira says, holding up the bag. "Wanna meet me outside? I can give you a ride home."

"Yeah, thanks."

I watch her go and pick up my bag from where it's hidden under the counter, double-checking all my stuff is in there. I turn off everything except the fridge, slip out under the counter, and head outside.

It's one of those nice summer nights where it's warm but not so hot that I'm sweating just by standing still. The sun is setting, and the sky is a beautiful shade of red orange. I reach for my phone and step into the parking lot, backing up until I can get most of Horizon in the shot with the sky. Surprisingly, it doesn't look half-bad. Before I can talk myself out of it, I send it to the Horizon work chat. I don't bother to add words. The photo speaks for itself.

"Why are you standing in the middle of the parking lot?"

I look up to find Amira staring at me. She's already removed her Horizon shirt, revealing a black spaghetti-strapped shirt underneath that hugs her curves.

So, maybe I find her attractive. That's fine. I can accept that Amira is nice to look at. That doesn't have to mean anything!

Still, I make sure to focus my attention on her face as I walk over.

"The sky is pretty, so I took a picture," I say. "I sent it to the group chat. The one with Glory."

Amira pulls out her own phone and looks at it, nodding.

"And so you did," she says. "You should post this on your Instagram and tag Horizon. We rarely get any engagement on there. We can use this."

I tilt my head. "There's a Horizon Instagram?"

"Yeah, see, that's the problem," Amira says with a laugh. "I think Glory made it ages ago, but no one maintains it. It just exists."

"But don't you like social media?"

I frame it as a question, even though I've scrolled through her IG and TikTok more times than I'd like to admit. She's not an influencer, I don't think, but she's gone viral a few times. Her videos are mostly vlogs, particularly on game days or when she has a dance competition. Come to think of it, it's kind of surprising that she doesn't have any Horizon content, at least not that I've ever seen, obviously. Though I guess if she's working, she doesn't have much time to film.

Regardless, from the one or two times I've somehow found myself scrolling through her posts, I can admit that she's good.

Her videos are often straightforward, with voice-overs narrating the video, and she has this pastel aesthetic that's pretty consistent. It works.

"I do," Amira admits. "But this is Glory's thing. Not mine."

It takes everything in me not to roll my eyes. Amira will throw down with me any day of the week, but when it comes to asking Glory to run an Instagram, she's not up for the challenge? She can't be serious.

"You just said no one's maintaining it," I say as calmly as I can. "Just ask them if you can step in and take over. Do you know how many more people we could get coming in if we build a solid social media presence? It could be a game changer."

"I can't just make the account blow up overnight," Amira says.

I can see the wheels turning in her head already though. She's considering it.

"Maybe not overnight," I hedge. "But posting would be better than not posting, and I'm sure if you give it some thought, you could come up with a strategy or something. Don't you have like thousands of followers?"

"Five K," she says, with a shrug that feigns nonchalance. I don't buy it for a second.

"Right, so anyway, clearly you know what you're doing," I say. "Just go for it."

"What, like right now?"

Now I do roll my eyes.

"Glory's still in there, right?" I ask. "Why not now?"

Amira chews on her bottom lip, which looks a shade pinker than when we were at the counter. Did she put on makeup?

"Okay."

I snap my eyes up from her mouth and focus on her forehead. Meeting Amira's eyes right now feels dangerous.

"Be right back," she says, turning on her heel and going back into the theater.

I inhale deeply once she's gone, trying to get a handle on myself. All these thoughts about kissing and Amira and Horizon are making my head swim. I feel like I need to lie down or scream. That's when my stomach decides to growl so loudly, I worry Amira can hear it inside.

"Hm, maybe I'm just hungry."

I pat my stomach gently, hoping to settle it until I get home and stuff my face. A moment later, Amira is running back out the door right toward me. I don't even have a chance to move.

She launches herself at me and next thing I know we're hugging, her arms wrapped around my middle and her chin resting on my shoulder.

"Glory said yes!" she practically yells in my ear.

"Oh."

Awkwardly, I pat her shoulder with my hand, unsure what else to do.

Amira pulls back and places her hands on her hips.

"Now *I* get to say it," she says.

My brows furrow. "Say what?"

"You were right. Or good call. Whatever it was that you said before."

"Good call," I say. "Though saying I'm right makes more sense in this case."

"Of course, you would say that."

The door to the theater opens again, and Glory steps out, pulling up short when they see us.

"You girls are still here?"

Amira moves so she's now standing next to me. "We were just about to leave."

"Good, get out of here," they say, waving us off.

We say our good nights, for real this time, and Amira and I start walking to her car.

"Wanna get pizza?" Amira asks.

I feel like I'm having so much pizza this summer, I'm going to turn into one, but my stomach growls again, and that pretty much answers for me.

"Sure, why not?"

FOURTEEN

DECIDING TO GET PIZZA, AND choosing where to get the pizza from, turns out to be two very different things.

Obviously, I advocated for Joe's, but Amira claimed that Gino's, which is closer to her house, had the better sauce. I pointed out that it didn't make sense for us to pass my house (and Joe's) to get pizza, when she'd have to still drop me off after we ate.

That settled things. Because as she already realized this evening, I'm always right.

It's a Wednesday night, but it's summer, so Joe's is surprisingly packed when we arrive. Every booth is filled, and it takes almost twenty minutes just for us to get a regular pie to go. I barely get to say hi to Joe before he's moving along to the next customer.

With nowhere to sit inside, I suggest we go to my house and eat there. I immediately regret this decision when we walk through the door and Ma absolutely loses it.

"Oh my goodness, I must have died and gone to heaven."

Ma hops off the couch, pausing whatever true crime show

she's watching today, and pulls Amira into a tight hug. You'd think Amira had just returned from war or something.

"Hi, Mrs. Coleman," Amira says. She's using that voice I hate, the sickly sweet one, and I decide to remove myself from this lovefest and bring the pizza into the kitchen.

I start pulling down plates and hear Ma ask, "What brings you over? And with my daughter no less? I thought I'd never see the day."

"You're the one that told me to play nice, Mother," I call out, but she ignores me.

"We just wanted to get some food after work, and there was nowhere to sit at Joe's," Amira explains. "No biggie."

"Well, I'm happy to see you two getting along," Ma says.

I pop my head into the doorway that separates the kitchen and living room.

"Do you want a slice, Ma?"

"Just one, please."

I nod and grab another plate, setting it down on the table.

"Do you need any help?"

Amira has appeared in the doorway, and I shake my head.

"No, it's just pizza, but thanks. Do you want something to drink?"

It feels weird having her here in my house. I can't even really remember the last time she was here, if ever. The few times we've had to hang out, it's been at her house. Luisa has popped by here once or twice, but Amira is never with her. Now, seeing her stand in my little kitchen, I can't help but wonder what she's thinking.

"What do you have?" Amira asks.

"I finished the iced tea earlier," Ma says, stepping around her and reaching the fridge before I can. "So it's just lemonade or water."

"I'll take lemonade, please."

"Coming right up!"

I frown. "I never get this kind of service."

"You're not a guest." She proceeds to boop me on the nose before grabbing a couple plastic cups. We have real glasses, but they never get used. Instead, it's always these random cups that seem to magically appear in our cabinets.

One is from a 5K I can't recall either of us running in, and the other two are from *The Lion King* musical, which Ma won lottery tickets for a couple years ago. Once everything's arranged on the table, I move the pizza box to the counter, so we have more space, and then we dig in.

The quiet is a clear sign of just how hungry we all are, and it isn't until Ma has cleared her plate that someone speaks.

"So, how's it been working at Horizon?"

Amira and I look at each other, both of us still chewing, as we attempt to determine who's going to answer this question.

I swallow first, so I answer. "It's good."

"Yeah," Amira agrees. "Rochelle just came up with the great idea of me running the Horizon Instagram, so that's going to be fun."

"Oh, did she, now?" Ma raises her brows at me, somehow looking both happily surprised and proud.

"She's the one who's going to have to do the extra work," I

say with a shrug. "It was no big deal."

"Still, I wouldn't have asked Glory about it if Rochelle hadn't pushed me," Amira says.

"Yes, well, you're welcome, I guess."

My face feels warm as I focus my attention back on my pizza.

"Is Glory the woman who was so loud on the phone?" Ma asks.

"Person," I correct. "They're nonbinary."

Ma nods. "Right, got it. So, it was them?"

"Yep," I say. "Though surprisingly, they're not as loud in person."

Amira snorts at this, and I feel a small twinge of pride.

The conversation continues with Ma asking us more and more questions about Horizon, and we catch her up on all that's been going on, though somehow without discussing it, we mutually agree not to bring up Horizon's financial troubles. For some reason, I don't want Ma to know that they're not doing well. It feels like something we, meaning the Horizon staff, need to work out for ourselves, and I know if I mention it to Ma, she'll try to get involved somehow.

Ultimately, if Amira and I can't come up with a plan and the situation gets dire, I'll bring Ma in as reinforcement, but I don't want to burden her with this. Not yet.

Once we finish eating, Amira volunteers to help me with the dishes, which of course makes her even more special in Ma's eyes. If I didn't hate washing dishes, I would've told her I could do it myself, just so Ma could remember that I'm her real daughter and the one she loves. But washing dishes is my least favorite chore, and Amira and I get through them in half the time, with her helping me dry.

Plus, it's kind of nice. We get into a steady rhythm of me passing her each clean dish, and she quickly figures out where everything goes after she dries. Benefit of having a small kitchen is that there are only so many drawers and cabinets. By the time we're done, Amira needs to head home.

"I do need to pee before I go," Amira says.

At some point, Ma disappeared into her room, so it's just us.

"Oh, sure, let me show you."

I take her down the short hallway and flick the light on for her.

"Here ya go." I hold out my hands like an usher directing her to her seat, and suddenly feel so awkward I could die.

"Thanks," Amira says, laughter lacing her voice, and she steps past me into the bathroom, closing the door behind her.

I sigh and lightly pound my fist on my forehead. Literally, what is going on with me today? I cross the hallway into my bedroom, so I'm not just standing outside the bathroom door like some kind of creep. I fall into my bed, resting my hands across my stomach, taking in my glow-in-the-dark stars as I replay all the events of the day, from the almost kiss that probably wasn't almost anything to me inviting Amira into my home.

I fear I've taken Ma's advice a step too far. This tentative friendship should've never left Horizon's walls, and now I'm in too deep.

"What are you doing?"

I sit up to find Amira at the threshold of my room, head tilted, watching me.

"Nothing," I say. "Just looking at the stars."

Amira's brow furrows, so I point up to the glow-in-the-dark stickers.

"Oh my God." Amira steps farther into the room to get a better look. "You still have these up?"

Now I must look confused, because when she looks back down at me, she laughs.

"Do you seriously not remember? We put these up ages ago."

"We?"

"Yes, we!" Amira rolls her eyes before plopping down on the bed beside me. "I think we had a sleepover or something, and I brought these over and we stuck them up there. Your mom was so mad."

And all at once, it comes back to me. "Because we couldn't get them off."

Amira nods. "Yep. It was like they were superglued or something. My mom was pissed too when we moved, because we put the leftover ones on my ceiling. I wonder if mine are still up there. Can you imagine?"

I'm too busy slipping back into a memory to really digest her words. I don't know how I'd forgotten. It was before Amira moved, so we couldn't have been more than five. We were tiny, but Amira was still taller than I was even back then, so we stacked up my pillows for her to stand on, and I held on to her ankles as she placed the stars all over. We stayed up half the night just looking at them glow.

Even though Ma was mad, it was totally worth it.

"Sometimes I forget how far back we go," Amira says.

"I think I literally forgot," I say, and Amira laughs.

The sound tickles in my ear, and I realize how close we're sitting. If I turn slightly, my knees will knock into hers.

"Do you think if I hadn't moved, you wouldn't have ended up hating me?" Amira asks, catching me off guard.

"I don't hate you," I say automatically.

"Maybe not anymore," Amira says. "But you made it perfectly clear you wanted nothing to do with me the moment we started at North, and I never understood why."

"I told you why," I say, defensive. "It wasn't personal. I just didn't think being friends with you would be conducive to me reaching my goals."

Amira shakes her head and pushes to standing.

"Rochelle, how could I not take that personally?"

"I—"

"Just forget it," Amira says, waving a hand. "I don't know why I even brought it up. I should go."

"Amira . . ."

I falter, unsure what I want to say, but Amira doesn't wait for me to figure it out.

"I'll see you at work," she says, and then she's gone.

FIFTEEN

DESPITE WHAT AMIRA SAID, I don't see her at work.

For the first time in maybe forever, she's not working the same shift as me. The first time it happens, I brush it off. Schedules change and people switch shifts all the time. But by the third time, I begin to suspect it's intentional.

I've considered texting her to ask point-blank if she's avoiding me, but I've refrained out of fear of sounding self-centered. How embarrassing would it be if there was a valid reason for us somehow not overlapping in our last few shifts, and I assumed it had something to do with me?

No, instead I sit and stew, running through our conversation (fight?) over and over again, wondering how I messed things up so badly. It wasn't like I said something she didn't already know. I thought we'd moved past this.

When I finally get another day off, I'm grateful when Taylor and Kerry practically invite themselves over to my house.

Between me working, Taylor dating Shawn, and Kerry spending half her time at Horizon as our undercover secret agent, our schedules have become even more chaotic than during the school year. At least when we're at school, we're guaranteed to see each other in class. I haven't been able to tell them any of the Amira stuff that's been going down.

"So, what's been happening?" Kerry asks.

She's sitting up on the couch, her legs tucked underneath her, a Blow Pop in one hand and her phone in the other. Taylor and I are sitting on the pillows on the floor on either side of her, trading packs of sour straws. We decided that today we could have candy for lunch.

I'm about to dive into my debacle, but Taylor speaks before I can.

"Nothing," Taylor says, way too nonchalantly to be believable.

Her lips twitch with the hint of smile, giving her away. Kerry points a finger at her, and she looks exactly like that one Leonardo DiCaprio meme.

"Uh-uh-uh," she says, wagging her finger. "Don't even try it. People keep coming to me asking what's going on with you and Shawn. You know people are calling you two the Goth and the Golden Retriever?"

Taylor stops mid-chew. "Who's calling us that?"

Kerry shrugs. "Everyone."

Taylor turns to me, eyebrow raised. "Have you heard us called that?"

"No," I say, truthfully. "But I don't hear much, so I'm not a reliable source."

"Exactly," Kerry says, smugly. "Meanwhile, I have been spending all my free time around Horizon, and so I hear all the things. And you, my friend, have a ship name."

"I thought ship names were supposed to be combinations of the couple's names," I say.

"Typically, but isn't the Goth and the Golden Retriever so cute? It kind of sounds like the title of a children's book."

Taylor lets out a long-suffering groan, which only makes Kerry laugh.

I poke Taylor's knee with my pack of strawberry sour straws, and she picks up the green apple straws she's been hoarding and hands them over in exchange for mine.

"So, to confirm, you two are officially dating now, right?" I ask.

Taylor nods, almost reluctantly, and Kerry squeals in a register that sounds unnatural.

"Have we still not figured out a way to turn the volume down on her?" Taylor asks me.

I shake my head. "Unfortunately, no."

"Do not speak of me as if I'm not right here," Kerry says with a pout.

"How could we forget you're right there when you make sounds like that?" Taylor asks.

Kerry, very maturely, sticks her tongue out at her.

"Anyway," Taylor continues. "Shawn actually took me out last night to see this really cool indie goth band that I won't even bother telling you the name of because I know you haven't heard of them. I was kind of shocked Shawn had, but he said he did his research."

Kerry sits back on the couch, beaming with heart eyes. I too am overcome with a warm fuzzy feeling, but I'm better at keeping that kind of thing under the surface.

"He did his *research*?" she says, though it's obviously not a question. "That's so romantic."

Taylor is looking everywhere but at our faces.

"It was pretty cool, yeah," she says. "And now he's my boyfriend, so that's cool too."

Kerry completely loses it now, but thankfully she has the thought to cover her face with a pillow before screaming into it. I can't help the laugh that escapes me at Kerry's theatrics, and when I look over at Taylor, she can no longer hide the grin on her face.

"Wow, I can't believe you and Shawn are really an item now," I say.

Taylor rolls her eyes. "An *item*? Really? What year is it?"

"Would you prefer we call you a couple?" Kerry asks, leaning forward with a grin like the Cheshire cat.

"Boyfriend girlfriend?" I ask.

"Looooverrrrs?" Kerry wiggles her eyebrows suggestively.

Taylor promptly hits her with a pillow, but that doesn't stop me and Kerry from bursting out laughing.

"I hate you both," Taylor says, but neither Kerry nor I believe her.

"Can we please talk about literally anything else?" Taylor asks.

"I think Amira's avoiding me," I say without preamble.

Kerry, for some reason, chooses to raise her hand.

"Permission to speak freely?" she asks.

"Were you not already doing that?" Taylor says.

"Permission granted," I say at the same time.

"Thank you," Kerry says. "You seem to be implying that Amira avoiding you is a problem."

I wait, struggling to find the question here. "Yes. And?"

"And I don't understand why this is a problem," Kerry says. "Last I checked, Amira was the bane of your existence."

"The thorn in your side," Taylor adds.

"Everything wrong with the world," Kerry adds on. "I know you two are committed to the 'Save Horizon' cause now, but I thought that was simply an alliance of mutual benefit."

"Wait, what cause are we talking about?" Taylor interjects, but Kerry waves the question away.

"I'll explain later. The point is, isn't Amira avoiding you like a dream come true?"

I blow out a breath as I realize they truly have no idea what's been going on lately.

"Okay," I say, "clearly there's a lot I need to catch y'all up on."

And so, I dive in, starting with my offer to be "amicable coworkers" with Amira all the way up to our fight the other day. I even tell them about the maybe-almost kiss, which gets a certified gasp out of Kerry. By the time I'm done, they both look shook, and Kerry has slid off the couch, squeezing in between Taylor and me on the floor.

"Let me see if I have this right," Kerry says, pressing her hands together like she's in prayer. "You and Amira agree to be friends, things are going well, so well you think there's a possibility she may even kiss you? Then she asks why you hate her, and your response is that you simply didn't think it was beneficial to keep her around. Do I have that right?"

"That's not exactly what I said," I grumble.

"Tomatoes, to-mah-toes," she says. "That's the general gist, then?"

I sigh. "Yes."

"Okay, cool." Kerry turns to Taylor. "Would you like to do the honors, or shall I?"

"I think you have this handled," Taylor says, as she chews on another sour straw. "Please proceed."

Kerry nods and then refocuses her attention on me. Smiling, she grabs the nearest pillow and bops me on the head before I even have a chance to dodge it.

"Ow!" I say, glaring at her.

"It's just a pillow," Taylor says. "You'll live."

"Exactly," Kerry says. "And more importantly, you deserve it. Rochelle, people are not obstacles in your way that you can just push aside. They have feelings!"

"I know that," I shout back. "I never intended on hurting Amira's feelings."

"Intent does not negate impact," Kerry says.

Taylor snaps her fingers. "Preach."

"Can you two be serious and focus, please?" I say. I'm beginning to get a headache, and I don't know if it's because of the pillow, this conversation, or a combination of both.

"Did you say you're sorry?" Taylor asks. "To Amira, I mean? That's probably what she wanted."

I sigh. "No, she ran out of here before I could."

"Mm, and she doesn't have a working phone or anything?" Kerry asks.

"I didn't consider that, thanks," I say sarcastically.

The truth is, it didn't even occur to me to apologize, which makes me feel like the worst person on the planet. Though in my defense, I thought explaining why I had to keep my distance from her would be enough, especially since this whole thing happened ages ago. I had thought we moved past it. I wasn't expecting Amira to bring it up again out of the blue. Not when it was beginning to feel like we could be friends after all.

"What I don't get is, you're friends with us," Kerry says. "Why did you think you couldn't be friends with Amira?"

"We've been friends for years," I say. "This may shock you, but I actually wasn't thinking about Wharton when we met at the ripe old age of seven."

"But you were thinking about it in ninth grade?" Taylor asks.

"Yes!" I throw up my hands, exasperated. Why do I still need to explain this? "We were starting high school. Our GPAs were finally going to matter. I was taking all AP classes for the first time, and it was terrifying. Everything was different and then in walks Amira, someone I'd barely seen or spoken to over the past decade, and she keeps talking to me and making me laugh while I was trying to do our first lab assignment.

"We barely got it done, and I think we scraped by with maybe an eighty percent at best. Don't you see? I couldn't have her around. She would've ruined everything!"

I'm breathing so hard, I can see my chest rising and falling.

I feel tears prickling the corners of my eyes, which irks me even more. Why am I crying?

"Whoa, all right," Taylor says.

She shifts closer and so does Kerry, until they're on either side of me, their arms wrapped around me in a protective cocoon.

"And here I thought you just hated her because she was annoying," Taylor says into my hair.

"She is," I say, but it comes out a laugh. "Very annoying. And frustrating. She's not supposed to be taking up so much of my brain space. This is what I mean!"

There's a beat of silence, and I can practically feel Kerry and Taylor have a silent conversation over my head.

"What?" I say, looking between them. "Just say it."

"Now, I don't have too much experience in the crushes department," Kerry begins, hesitantly.

"But you definitely sound like you have a crush on Amira," Taylor finishes.

"Which would explain the whole kiss thing," Kerry adds. "You probably just *wanted* her to kiss you."

"I . . . what . . . no," I stammer. "No. We're just friends. I like her as a friend now. That's all."

"Right, except that we're friends," Taylor says. "And you have no problem juggling being friends with us and everything else you do. Sure, we became friends a long time ago and circumstances were different, but you were so undone by Amira, you made her enemy number one."

"And, for all your concerns about her distracting you from your goals, you've still ended up spending the majority of these last three years with that girl living in your mind rent-free," Kerry adds. "Plus, you know what they say. There's a thin line between hate and love."

Taylor nods in agreement. Meanwhile, I feel like my head is going to explode. It's one thing when the possibility crosses my mind, as a total hypothetical, of course, but it's another thing entirely to hear it from my two best friends.

"Oh my God." I bring my hands up, covering my face. "Oh my God. Oh my God. Oh my God."

"Yeah, girl," Kerry says, patting my back gently. "You're in trouble now."

SIXTEEN

WHEN I ARRIVE AT HORIZON for my next shift, Amira is there.

I do a double take when I see her at the register, and a part of me wants to flee. But I've never bailed on work before, and I'm not about to start now. It's the first time I've seen her in almost a week, and I was beginning to worry I may never see her again, which is ridiculous since we literally go to the same school.

Still, the fear that I'd wrecked everything between us lingered, making it quite obvious that if I don't have a crush on Amira, at the very least my strong feelings should probably be addressed. Maybe not with her yet. That feels like way too much. But I can at least acknowledge to myself there's something LGBTQ going on here.

I approach concessions cautiously, as if Amira is a skittish cat that might run as soon as I reach her.

"I can see you, you know."

Amira looks up and when our eyes lock, I'm not sure what to make of her expression. She doesn't look mad per se, but she definitely doesn't look happy to see me either.

"Right, well, hi," I say, because I am a competent person who knows how to speak in complete sentences.

"Hello."

"Hi!"

Jennie pops up from behind the counter, nearly giving me a heart attack.

"Jeez, how long have you been down there?" I ask, clutching my chest.

"Not long," she says. "I was counting the cups."

"Right." I look away from Jennie back to Amira. "Can we go somewhere and talk for a second?"

Jennie looks between the two of us, and then turns her attention to the soda machine as if she's never seen it before.

"Sure, we can go into the office," Amira says. "Glory just popped out."

I sigh with relief. I don't really have a plan for how to fix things with Amira, but I know I won't be able to work a whole shift with her without at least saying something first.

I step aside so she can step out from behind the counter and follow her into the office. Once we're inside, I close the door behind us, not really wanting anyone to overhear this.

"So," Amira says. She's standing in front of Glory's desk, arms crossed, watching me. "What do you want to talk about?"

I swallow, a lump of nerves caught in my throat. I hate that she makes me feel like this. Why does it feel like whatever I say right now may be the most important thing I ever say in my life? This is just a conversation with Amira. It shouldn't be this dire.

And yet . . . !

"I'm sorry." The words tumble out of me as I exhale, and Amira quirks a brow.

"That's it . . . ?"

"No, I mean." I pinch the bridge of my nose, closing my eyes, and then open them.

"I'm sorry for what I said back in ninth grade and for not realizing that I owed you an apology in the first place. I thought I was doing the smart thing by pushing you away, and I should've considered how that'd make you feel. And I'm sorry."

"You said that part already," Amira says. Her arms are still crossed, but her face has softened a bit.

"I think it bore repeating," I say with a hesitant shrug.

Amira's lips twitch and she shakes her head like she doesn't know what to do with me.

"Apology accepted," she says. "Though I maybe also owe you an apology."

This surprises me, and it must show on my face. Amira adds, "Don't look so shocked. I just mean it's possible you're not the only one to blame for us not getting along all these years. You pushed me away, and I pushed back by trying to beat you in any class we were in together. Which, honestly, has been really exhausting. You're very smart. Most of the time anyway. Though your emotional intelligence could use some work."

That shocks a laugh out of me, and Amira grins.

"So, does this mean we're good now?" I ask.

This almost feels too easy. Too good to be true.

"That depends, are we actually friends now?"

There's a small voice inside of me that wants me to ask for more than that, but I'm not willing to open that can of worms yet. I hold out my hand.

"Friends," I say.

Amira rolls her eyes but takes my hand, giving it a quick up-and-down pump before letting me go. As soon as her hand falls away, I miss the feel of her skin against mine.

"All right, well, now that that's settled, shall we get to work?" Amira says.

"Oh, right, I kind of forgot about that part for a second."

Amira gasps so dramatically, Kerry would be proud.

"Rochelle Marie Coleman forgot about work? Am I dreaming?"

I gently push her as we make for the door.

"Ha ha, whatever. And why do you know my middle name? Let me guess, my mom told you."

"Nope," Amira says, turning so she's walking out the door backward, looking at me with a playful grin. "You told me once. Your middle name is Marie and mine is María.

"You see, Rochelle, I haven't forgotten a single thing about you."

She then has the audacity to wink at me and walk away.

We make it through our shift without a hitch, and it feels like things might be moving in the right direction at Horizon.

In the midst of our work, Amira has Jennie and Brigit do these "Staff Pick" videos for the Horizon Instagram. They have to recommend what movie people should see. Thankfully,

I avoid the camera, because I haven't actually seen any of the movies that are currently showing at the theater.

"You know," Amira says. She's standing next to me, monitoring me as I handle the register.

"We could watch a movie together," Amira continues. "That way you won't have to lie for your Staff Pick video."

I turn to her. "You were going to make me lie for the video? I thought I simply wasn't going to do it."

"Everyone has to make a video, Rochelle," Amira says, like it's obvious. "It's mandatory."

"Legally, I don't think you can force me to participate."

"What are you gonna do?" She steps closer, hands on her hips as she towers over me. "Sue me?"

I swallow. "Well, my mom is a lawyer after all."

"Your mom loves me; she would never agree to represent you in a case against me."

Unfortunately, even in this hypothetical scenario, I know this is true.

"Like I was saying." Amira smiles, triumphantly. "We should pick a day when we're both off and see a movie."

"You didn't want to go to Green Acres on our day off, but you'll actually come to our place of work instead? Seems sus."

"What seems sus?"

Amira and I both jump at the sound of Brigit's voice, coming from the other side of the counter. Her shiny blond hair is pulled up again in a sleek ponytail, and I'm beginning to be concerned about her edges. She's giving off JoJo Siwa at this point.

"Brigit, you're supposed to be over there," Amira says with an exasperated sigh, pointing toward the red velvet rope that sections off the path to the theaters.

Brigit shrugs. "No one's coming in right now, and if they do, I'll see them from here and run right over. It's boring just standing over there by myself."

Amira looks like she's about to argue the point, but then Jennie returns from break, beaming.

"Aw, look at this all-lady shift," Jennie says, draping an arm around Brigit's shoulders. Brigit appears to flinch at the contact, and Jennie quickly drops her arm.

"Sorry, Bridge," Jennie says.

I exchange a look with Amira. *Since when do we call Brigit, Bridge?*

Amira rolls her eyes. *Since always, you just don't pay attention.*

Oh, cool, I guess we can speak with our eyes now.

"It's fine," Brigit says with a wave of her hand. "You're just sweaty is all."

Jennie's smile falls and I see her pull her shirt away from her a bit, giving it a little sniff, before wrinkling her nose. We have been here for hours now, and though the AC is allegedly on full blast, the July heat has still managed to sweep in. Moving around all day serving food certainly doesn't help the BO situation. And yet Amira seems unaffected. How does she do it?

"Anyway, what were you two talking about?" Brigit asks, focusing her attention back on me and Amira.

"Nothing," I say, as Amira interrupts me. "Rochelle hasn't seen any of the movies playing," she says.

Jennie and Brigit both gasp as if I've committed a crime. Seriously, the theatrics of these people.

"Rochelle, you know we can see movies here for free, right?" Jennie asks.

Her face is filled with such genuine concern, I have the absurd need to assure her I am well aware of this one perk from our job.

"Yes, I know," I say. "We spend so much time here already, it just feels silly to come and watch a movie here as well."

"So, you'd rather go somewhere else and pay to watch a movie instead?" Brigit asks.

It takes me a second to realize this is not rhetorical.

"No," I say, drawing out the word. "I just don't go to the movies. I definitely mentioned this during orientation."

"That feels like a lifetime ago," Jennie says, almost wistfully.

"Yeah, I remember nothing from that day," Brigit says.

"Well, I said I don't go to the movies that much," I say. "And that was the truth."

"So, why did you want to work at Horizon?" Brigit asks.

"I . . . didn't," I say.

Brigit and Jennie look like I just kicked a puppy, and I turn to Amira, who's grown incredibly quiet. She holds up her hands as if to say, "You're on your own, kid."

Great.

"I just mean, it wasn't my first choice," I explain. "But I love working here with everyone now, obviously. I couldn't imagine working anywhere else. That's why I want to save Horizon."

"Speaking of which, where are we on the plan?" Jennie asks

excitedly. "Did you talk to Glory about the renting thing you mentioned the other day?"

The twists and turns of this conversation are giving me whiplash.

"I did," Amira says, finally jumping in. "They said they'll need to run through the idea with Derek and Eric and figure out logistics, but that it could certainly work. Though they didn't seem confident that would be enough to change things, so I'm still brainstorming."

"*We're* still brainstorming," I correct. "We'll think of something. I'm sure of it."

"Okay, I'm also thinking too," Brigit says.

"Me three!" Jennie adds.

"Perfect, the more brains the better," Amira says, grinning at me in a way that makes it impossible for me to look away.

Thankfully, that's when the doors up front open, and a couple steps through.

"Back to my station I go," Brigit says, deflated.

Jennie makes her way back under the counter, looking between Amira and me suspiciously.

"What?" I finally say.

"Oh, nothing."

Except she's smiling, and I know without a doubt I've somehow been caught.

SEVENTEEN

MY FEARS ARE CONFIRMED DURING my next shift.

Lisa, Jennie, Shawn, and I are running concessions and Danny's doing tickets. Amira is off today, but this time I know it's because she has a dentist appointment. She's actually going to be by later so we can watch the new Marvel movie together. Thanks to the help of our coworkers and her reframing of this assignment as homework, I've agreed to finally experience Horizon from the customer's point of view.

Also, the fact that this seems like a date may have swayed my decision as well.

I'm so busy thinking about seeing Amira tonight, it takes me a second to realize Lisa is asking me something.

"So, how's Amira?" Lisa singsongs into my ear.

She's saddled up on my left, and Jennie has appeared on my right. They're extra twinning today, their hair pulled up in somehow identical messy buns, and they're wearing the same khaki capris and black Fila sneakers. The only slight difference between them is Jennie appears to be wearing a little makeup, which is weird since I don't think I've ever seen her wear makeup before.

"She's fine, I guess," I say, fighting to take off my gloves.

It's been a slow day, which isn't too unusual since this is a weekday morning, but I can't help but feel a little concerned about the pace of business, now that I understand how much it matters.

"It seems like you two are BFFs now," Jennie says. Out of the corner of my eye, I can see a mischievous glint in her eyes, which puts me on high alert.

I've told no one at work about my feelings for Amira, and I plan on keeping it that way. Especially with Amira's bestie Shawn being here today. The last thing I need is for Shawn to go blabbing to Amira that I'm into her, especially when I don't necessarily know what to do about this new development yet myself.

"We're friendly," I hedge.

"Interesting," Lisa and Jennie say in unison.

I step out of the sandwich they've put me in and grab a rag, wiping down the already clean counter to give my hands something to do. Lisa and Jennie aren't dissuaded, of course, and come to stand behind me, following me as I make my way around the counter.

"What caused the change?" Jennie asks.

"Nothing caused it," I say. "We just decided to call a truce while we work together."

This at least is true. Jennie and Lisa aren't buying it though.

"And that's all?" Lisa asks.

I nod. "That's all."

They both hum in disbelief and I roll my eyes. Why is everyone so nosy? Just this morning, Ma asked me how things are going with Amira. I said, "Fine," and she answered, "That's it?" As if I was supposed to have a whole story to tell. She just saw the girl at our house not too long ago, and I know she and Luisa have been gossiping about us whenever they get together. Ma just wants the tea.

"Look, I don't get what the obsession is," I say, turning to the twins. They both jump back a bit, which fills me with a little satisfaction. "Amira and I are cool now, and that's all you need to know. What we should be talking about is why Jennie is wearing makeup today when we have basically no customers."

Lisa and Jennie both blink, startled, and then Lisa turns and looks over her sister's face. She proceeds to speak in Korean, reaching out a finger to swipe at Jennie's face, but Jennie swats her hand away.

"I'm just wearing a smidge of blush and a little gloss," Jennie says in English, presumably for my benefit. She steps out of Lisa's reach as she tries to poke at her again. "It's not a big deal, obviously, since you didn't even notice."

"But why?" Lisa asks. "We're only going home after this."

"I just wanted to look nice, that's all."

Now it's my turn to grill someone. "Nice for who?"

Jennie opens her mouth to respond but closes it again when Kerry appears. I raise my eyebrows at my friend, who, when last I checked, was spending a solid three hours watching the movie I'll be seeing later.

"There's no way the movie's over," I say. Then I remember the whole reason she's here. "Wait! Did something happen?"

She waves her hands. "No, no, everything's good. I am just tragically bored. That movie blows."

I'm about to ask Kerry what she didn't like about it, but for some reason, Jennie bursts out laughing. I look from her to Kerry, confused. Kerry can be funny, but nothing about what she just said deserved a laugh that big.

"Uh, you can probably just head home, then," I tell Kerry. "No reason to stick around today. Everything's been good lately."

"Knock on wood," Lisa says, though nothing around us is wood to knock on.

"Or you could hang with us," Jennie suggests. "We're off in about an hour."

I raise a brow at Jennie, but she ignores it. While I'm not opposed to my friend groups intermingling, Jennie has only interacted with Kerry in our group chat, and they've only seen each other in passing here at the theater.

"Oh, sure, I can kick it for a bit," Kerry says. She places her hands on the counter and hops up.

"Absolutely not," I say, gently pushing her off. "I just cleaned that."

"Oops, sorry," Kerry says, and I just roll my eyes, spraying down the counter.

"Actually, I should probably go home and review my scripts," she says. "I need to be off book for our next rehearsal of *Annie*."

"You're doing *Annie*?" Lisa asks. "Where?"

"Just at the Birdwell Theater, out in Suffolk. It's a bit of a ways away, but they've let me perform there since I was little, so I'm committed to making the journey," Kerry says.

"Who are you playing?" Jennie asks.

"One of the orphans, of course," Kerry says. "Not a big role, but I have a few key lines that I want to get just right."

"You're so dedicated to your craft," Jennie says with a sigh.

Kerry glances over at me, a questioning look on her face. I shrug, though I'm starting to get a bad feeling I know what's happening here. Why is everyone crushing on my friends?

"Yeah, I . . . guess I am," Kerry says, finally. "Anyway, I'll catch up with you all later. Let me know if you need me to spy again. We will catch this prankster even if that means I have to hide in the rafters or install listening devices in the halls. There's nothing I won't do."

I laugh. "All righty, soldier, at ease."

I wave her off, and she gives a mock salute as she makes her way to the door and heads out.

"So, Rochelle . . ." Jennie has slid over to me, and I'm already dreading where this is going. "I've been meaning to ask. Is Kerry single?"

Even though I knew it was coming, the question still catches me off guard.

"Uh, yeah," I say, then quickly add, "But she's not looking to date anyone right now."

The truth is Kerry probably wouldn't be looking to date anyone ever, though people love to tell her that she may eventually change her mind. She doesn't love labels, but currently she's been describing herself as aroace, which for her means she doesn't feel romantic or sexual attraction to people.

It's not my place to tell Jennie all that though. Unfortunately, Jennie isn't deterred.

"That's okay. We can be friends-to-lovers," Jennie says. "I've already begun laying down the groundwork. We'll keep hanging out, and then she'll fall for me over time."

"Jennie, for the last time, we are not in a K-drama," Lisa says. "You cannot *make* Kerry like you."

"Yep, you definitely cannot do that," I agree.

"You guys just lack vision and drive," Jennie says, which makes me guffaw. Seriously, I have the *most* vision and drive, thank you very much.

"There's something there," Jennie continues.

"How could something possibly be there?" I ask. "You barely know her."

I try to hide it, but I'm a little annoyed now. It took me ages to realize I like Amira. How could Jennie like Kerry this quickly?

"That's not true!" Jennie says. "We've been texting! She's watched all my drama recs and lets me know all her thoughts, unprompted. Clearly there's potential here. I just need more time with her."

I blink, surprised. This is the first I'm hearing of this new friendship, and now I'm curious why Kerry hasn't mentioned it. Taylor and I did kind of dominate our last catch-up sesh, so perhaps that's it. Regardless, I know Kerry well enough to know that whatever Jennie thinks is going to happen here, it won't.

"I don't think time is going to help," I try to say, but Jennie's clearly not listening.

"I'll text her and see if she needs help running her lines." Jennie pulls out her phone and starts typing. Lisa exchanges a concerned look with me, but I'm not sure what I can do or say in this situation. Jennie has obviously made up her mind to pursue Kerry, and I'm not going to out Kerry to protect Jennie's feelings.

The best I can do is warn Kerry that Jennie has a crush and hope Kerry can handle it.

Besides, how serious can Jennie's feelings even be?

EIGHTEEN

IT WOULDN'T HAVE MADE SENSE to go all the way home to shower and change before Amira got here, so after I clock out, I run into the gender-neutral bathroom to do what Ma likes to call a bird bath.

Essentially, I take a washcloth I brought from home and the travel body wash I got while on break and wipe down the most important body parts. I then swap my uniform for the ombre purple fit-and-flare dress I stuffed into my bag this morning. I take my braids down from their standard ponytail and shake them out a little, so they fall around my shoulders, and slip back into my sneakers. And voilà! I check myself out in the mirror and I don't look half-bad.

When I step back out, Shawn, Jennie, and Lisa all hoot and holler like I've just won a contest or something.

"All right, all right, all right," I say, waving them off. "It's just a dress."

"You look cute though, Rochelle," Lisa says. "I like this look on you. It's like you're glowing."

My face warms, and I simply mutter, "Thanks."

"Are you going on a hot date?" Jennie says, wiggling her eyebrows suggestively. I low-key admire her commitment to assuming everyone is in the middle of a love story.

"No," I say, though I already know what I say next will have her losing it. "Amira's coming and we're going to watch a movie. The Korean one. Which looks good, I think. I don't really know what it's about. We were gonna do Marvel, but I trust Kerry's opinion enough to skip it."

I feel like I'm rambling now, so I force myself to stop talking.

Lisa, Jennie, and Shawn are all quiet as they stare at me. And then, with no preamble, Shawn shouts, "Finally!"

Next thing I know, he's hopping over the counter and pulling me into a hug that lifts me off my feet.

"What is happening here?"

Shawn and I both turn at the sound of Amira's voice. She looks great but very casual. Her hair is pulled back in two tight cornrows with yellow rubber bands at the ends, presumably to match the yellow crop top she's wearing with gray denim shorts. Perhaps I overdressed for this.

Shawn releases me and once my feet are back on the ground, I move over to Amira to . . . give her a hug, maybe? I'm not sure what my plan was, but I pull up short and raise my hand and give an awkward wave.

"Hey."

"Hi," Amira says, though it comes out sounding a little like a question. She has a bemused look on her face that I cannot look at for too long or my stomach will never stop flipping around. "Why was Shawn hugging you?"

"That's a great question," I say. "And I honestly don't know."

"No reason," Shawn says, though he's beaming. "Sometimes I just want to hug my friends and show them love, that's all."

Amira and I both stare at him.

"All righty, then," Amira says. "Shall we go in? Movie starts in ten."

"Yeah sure," I say. "Do you want a snack? Twizzlers and popcorn?"

It takes everything in me to hide my smug smile at Amira's surprised expression.

"You remembered that?"

I shrug. "You're not the only one with a good memory."

"Apparently not. All right, let's—"

We're both surprised to find Lisa, Jennie, and Shawn all staring at us. I kind of forgot they were there for a second.

"What?" I ask.

"Oh, nothing," Jennie says, though she's grinning like the Cheshire cat. It's a little scary.

"Twizzlers and popcorn you said?" Lisa asks, stepping around her sister.

Amira exchanges a "What the fuck?" look with me before saying yes.

We wait patiently as our friends put together our order, and the whole thing feels a little weird. It gets even weirder when Amira pays for all of it, including the large soda she decides we can share since it's cheaper than buying two small drinks.

"You know you don't really need to pay for all of this," Shawn says, more to Amira than to me. "We can just comp all of this."

I've learned recently that comping is something we do for friends and family, or when the inventory and cash bag don't match but the difference is the exact price of one item. It basically means someone got something on the house, so even though we lost the inventory, we didn't make money off it.

"I know, but I like to support Black businesses," Amira says. "And the last thing we need right now is comping things willy-nilly."

"You're right, you're right," Shawn says. He passes over our stuff, with a wink. "Enjoy your show and thank you for being a loyal customer to Horizon."

"Is that something we say now?" Lisa asks.

"No, but maybe we should," Amira says. "I like it."

"See what you did, Shawn," I say, grabbing the soda. "You can't just say things around Amira. She's not one of us. She's a *manager.*"

"Assistant manager but, yes, thank you for finally putting some respect on my name," Amira says. "Now, let's go before we miss the previews. Bye, guys!"

"Bye!" they all call out after us.

When we approach Danny, he barely glances up.

"Tickets?"

Amira pulls out her phone and shows him the barcode to scan.

"Thanks," he says, unhooking the rope.

"Do you think he even realized it was us?" I whisper as we head to theater 4.

"There's a solid chance he did not, and that is quite concerning," Amira says.

I laugh easily. This is surprisingly nice. I was expecting to feel nervous about this, because despite what I said to Jennie, this does feel like a date. Maybe not a hot one, but I don't even really know what that means. It's a date, nonetheless. And yet I feel comfortable.

We sit down right as the previews begin, and I swear I've heard nothing about any of these movies that are supposedly coming soon. Do I live under a rock? Amira, on the other hand, keeps dropping little tidbits about each one.

"This is clearly Oscar bait, but it's going to be so good.

"I can't believe they got Meryl Streep to come back for this.

"Have you seen the original version? It's so much better than whatever this is going to be."

As she goes on, a part of me feels like she should be here with Kerry. I know Kerry would know all about everything Amira is saying, but all I can offer her are little nods. It's fun seeing Amira this animated though. This is clearly what she loves, and I can see why Horizon is so important to her.

"Do you want to try it?" Amira asks, as the theater starts to darken. The movie is starting soon.

"Try what?" I whisper.

There are only a handful of other people in here with us, but how embarrassing would it be to have someone complain to our coworkers about us talking during a movie?

"The Twizzlers and popcorn," she whispers back. I can see now that she's holding out a Twizzler. I've been holding our bucket of popcorn in my lap, our soda in the cupholder between us.

I hesitate for a second before I grab a Twizzler. "Sure."

"Okay, now the key is to put a handful of popcorn in your mouth, chew a little bit, then add the Twizzler," she whispers. "It maximizes the salty-to-sweet ratio."

This sounds like a disgusting idea to me, but when in Rome, right? I do as I'm told, using my free hand to grab some popcorn, chewing a little, and then taking a bite of the Twizzler.

"Well?"

Amira's eyeing me and I keep chewing slowly, trying to figure out what I think.

"It's not bad," I say once I swallow. "Not great, but not bad."

"I'll take it," Amira says. "Now, hush, the movie is starting."

"You're the one who—"

"Shh," she says, holding a finger to her lips.

I grab some more popcorn and throw it at her, most of it landing in her lap or on the floor.

"You're cleaning that up, you know," she says, though I can hear the hint of a laugh in her voice.

I shrug. "Worth it."

NINETEEN

DESPITE US MISSING THE OPENING of the film, thanks to Amira's shenanigans, we both loved the movie.

I'm typically not into violent movies, but watching this single mom who doubled as an assassin throw a bunch of dudes around was pretty cool.

"So, I'm guessing this will be your Staff Pick," Amira asks as we walk out of the theater. She did actually make me clean up the popcorn, but I would've done it anyway. I've swept these floors before; I'm not going to make more work for someone else.

I nod. "Yes, but not just because it's the only one I've seen. It was really good."

"Think you could talk about it right now?" she asks.

We wave at our friends on our way out. Brigit has now swapped out for Shawn, and she does a double take when she sees us. She doesn't have a chance to say anything, since the place is way more packed now than it was earlier.

"Is this just a question, or are you saying I'm actually going to have to talk about it now?" I ask once we're outside.

"I would never make you do anything you wouldn't want to do, Rochelle," Amira says in that "I'm totally innocent" voice of hers. She even bats her eyelashes for good measure. I roll my eyes but do a poor job of keeping the smile creeping up my face at bay.

"Fine, where do you want me?"

I hear the innuendo as soon as I say it, and my face warms. But if Amira thinks anything of it, she doesn't show it. Instead, she takes my hand, leading me away from the doors and in front of the brick wall.

"Right here," she says.

She lets go of my hand as soon as I'm situated, and I miss the soft touch of her skin against mine. I lace my hands together in front of me, as if that'll help.

"All right, so we probably only have like ten or fifteen minutes of this perfect twilight hue we've got going on right now," Amira says, phone already out and pointed at me. "So, let's see if we can do this in one take."

"So, I just say what movie I like?"

"First, introduce yourself, then say why you think everyone should watch the movie," she says. "Have you not watched any of the videos I've posted?"

She sounds almost incredulous, but when she looks up from her phone, it's disappointment in her face.

"No," I say quickly. "I mean no, I haven't not watched your videos. I mean . . ." I pause, take a deep breath, and try again. "Of course, I've watched the videos. All of them. And I liked them too. Engagement, amirite?"

Seriously, what is wrong with me?

"Right . . ." Amira says, and I can't tell if she doesn't believe me or simply thinks I'm losing it. "Okay, well, then do like everyone else and you'll be fine. Ready?"

I shake out my limbs a bit and then nod.

"All right, we're rolling in three . . . two . . . one!"

Despite my best efforts, it takes three tries before we get it right. In my defense, we were interrupted when a couple stormed out of the theater arguing so loudly there was no way the audio could pick up anything I said. Thankfully, the third time was the charm.

"Perfect," Amira says, clicking off the camera. "See, easy peasy."

"Yeah, sure, easy to say when you're the one behind the camera."

"Excuse you, I already filmed one of me too. I just haven't posted it yet."

"Sure, likely story."

"Wow, you are about to feel so dumb right now."

She closes the short distance between us, standing beside me so her shoulder is slightly pressed against mine.

"Here," she says, thrusting her phone practically under my nose. I can see a video of her talking about how much she loves the Marvel movie we were supposed to see tonight.

"Wait, if you've already seen it, why did you suggest we see it tonight?" I ask.

Amira shrugs. "It seemed like something you'd like. Plus, it's three hours."

I attempt to understand her logic. "And a three-hour movie is a good thing?"

"Yeah." Her voice is completely calm and measured. "If it means spending three hours alone in a theater with you."

TWENTY

"WHAT?"

This is the eloquent response I give Amira. If I'm not mistaken, she's just told me she wanted to spend three hours alone with me in a dark room.

Sorry, dark theater.

Same difference though, right?

Amira chuckles as if this is a ha-ha kind of moment, when in reality it feels like the Earth has shifted on its axis.

"I said a three-hour movie is a good thing if it means spending three hours with you."

"Ah, yes, that's what I thought, just needed to confirm."

"Any further questions?"

"Just one," I say, turning so I'm fully facing her. "Did you mean it?"

Amira seems taken aback by my question, but I have to know. Because if this is a joke, if she's just teasing me again, or this is some long con to mess with my head so she can dominate in our classes this fall, I don't think I can take it.

She must see it on my face, because her voice softens as she takes my face in her hands.

"Yes, Rochelle," she says, leaning so close I can almost taste the mix of sugar and salt on her lips. "Of course, I meant it."

Then, as if to prove it, she presses forward and kisses me.

And oh wow, I can feel them now.

The sparks.

When we pull apart, Amira doesn't go far.

She laces her fingers through mine, and without a word she leads me to her car, where she kisses me again.

And then again when we reach my street. She parks a few houses down in case Ma is home. This kiss is slower and lasts longer, and it makes me feel like my insides have turned to liquid. I don't even know if I'm doing this right, and it takes me a second too long to remember to close my eyes, but Amira doesn't seem to care, and quite frankly neither do I.

When we're finally forced to come up for air, Amira giggles, and she's still so close I can feel the vibration of it on my lips. That makes me laugh too, and then we're both laughing—it's stupid, because nothing about this is funny. Except maybe the fact that it took us so long to get here. Or that I ever thought being around Amira would push me off course. Being with her feels like I've landed exactly where I'm supposed to be.

A few days pass before I see Amira again.

Between us working different shifts at Horizon, me trying to find time to keep up with Kerry and Taylor, and Amira going to her dance classes, we're both really busy. Still, if it weren't for the fact that we text every day, I might begin to think the kissing was a very vivid fever dream.

Our texts are mostly stupid stuff—she'll send me pictures of a weird snail she saw on the street or an endless number of TikToks, and I send her long paragraphs about some of the movies she's demanded I watch. So far, my favorites have been *Moonlight* and *If Beale Street Could Talk*, which she claims she knew I'd love.

She also says this makes me a Barry Jenkins stan now, as if that could ever be a bad thing.

We're finally reunited when we're put on the schedule together again exactly four days after The Kiss™, but things are so busy that I don't really get a second to talk to her. It's like every day camp in the tri-state area has decided that this Tuesday was the day to bring their kids to the movies. The day flashes in a blur of colorful branded T-shirts, and if I never see another child's hand covered in some kind of mysterious gunk, it'll be too soon.

"Is it over yet?" Jennie asks, as she face-plants on the top of the counter. "I don't think I can keep standing any longer."

Amira shoots me a look of amusement.

"It's over for now, I think," Amira says, tapping her shoulder sympathetically. "Why don't you go sit on a bench over there?"

"Nope, not so fast, Ms. Choi," Glory says, approaching us, seemingly from nowhere.

I realize I haven't actually seen Glory around much since they kind of had that little breakdown in the office two weeks ago. Today they seem more chipper, albeit still a bit messy.

Their red locs are pulled up into a bun that's tilting slightly to the right, and they're wearing a T-shirt that says "Be Gay. Do Crimes," instead of one with the Horizon logo.

As I lean over the counter, I can see they're also wearing flip-flops with socks, which besides probably being a health code violation is also a crime against fashion. Even to me. But I keep my mouth shut.

I'm starting to get better at keeping my inside thoughts inside.

"I need two of you to head down to the basement and grab a couple of things for me," Glory says.

Jennie lifts her head just enough to say, "We have a basement?"

"That we do!" Glory has way too much enthusiasm for a basement.

"What do you need down there?" Amira asks.

"Letters for the marquee," they say. "It seems someone thought it'd be funny to take some off our board to make some ridiculous phrases."

Amira, Jennie, and I all exchange looks. We'd gotten too comfortable thinking whoever was causing havoc at Horizon was done with us. Nope, now they were stealing. Awesome.

"I pulled it all down this morning," Glory continues. "So now it's blank, but we should have extra letters down there."

"Rochelle and I will go," Amira says, and I blink at her.

"We will?"

She gives me a pointed look that clearly says, "Yes, shut up."

"I mean, sure, yeah, we will," I say to Glory. "Do we need keys or . . ."

Glory somehow manages, with one hand, to detach a set of keys from the ridiculously large key ring hooked to a belt loop on their pants. They throw them to Amira, who catches them in the palms of her two hands.

"Are they in a box or something?" Amira asks.

"Yeah, they should be in a black box, I think," Glory says. "I haven't been down there in a while, but it should be pretty close to the stairs. If you can't find it, don't worry about it. We'll just have to order more."

"We'll find them," Amira says, with a confidence I do not share. I didn't even know we had a basement until today.

"Thanks, girls," Glory says.

They turn on their heel and instead of going into the office, they bound over to Shawn, who's been doing various poses that could be anything from karate to yoga.

"Come on. Vámanos," Amira says, looping her arm through mine.

"Aw, y'all are so cute together," Jennie says, causing me to freeze. Rationally, I know there's no way she could know me and Amira are . . . whatever we are. I haven't even had a chance to tell Kerry and Taylor yet, since I feel something of this magnitude needs to be discussed in person. And I don't think Amira has told anyone, although perhaps she told Shawn, who told Jennie?

I shake the thought away. Even if Amira did tell Shawn, I don't think he would've blabbed. Not about this.

Jennie clearly thinks nothing of her innocuous comment. She's now resting her head on her hand, elbow on the counter, bent at her waist. I don't understand how this could possibly be comfortable, and yet she looks like she's about to fall asleep. Amira must think the same, because she pulls away from me to clap three times right by Jennie's ear.

Jennie says a string of words in Korean that I don't have to understand to know are swears.

"No falling asleep on the job," Amira warns.

I still sometimes forget that Amira is technically the boss of the rest of us, but in moments like these, it's quite clear she takes her position seriously. Jennie must sense the shift as well, because she straightens up.

"Yes, ma'am," she says.

I snort, but Amira throws me a glare that has me quickly fixing my face.

"We'll be right back, but if things get busy again call me," Amira says. "Cell reception is spotty in the basement, but it usually at least goes through enough for me to see someone called."

"Will do," Jennie says, still standing with the posture of someone in the military.

Amira turns her attention back to me. "Let's go."

The command of it all should make me bristle, but I think it's maybe . . . hot? I don't know. It makes me feel things, and I purposely hurry after her so Jennie doesn't see whatever I'm feeling written all over my face.

TWENTY-ONE

AMIRA TAKES US OUT THE main entrance and around to the back of the building.

"Are you going to kill me?" I ask her. "This looks like the kind of place where someone gets whacked."

She smirks. "If I wanted to kill you, I would have a much better plan than this."

"Can you believe that's not at all comforting?"

We reach the dumpsters, which smell as gross as always, and beyond them is a rusted metal door that I've never once paid attention to.

"This leads to the basement?" I ask.

"No, it goes to Narnia, but we like to call it the basement," Amira says, grinning.

I reach out to flick her, but she grabs my hand, pulling me close until we're practically nose to nose.

"Hi," she says.

"Hi," I say back. I'm smiling now too.

She brings her lips down to mine, and everything else

around us fades away as she kisses me. I was worried that maybe the other day was a fluke. That we were just so caught up in the moment, and that's why it felt so amazing.

But I'm happy to discover I was totally wrong. This kiss is just as wonderful as the last, and my stomach feels like it's doing backflips. I can only barely register the gross trash smell a few feet away.

When we pull apart, we're both breathing hard.

"Going forward let's not wait so long to do that again," Amira says. "I can skip a dance class or two."

I shake my head. "Nope, nope. Kisses only come when we do the work we're supposed to."

Amira pouts. "But that's no fun."

"Where is the bossy girl from five minutes ago?" I ask, laughing.

"She melted away with your kisses," Amira says, before pressing her lips back against mine again. Despite what I just said, when she pulls away a moment later, it feels much too soon.

"Okay, back to work mode," she says. She steps away from me, as if distance will make this thing between us feel less all-consuming than it is.

"I may need your help pulling this open," Amira adds, moving to the door. "It can be tricky."

"Sure, okay."

I hover behind her as she inserts the key and gives it a turn while pulling on the metal handle. The door budges a smidge but doesn't open all the way. Amira makes room for me, and I come up around her and also grip the handle, my hands resting above hers on the bar.

"One, two, three . . . !" she says, and we pull hard.

The door jerks back and Amira falls into me, but I instinctively grab her waist, steadying her.

"Nice catch," she says, patting my hand that has somehow come to rest on her stomach. I quickly pull it away, before I do something stupid like hold her there against me, her back to my front.

"No problem," I choke out.

Amira pushes the door open a bit more until there's a sizable gap for both of us to slide through. The steps lead down into darkness, and I feel like I'm at the start of a scary movie.

"Quick question," I say. "If two Black girls are in a horror movie, who dies first?"

"I think the virgin always lives, so you should be safe," Amira quips.

"Ha ha," I say, though now my head is swimming with questions. Does that mean she's *not* a virgin? She's hooked up with someone? Who? When? How?

But I voice none of these questions and say, "Is there no light?"

Amira reaches inside and then flicks a switch that casts the steps in an orangey glow.

"Any other questions?" Amira asks, raising her brows to me.

"Nope, just tell my mom I love her if I don't make it out of this alive," I say.

Amira rolls her eyes and proceeds down the stairs. I reluctantly follow. When we reach the bottom, Amira stretches up and pulls a string that has another light bulb flickering on, casting the space in strange shadows.

The basement is really more of a long hallway filled with boxes and junk from what I can see. I pull my phone from my back pocket and click on the flashlight, and Amira does the same.

"What did Glory say we were looking for again?" I ask, flashing my phone around.

"A black box," Amira says.

"Oh, good, something easy to find in a dark room."

Amira snorts, and I grin.

"Did you just *snort?*"

I turn and she covers her face with a hand.

"Rochelle, my eyes," she says, and I lower my phone.

"Sorry."

"Wait, what's that behind you?"

Immediately, I'm jumping away from whatever it is she's talking about and standing by her side. I wave my phone around.

"What? What is it?"

Rather than answer, Amira bursts out laughing, hands on her knees.

"I literally hate you," I say, flipping her off.

"You do not," she says, between fits of laughter.

I roll my eyes and walk away from her. A quick scan with my phone reveals only a clutter of brown boxes that look like the ones people use when they're moving, but no black boxes. Odds seem high that the black box is actually packed away in one of these boxes, so I pick one at random and open it.

Instead of a black box, it's filled with a bunch of round silver canisters stacked on top of each other. They all have various writing on them like D73504 and D30024, but I have no idea what it means.

"Hey, Amira, do you know what this is?"

Amira, who's been looking into her own box, comes over and peers into the box over my shoulder.

"Oh my God, they're film reels," she says.

She reaches in and grabs one, flipping it over in her hands. She brushes the dust off and holds her phone's light over it.

"It looks like there was a title on here once, but it's faded," she says. "I wonder what it is." She looks up at me, her face excited. "What if this is, like, a long-lost film, and we can sell this for millions?"

I take the canister back from her. "What would a long-lost movie be doing in the basement of Horizon?"

"What are any movies doing in the basement of Horizon?" Amira says. She looks around the long row of boxes leading down what I'm beginning to fear is an endless hallway. "Let's see what else is in these."

"Amira, we're supposed to be looking for the letters for the marquee," I say, but she's clearly not listening.

The only way to find the letters for the marquee is to keep going through the boxes, so I leave Amira to her own devices and continue riffling through my own boxes as well. I push aside the box with the film canisters and open the one underneath it. I jump back with a scream.

Amira comes running over instantly. "What? What is it?"

I put a hand to my chest, feeling the quick rise and fall as I try to remember how to breathe properly. Meanwhile, Amira reaches into the box and pulls out the weird mask that almost gave me a heart attack.

"Oh, it's Michael Myers," she says, holding it out as if to show me.

"Who?"

"*Halloween*," Amira says. The "duh" at the end of that sentence is heavily implied. "One of if not the greatest thriller franchises ever."

"I don't watch scary movies," I say. "But sure, that sounds familiar."

I look back into the box and see it's filled with a number of other masks and costumes from various movies. I move that box aside and reach for the one on the bottom.

"Oh wow, some of these are really good," Amira says, her attention still focused on the previous box. "They feel real. Not like the ones you'd get from Party City."

The other box is more of the same, so I push it aside and move around Amira to a bigger box pushed against the wall. I give it a little push away from the wall, but it doesn't budge.

"What is this?" I mutter to myself.

The top is only folded closed, so it's easy to open, but looking down into it, all I see is a glass case. It's obviously not what we're looking for, but now I'm curious. Since I don't think I'll be able to pull it out of the box, I decide to rip the box open down the side.

"Rochelle!"

"What?"

I say this as I continue to rip the box open. When I get to the bottom, I can't keep my balance and end up falling backward onto my butt.

"Ow."

"What did you just do?" Amira says, looking from me to the now torn-open box. And then she does a double take. "Wait, what *is* that?"

With the box now open, we can see a glass case that comes up to Amira's waist and what looks like an old pay phone. The box and handle are black, but the place with the buttons and where the handle sits are all silver. There's a spot up top for coins to go in and another on the bottom for them to come out.

"I didn't know these still existed," Amira says.

"Why is it in a glass case?" I say at the same time.

Amira feels her way along the glass box, until she stops near the bottom.

"There's something on it," she says. Then she proceeds to completely remove the front of the box, and I raise my brows at her.

"What?" she says. "You already destroyed the box anyway."

Taking her phone, she flashes the bottom of the glass case with light and she's right. Down on the bottom there's a little engraved plaque.

"'Pay phone used in *Candyman* (1992),'" Amira reads. "Whoa."

"Oh wow, *I* even know that one," I say.

Amira stands and looks around the room. "What if there's

more stuff in these boxes?"

"Yes, I would think there is, in fact, stuff in the boxes," I say.

Amira rolls her eyes. "No, smart-ass. I mean stuff like this. Memorabilia. Props. Things that we could display in Horizon. We could have different exhibits each month. Become, like, a museum or something!"

I look around at all the other unopened boxes. There must be at least a hundred of them.

"You really think this basement is full of this stuff?"

Amira nods with the quick succession of a bobblehead. "Easy way to find out. Oooh! I can even post about this on our Instagram."

I chew my lip, thinking. It would be a cool promotional tool for the theater. I can already imagine Kerry losing her shit over this pay phone alone. If Amira's right, and there's more where this came from, this could be a huge deal.

"Okay," I say, finally pushing myself up. "Let's open some boxes."

Amira squeals and we get down to business.

TWENTY-TWO

WE LOSE TRACK OF TIME, opening box after box, discovering more props encased in glass. There are also items that tell the whole story of this place, from all the way back in the day.

Like someone put together a photo album of newspaper clippings about its opening in 1953 and the backlash that ensued. People like to think that only the South has issues with racism, but Long Island is just as segregated as down there, and while Horizon is in one of the more diverse areas now, it still clearly bothered people that a Black couple was able to buy prime real estate right by a mall that would open three years later.

That didn't stop the Handlers, though, or the community, who came out to support the theater. Horizon was even chosen as the location for a couple of movie premieres, attracting Black Hollywood to see what Long Island was all about. Some even stayed, increasing the Black population in places they'd previously been shut out of.

This of course pissed off white people even more, but still Horizon prevailed.

"This is incredible," Amira says.

She finds another album filled with black-and-white photos of Horizon and the events that took place here.

I look over her shoulder. "It really is."

Amira's phone begins to vibrate in her hand.

"Oh shit, it's Jennie," Amira says. "We've been down here for half an hour."

"And we never found the letters for the marquee," I say with a grimace, but Amira just waves her hand.

"It's fine, this is even better."

She closes the album she's holding, along with the one in my lap.

"Grab that and let's go."

She heads for the stairs, and I quickly follow.

When we get back inside, Lisa has joined her sister at the food counter, and Danny has replaced Shawn by the ticket rope.

"Where have y'all been?" Jennie asks.

"We got distracted," Amira says.

"Oh?" Jennie wiggles her eyebrows suggestively, which is hilarious because she barely has any eyebrows to begin with.

"Not like that," I say.

I'm too thrilled by our discovery to even take her little pokes at whatever she thinks she knows about me and Amira seriously.

I place my album on the counter, and Amira does the same with hers. Lisa and Jennie both step closer, scanning them.

"What are these?" Lisa asks.

"History," Amira says.

"Photos and news clippings about Horizon," I clarify. "Is Glory around? They should see this."

"In the office," Lisa says.

"Did they say anything about us being gone for so long?" Amira asks.

Jennie shakes her head. "No, they either didn't notice or figured it'd take you a while to find . . . whatever it was you were looking for."

Lisa, who's begun flipping through the photo album, gasps. "Is that Vivica A. Fox?"

"Respectfully, how do you know who Vivica A. Fox is?" I ask.

"She's in *Kill Bill*," Lisa says, like it's obvious.

"You've seen *Kill Bill*?" Amira asks.

Jennie rolls her eyes. "Ugh, yes, she loves all those fighting kind of movies. It's our dad's fault. He's a Bruce Lee stan. Very into the conspiracy surrounding his death and the death of his son too. One might even say he's obsessed."

"You're one to talk," Lisa says. "All you ever talk about are your dramas and Wi Ha-joon."

"When you find the love of your life, you will do the same, and I won't judge you," Jennie says.

I can't help but tilt my head in curiosity, thinking of what Jennie said about Kerry. She must be bi, then, or pan.

"I feel like we've lost the plot here," Amira says. She shuts the album, pulling it to her chest, and turns to me. "Let's find Glory. You two good here?"

The twins nod.

"Cool, we'll be back in a flash this time," Amira tells them.

"No worries," Lisa says, with a wave of her hand. "No one's here. It seems like a chill day."

"Oh, shut up," Jennie says. "You can only say that because you missed the camp rush. Today was brutal."

"Regardless, we'll manage," Lisa says.

"All right, let's go, then," I say.

We make the short walk to the office, and I knock on the door.

"Come in!" Glory calls.

I open the door and find the office slightly more cluttered than usual. The filing cabinet in the corner is open, and there are folders on top of folders covering Glory's desk.

"Hi, girls." Glory has to move one pile of folders to the left so we can see them. "Did you find the letters?"

"No, but we found something even better," Amira says, then she looks to me as if it's my turn. I guess it was my idea to try to find a way to save Horizon.

Well, here goes nothing.

"Did you know that there's a bunch of memorabilia from the golden days of Horizon in the basement?" I ask. "There are photos, news clippings, and, most interesting, props from old Black films."

"Classics," Amira prompts with a cough.

"Yes! Classic Black films," I say. "All of this incredible history, just sitting in the basement collecting dust."

"I knew there was stuff down there, yes," Glory says, almost hesitantly, as they look between the two of us. "But what about it?"

"We're looking for ways to bring people in. To breathe new life into Horizon, right?" I ask, again rhetorically. "This could be it. We can set up a display with all this cool stuff and remind people that Horizon isn't just a movie theater, it's history."

Truth be told, I didn't know where I was going with this speech when I started, but by the end I'm feeling impassioned. This is a good idea. A great idea even. I can already see the display case. We can have it over by the benches in the lobby, maybe even set up the telephone in between the restrooms. It'll be vintage decor to go with the incredible art on the walls.

"This sounds great," Glory says. "But I'm not sure we have money in the budget for display cases, or really anything extra right now."

"We could set up a table to start," Amira says. "Someone can monitor it so nothing gets lost, but we can have something out with maybe a sign that says 'Explore Horizon's History.' I can make videos to post on social to gauge interest. If it blows up, we can think about investing in a real display. We could even position some of it so people could see it from outside too, so it draws them in."

"Oh, I like that idea," I say.

Glory and Amira both look at me, a mix of surprise and disbelief on their faces.

I frown. "What? I've liked Amira's ideas before."

"Yes, but it's always so wonderful to hear," Amira says, with a deliciously wicked smile that I have the weird urge to kiss.

I look away, focusing my attention back on Glory.

"So, what do you think?" I ask.

"It's an . . . interesting idea," they say, hedging. "I'll need to go down and look at the stuff myself, and run it by my uncles, but if you two are willing to handle the setup and figure out how to add in this new role in the rotation schedule, then I don't see why not. It couldn't hurt, right?"

Amira turns to me, beaming, and I can't help grinning too.

"So, that's a yes, then!" Amira says.

Glory holds up their hands. "That's a strong maybe. Let me call my uncles and I'll get back to you, all right?"

"All right," I say. I put the album down on their desk, and Amira puts hers on top of mine. "You can start with these. They're really interesting. And I'll do research as well. There may be even more Horizon history online that we don't know."

"That sounds great, Rochelle, thank you," Glory says, a pleased look on their face.

"No problem."

"Now, please get back to work before I have to explain to someone why there are only two newbies running concessions," Glory says.

Without hesitation, Amira and I both give mock salutes and say, "Aye, aye, captain," in unison.

Glory rolls their eyes and waves us off, a clear dismissal.

We scurry away back to Lisa and Jennie, who are expectantly waiting.

"Well, what did they say?" Lisa asks.

"A strong maybe," I say.

"Which is basically a yes," Amira says.

"Amazing," Jennie says. Then adds, "So what exactly is it that we're doing again?"

I meet Amira's gaze and grin.

"We're saving Horizon."

TWENTY-THREE

THE NEXT DAY GLORY TELLS us we're a go, and we immediately get to work.

Amira sends Danny and Shawn down to the basement to bring up enough stuff to fill up the long plastic tables Amira's cousins have loaned us. Brigit gets us some fancy gold tablecloths from home to cover the table, making it look more official, and we start setting up.

Amira records it all, cutting and editing the footage into content that she uses to promote our new historical display. And it works.

We ask people to share their stories about visiting Horizon, even posting on the mostly defunct Horizon Facebook page, since we know that's where the old folks live these days, and people actually respond, sharing their stories.

"Back in my day Horizon was the spot," Jerrod A. Brown writes. "If our parents wanted to get rid of us, they'd drop us off right there at the theater and that's how we'd spend the day, slipping in and out of theaters seeing multiple movies with one ticket. I'm sure Mr. Handler turned a blind eye to us kids, but we felt like we were really getting away with something."

"Oh, I'm so glad Horizon is still around," Ashley Carmichael writes. "These new theaters don't have the same vibe as Horizon did. It wasn't about all the flashy stuff, it was about supporting the community and showing movies that mattered."

"I'll be there on Sunday," Eric Brown posts. "My son ain't never seen the OG *Blade* but now that he's old enough, it's time to introduce him to a classic."

And on and on it went.

"Our social traffic has never been this high," Amira says, her words a bit jumbled since she has a Blow Pop in her mouth.

We're having a sleepover at her house, which feels illicit, except for the fact that Brigit, Jennie, Lisa, Taylor, and Kerry are here too. It still amazes me that Amira's room is big enough to hold all of us, but she's laid out an obscene number of pillows and blankets on the floor in front of her bed, and so far we've all made ourselves comfortable down here.

I've been to Amira's house a number of times over the years thanks to our moms, but it's been a long time since I've had reason to come up to her room. It looks just as bougie as I remember. Her walls are painted sky blue with swirls of white stenciled in, giving it a sort of whimsical vibe. The white canopy over her bed also helps with that.

Her floor is covered with the softest carpet I've ever felt in a blue-gray color that goes nicely with the walls. All the furniture in the room is white, and I don't know how everything still looks this clean and put together. Maybe she cleaned it in preparation for us?

Regardless, I've always thought this room didn't feel like Amira. When I think of Amira, I see bright colors and random items from all her various activities that Ma is always telling me she does. Trophies, her dance uniform—things like that.

Instead, Amira's room looks like something spit out from those renovation shows Ma loves to watch on HGTV.

Still, as soon as we walked into the room, the vanilla scent in the air went straight to my head. She was burning a candle apparently, but blew it out because Taylor said the smell was tickling her nose.

Kerry and Taylor still don't know that Amira and I are more than friends now. While I could say it's because we've all been so caught up with our own stuff, Kerry doing the musical and Taylor with Shawn, the few moments I've had to say something, I couldn't. For starters, I'm not even sure what I would say.

Calling Amira my girlfriend doesn't seem right, especially since technically I'm not sure we've even been on a real date yet. But saying we're just hooking up doesn't feel right either.

So, my compromise has been simply to say nothing at all.

Now we're all laid out on Amira's floor, *The Princess and the Frog* playing on the TV atop Amira's dresser, and no one in this room knows the truth about me and Amira except the two of us.

Whatever that truth may be.

"Okay, but how does social traffic translate to money for Horizon?" Taylor asks from my left. I'm currently sandwiched between her and Kerry, with Jennie on Kerry's other side, then Lisa, Brigit, and Amira. Together, we form a little circle on top of the blankets and pillows. I would've liked to sit next to Amira, but my annoying best friends surrounded me while Amira was out of the room grabbing pizzas. There was no way for me to stealthily move to her side.

I keep hoping someone will get up to use the bathroom or something, but we've made our way through all the pizza and now the candy, and the most anyone has done is turn their legs around and switch positions. These people have bladders of steel.

From the way Taylor's currently sitting beside me, I can't really see Amira, but I'm too full on pizza and chocolate to reorient myself.

"It hasn't . . . yet," Amira says with a grimace. "But we're off to a great start. We only put up the display two days ago, and people are definitely coming to check it out. And I think I'm going to turn all these stories into another video or something to keep the momentum going."

"That's a good idea," I chime in. "I think anything that keeps people talking about Horizon is good. Word of mouth is one of the best business strategies. It's organic marketing!"

"All right, calm down, nerd," Taylor says, and the other girls snicker.

"Takes one to know one," I shoot back.

Taylor sticks out her tongue, and I whack her with a pillow in retaliation. Taylor reaches for her own pillow, but Amira leans over and snatches it out of her hand.

"Ah, no," Amira says. "We will not be having a pillow fight and destroying my room. Not on my watch."

"You know you're off the clock, Amira," Brigit says. "You're not the boss of us right now."

Jennie's eyes widen. "Oh my God, Bridge. That was maybe the snarkiest thing I've ever heard you say."

"It's always the quiet ones," Kerry says, with a shake of her head.

Brigit blinks with what looks like genuine confusion. "I'm not quiet. I'm a cheerleader!"

"Are you really?" Lisa asks. "So am I!"

"Really?"

Brigit's face literally brightens, and they both squeal as they grab hold of each other.

"No one told me cheerleaders walked among us," Taylor whispers.

Lisa and Brigit stop their celebration to turn and glare at Taylor.

"Is that a problem?" Brigit asks.

Taylor holds up her hands. "Absolutely not. Kerry's my best friend, and she's as bubbly as any cheerleader."

Kerry perks up at this. "It's true! I have no off switch."

"Right," Taylor says, with a roll of her eyes. "Anyway, I just never expected to be dating a football player and hanging out with cheerleaders. It wasn't on my Bingo card for senior year."

Jennie stretches out, so her head is not too far from Taylor's lap. "So, you two are officially dating, then? The Goth and the Golden Retriever?"

Taylor leans forward so she can see past me and glares at Kerry. "Did you tell her to call us that?"

"I did no such thing," Kerry says with the face of a kid caught red-handed.

Taylor rightfully looks at her with disbelief, but Kerry attempts to fix her face into one that only shows innocence.

"Anyway, I think we're off to a great start," Amira says, putting her phone down. "I'm excited. Especially since Derek and Eric are coming in next week. I think they'll love it."

Kerry's mouth falls open. She'd just filled it with a bunch of peanut M&M's like a chipmunk trying to store up for winter, so they all fall out of her mouth and into her lap.

"Gross," Taylor and Brigit say at the same time. They exchange a look that seems like solidarity or mutual understanding.

"Derek and Eric are coming into Horizon *next week*?" Kerry asks.

Now I can see Amira again, and she looks just as cute as she did when we first arrived. She's wearing a matching pink pajama set, the top a short-sleeve button-down with a collar and shorts that stop a few inches above her knees. Her curls are braided back into two perfectly neat cornrows again, this time with pink rubber bands around each end.

I came in my favorite *Among Us* pajama pants and my comfiest black T-shirt that has a slight V-neck, so I don't have a uniboob situation. I am slightly worried about how I'm going to sleep though. I cannot sleep in a bra, but if my bra is gone, my boobs are going to run free, and while I don't care when that happens around Kerry and Taylor, I don't want to feel exposed that way in front of everyone here.

Especially Amira.

"Please do not leave those M&M's there," Amira says, sounding incredibly exasperated.

Brigit's right, I don't think Amira knows how to turn off her boss voice anymore.

Kerry starts picking up the M&M's, putting them back into her mouth one by one, much to our disgust. Even Jennie, who's been looking at Kerry with heart eyes for most of the evening, grimaces.

"Okay, but what day?" Kerry asks again. "I need to be prepared."

"Prepared for what?" Brigit asks.

"My first big break," Kerry says, midchew.

Taylor and I both groan.

"Your what?" Brigit unfortunately asks.

"Here she goes," I say, lying back down.

Taylor lies down beside me, our heads sharing a long pillow.

"Wake me up when it's over," Taylor says.

"Oh dear," Lisa says.

"They're being dramatic," Kerry tells her.

"That's rich coming from you," Taylor says, her eyes closed.

Kerry ignores her. "Basically, getting my first big break is step one in my short plan, leading to my long plan of getting my *big* big break."

There's a beat of silence before I hear Amira say, "Come again?"

"She hopes that she can persuade Derek and Eric into getting her some kind of role on Broadway," I start.

"Which will be her first big break," Taylor adds.

"And once I get my Tony, I'll be one step closer to my EGOT," Kerry finishes. "So, *what day will they be at Horizon?*"

"Um, I think they're coming on Monday," Amira says, hesitantly. "But they'll be around all week, I think."

"Perfect," Kerry says.

I don't have to look at her to know she's wearing a devilish grin and rubbing her hands together like a Disney villain. Of course, that's when "Friends on the Other Side" starts playing on the TV. Everyone dissolves into chatter after that. I hear Jennie asking Kerry follow-up questions about her plans for being a star, and Lisa and Brigit are back to discussing the world of cheer. I think Taylor might actually be falling asleep beside me, and I'm almost halfway there myself. This pillow is very comfortable.

Just as I'm about to give in to my drowsiness, I feel someone hovering above me. I don't have to open my eyes to know it's Amira.

"Should I be worried about Kerry trying to ambush the uncles?"

I start at the sound of her voice and find her big brown eyes staring down at me. It takes everything in me not to reach up and pull her lips down to mine—a ridiculous impulse since I do not know how to kiss someone when their mouth is upside down.

Also, that's not exactly how I'd like to reveal what's going on to everyone in this room.

I swallow and force myself to speak.

"Probably," I say. "But that can be a Future Amira problem."

She smiles at that, and then as if it's just the two of us alone in her room, she lowers herself down to my other side so her mouth is right by my ear.

"I really want to kiss you right now," she whispers.

I'm pretty sure my whole body shivers, and I pray the other girls are still focused on whatever it is they're talking about.

"Ditto," I say back.

"Want to go to the bathroom?" she asks. "I can meet you there."

I glance at her sideways, unsure if she's serious.

"For real?"

Amira nods, the corner of her mouth pulled up in a daring smirk.

"Unless you don't want to," she says.

I think the only thing I want more right now is to get into Wharton, and that's by a very small margin.

"Where's your bathroom again?" I ask, loud enough for everyone to hear.

Amira rolls her eyes, and I don't know if she thinks my acting is absurd or if she's leaning into the bit.

"Where it always is, silly," she says. "Make a right and it's at the end of the hall. You can't miss it."

"Thanks."

I jump up probably faster than I should, based on the way my stomach reacts. Maybe that third slice of pizza and the two Kit Kat bars were a mistake. Thankfully, I've recovered enough by the time I reach the bathroom. When Amira arrives soon after, the only feeling in my stomach is butterflies.

TWENTY-FOUR

WHEN AMIRA AND I WALK in for the opening shift on Monday morning, the energy feels off.

For starters, Glory, who typically arrives after we do when it's opening shift, is not only here but running around like a mad person.

"Oh, girls, thank God you're here," they say, pulling up short in front of us as we make our way to concessions.

"What's going on?" I ask.

"Didn't Amira tell you?" Glory asks. Somehow, they look even more stressed than they did a second ago. "My uncles are coming in today! They haven't been here in almost six months, thanks to their beautiful but very needy baby! Everything needs to be perfect!"

"I understand that, but you don't need to yell," I say as politely as I can. Amira still elbows me in the side.

"I did tell her," Amira says. She gives Glory one of her patented teacher's pet smiles that makes all adults bend to her will. "All the staff knows, Glory. You also sent an email, remember?"

Glory lets out a breath of relief. "Oh, right, yes. I did do that."

Amira smiles and nods at them. "Yes, you did. Now, what do you need help with?"

Glory has the audacity to look between us, confused. "I don't need help with anything."

I exchange a look with Amira and say, "Then why are you so glad we're here?"

"Because you're on the schedule to work," Glory says as if it's obvious. "Can you call Danny and Shawn and make sure they're en route, please? I need everyone to be on time today."

They scurry off before either of us can respond.

"When are any of us ever late?" I ask Amira as we pop into the office to clock in and grab the money bag.

Amira rolls her eyes. "Don't mind them. They become a completely different person when their uncles get involved. They'll be like this all day, hovering and making sure everything is running smoothly. Hopefully, whoever or whatever was causing all those shenanigans at the start of summer is now officially gone. Glory will lose it if a single mishap occurs."

"I think we're in the clear," I say. "It's been great these past few days, and the display table has been working to draw people in. We've got Horizon moving in the right direction. The uncles will definitely see that."

Amira nods as we walk back out the office to concessions. She holds up the countertop for me to walk through, and when I slide past her, she doesn't look entirely convinced. For the first time, I realize Glory might not be the only one who's really worried about Horizon's future.

"Are you okay?" I ask.

Amira's already made her way to the register, using her key to open it and slipping out the money bag.

"Yeah, I'm good, why?"

She doesn't look up at me when she says this, which only makes me more worried.

"Well, for starters, you're not looking at me," I say. "And I'm pretty sure you just put the twenties where the ones should be."

Amira's hands pause, and she looks down into the register before releasing a groan and rearranging the bills.

She closes the register and turns to me.

"Okay, it is possible that I am also a little nervous about Derek and Eric coming," she says, arms crossed, eyes locked on the ceiling.

I look around to make sure Glory is still off somewhere and Danny and Shawn haven't arrived yet. Once I'm sure the coast is clear, I place my hands on Amira's elbows, gently pulling her closer to me.

"Can you tell me why you're nervous they're coming?" I ask. "You're not planning to audition for them too, are you?"

That thankfully makes her laugh. "No, definitely not."

"Okay, so what's going on?" I ask. "You don't get nervous."

Amira finally brings her eyes down to me, a look of disbelief on her face.

"You think I don't get nervous?"

"I mean I'm sure you're constantly worried about the embarrassment you'll feel when it's announced that I'm valedictorian,"

I say. "But otherwise, no, I didn't think so."

Amira looks like she maybe wants to flick me or something, but only rolls her eyes.

"I get nervous all the time," she says. She bites her lip for a second, contemplating something before she adds, "And I know you're joking, but I do get nervous about school, for the record."

I open my mouth, and she puts a hand over it, silencing me.

"Not about our rank," she says, removing her hand from my mouth. "Though blindsiding you and becoming valedictorian does still give me a bit of a thrill when I think about it."

I don't even dignify that with a response. Amira keeps talking.

"But I mean in general," she says. "I'm guessing your mom never mentioned that they put me in special ed when I changed elementary schools?"

I shake my head. "No, she definitely did not."

"Yeah, well, it's true." She shrugs. "I have the tools and everything I need to succeed now, obviously, but it was like the move from kindergarten to first grade was this huge leap and I couldn't make the jump. Maybe it was also because we moved and everything was different, but school became really hard for me. They were even thinking of holding me back one year, but my mom pushed back and told them it was their job to help me learn better. And so, they did."

I nod as if I understand, but I don't. I've always been the smartest kid in my class, which has had its advantages and disadvantages, of course, but being at the top of my class has always felt like a given. I still study and work my ass off to succeed, but it's also second nature to me. I know how to get A's. I thought Amira was the same way.

Out of all the marvelous things Ma has to say about Amira, it's interesting that this somehow never came up. Then again, maybe that was for the best. I'm not sure I would've trusted my past self with that information either.

That version of me wasn't always kind to Amira, I can admit.

"Anyway," Amira says, obviously ready to pivot away from this conversation. "I'm nervous because I became assistant manager and then Horizon started going to—well, for lack of a better word—shit."

"But that's not your fault," I say, giving her hands a squeeze. I pause and quirk an eyebrow. "Unless there's something you'd like to tell me."

This time she does punch my arm, albeit lightly.

"Obviously not," she says. "But still, it's weird that everything started as soon as I got promoted. What if Glory made a mistake and promoted the wrong person?"

I squeeze her hands again, lacing my fingers through hers and tugging her closer until she finally looks at me again.

"Respectfully, if the options were you and the other returnees, I think Glory made the right choice," I say. "You're perfect for this."

"That's not—"

Amira cuts herself off. Shutting her eyes, she takes a deep breath, and I wait while she tries to gather her thoughts.

"Someone else was supposed to be assistant manager," she says finally. Blinking her eyes open, she adds, "Pete. Danny's friend."

I nod, confused. "Okay, so what happened? I thought you guys said he was worse than Danny, right?"

"Yeah, but he'd been here the longest," Amira says. "He's like two years older than us and everyone expected him to be the assistant manager, but then Glory announced that they'd fired him. Apparently, he'd been MIA one too many times, and so they finally got rid of him. This was right before you started—that's why they were so desperate to hire someone."

Though I knew Glory only hired me out of desperation, hearing that now stings. But I push those feelings aside and focus on what Amira's telling me.

"I don't think they planned on firing Pete," she goes on. "I think it kind of just happened, and then next thing I knew, Glory was offering me the position of assistant manager."

"Amira, just because Pete was supposed to be the assistant manager doesn't mean you don't deserve this."

I take her by the shoulders and give her a little shake until she meets my eyes.

"You've been killing it this summer," I say. "And if I'm saying that, you know it must be true."

Amira laughs at this just as I'd hoped.

"It doesn't matter how or why you got the position, all that matters is what you've done with it," I say. "And what you've done is revive our social media accounts and make a mostly fascinating history display."

Now she rolls her eyes, but I push on before she can say anything.

"My point is, besides Glory, no one knows Horizon or loves it as much as you do," I say. "And whoever's been causing havoc, it has nothing to do with you. They're just an asshole."

Amira's big eyes go even bigger and she gasps.

"Asshole?" she repeats. "Wow."

I nod solemnly. "I know. I like to limit myself to one swear word a week, and I've wasted it on someone I don't even know. Alas, it had to be done."

"Oh my God," she says, laughing, and then she's pulling me into a hug. The feel of her pressed against me is a surprise, but I embrace it, hugging her back until she's ready to let go.

"Okay," she says. Then she says it again as if to really convince herself. "Okay, you're right."

I grin. "My two favorite words."

Amira smirks and pushes me away, returning to the register.

"Go start taking inventory, and text the boys, please?" she says. Boss mode reactivated. "If they're late, Glory may actually combust."

"Isn't Brigit also coming in today to do the table?" I ask.

Amira actually slaps her forehead. "You're right. Text her too. Although she's probably with Danny. But maybe text her anyway. She's more reliable."

I nod and pull out my phone. Before I can even unlock it, the doors of the entrance open. Instead of Danny, Shawn, and Brigit, it's two Black guys who look about my mom's age, and one of them is pushing a stroller.

"Oh my God," Amira says, dollar bills hanging limply in

each of her hands as she pauses her counting.

I lean over and flick a glance between her and the approaching couple, who, for what it's worth, look positively thrilled to be here.

"Derek and Eric?" I guess.

"Eric and Derek," she agrees.

And so, it begins.

TWENTY-FIVE

THANKFULLY, DANNY, SHAWN, AND BRIGIT all arrive about a minute after Derek and Eric do, which means they're right in time to see Glory walk out of the gender-neutral bathroom with a trail of toilet paper stuck to their shoe.

"Uncles," Glory says, their arms outstretched as they stroll over to us.

Brigit, God bless her, sidles up to Glory and stomps on the toilet paper, catching it before Glory reaches their uncles and pulls them in for a group hug.

At this point, I'm not sure who's Derek and who's Eric, but I can guess the one on the right is the uncle Glory is blood related to. They have the same full cheeks and lips, and when Glory pulls back, his smile is just like theirs.

"Hello, Glory," he says. His voice is deep and serious, kind of like the guy who does the voice of Mufasa in *The Lion King*, and it takes me by surprise a little bit. In contrast, the second uncle's voice is higher and much more chipper.

"Hi, Gee," he says, pulling Glory in again for another solo hug.

I look at Amira and mouth, "Gee?" Amira simply shrugs. We're still standing behind the counter, and Brigit, Danny, and Shawn circle our group on the other side.

"And who is everyone?" Uncle #2 says, finally freeing Glory from his embrace.

"Oh, yes, intros," Glory says, clapping their hands. They back up, leaving room for the three newcomers to get even closer, the stroller being pushed nearer to the counter while everyone surrounds it. I lean over to get a peek. Inside is the cutest baby I've ever seen, though admittedly I haven't seen many.

Her skin is light brown, and her head is full of dark curls that are currently pushed back from her face with a soft pink headband that has a bow in its center and matches her pink onesie. Her lips are bowed and set in this perfect little pout as she sleeps soundly, not the least bit bothered by all the chatter happening around her.

I've never wanted a younger sibling. I've seen the hell Kerry's little brother puts her through sometimes, but maybe a baby sister wouldn't have been awful. I would only want her around when she's like this though. Changing diapers is not in my wheelhouse.

"This is my uncle Derek," Glory says, pointing to the man that looks like her. "He/him pronouns. Then we have Uncle Eric, also he/him, and down in the stroller is baby Gracie. She/her until she's able to tell us otherwise."

Glory then turns to us. "Shawn, Danny, Brigit, and Amira

you've met before. And one of our new team members here is Rochelle, she/her."

I lift my hand in a tiny wave. "Hi, nice to meet you both."

Eric smiles brightly. "Likewise!"

Derek only nods, but his lips are still turned up in a slight smile. I get the feeling that if opposites attract, Derek is the quiet one in this relationship and Eric does all the talking. I guess I would be the Derek in my relationship with Amira. Although I'm not sure if we are in a relationship. Not yet anyway.

"Why don't I take you three into the office and let these guys finish setting up for the day," Glory says, already ushering her uncles away.

"Sure," Eric says. "And then we should do a tour. I want to learn more about this display you all put together. Though I don't see it. Where is it?"

He turns his head around looking.

"We put it all away at the end of each night," Amira says. She ducks under the counter and starts pulling out the props and albums, placing them on the counter.

"The only one we keep out all the time is the *Candyman* pay phone," I add, pointing to where it now comfortably rests on a little shelf between the woman's restroom and the single-stall all-gender bathroom. Glory was able to use their power drill, something they just happen to keep in their car for some reason, and with the help of their friend Joseph who does carpentry, they were able to nail a sturdy enough slab of wood to hold the heavy glass case.

"Oh wow," Eric says, noticing it for the first time. He quickly abandons us to get a closer look and Derek chuckles.

"Oh dear, he might want that one for our house," Derek says. He looks around, his eyes stopping every so often as he takes in the whole place. Then he places a hand on Glory's shoulder, giving it a gentle shake.

"You did a good job, kid," he says. "Looks great."

Glory beams and they look how I feel when I ace a test. A feeling of warmth envelops me as I take in Horizon too. I remember my first day, thinking this would be the worst summer ever because Amira was here. Now, when I glance over at her and everyone else in our circle, I can't imagine working anywhere else.

Horizon feels like home, and I can see by the way Eric practically bounces back over to us, that he and Derek feel the same. Under the counter, I reach for Amira's hand and give it a light little squeeze to tell her everything will be okay.

Unfortunately, there was no way to know how wrong I was.

TWENTY-SIX

EVERYTHING STARTS OFF FINE.

Glory takes Derek, Eric, and Gracie into the office while we're getting ready for the day, and then, as per usual, people start showing up for the matinee shows, and we're off to the races.

I work concessions with Amira and Danny, Shawn handles ticketing, and Brigit is monitoring the history table, as we like to call it. Eventually, Derek and Eric come out to walk around and take Gracie to see the new Pixar movie, though she sleeps through most of it.

After the movie, Eric takes Gracie to the bathroom to change her diaper—and that's when all hell breaks loose.

A group of kids not too much younger than us comes in with various different orders. Danny handles getting the food, and I go to the soda machine and start pouring their drinks, except that when I press to get some Coke, nothing comes out. I press the cup against the black lever again, holding it down, but still nothing.

"Uh . . ."

I look around. Amira is still at the register ringing up the kids' orders, and Danny is sliding hot dogs into buns. I look back at the soda machine, biting my lip. I've only set it up once or twice, so I'm not confident I know how to fix it, and the last thing I want to do is make a mess. However, I hate having to ask for help. Beads of sweat are starting to form at my hairline, so I give up and turn to Danny, tapping his shoulder as he slides hot dogs over to two kids.

"The soda machine isn't working," I say.

He glances from me to the machine. "What do you mean it's not working? I refilled it this morning. There's no way it's done already."

I shrug. "When I push nothing comes out."

"Nothing comes out?" he says, as if repeating what I say will help make sense of it.

"Nothing comes out," I say again.

He sighs. "All right, you handle food, I'll fix the machine."

He passes me the tongs we use for the hot dogs and steps around me. Amira looks up from the register and glances between us.

"What's wrong?"

I'm already moving, working to put more hot dogs in buns.

"Soda machine is being stupid," I say. I try to brush it off like it's a silly thing, but I'm not sure I hide my growing fear that something's wrong. "What else do you need? For food, I mean."

I can feel her eyes on me as I put one of the hot dogs into a container and pass it to one of the guys.

"I also got a Coke," he says.

"It's coming," I lie, and glance over at Danny, who's now opening the soda machine.

"What's next, Amira?" I ask her.

She looks down at the receipt that's still in her hand. "Four hot dogs, three bags of popcorn, and—"

One minute I'm listening to Amira rattle off an order, the next one side of my body is getting sprayed.

"What is happening?" I sputter as the liquid pours down my face. I turn so my back is fully facing the onslaught, and I can see Amira's eyes widen in surprise and then outrage.

"Danny!" Amira yells.

She steps around me, and I move out of her way, turning again so I can try to see what's happening, but I'm genuinely not sure what I'm looking at, at first. A tube looks like it's risen out of the soda machine and is dancing around spurting out dark liquid while Danny attempts to grab ahold of it.

"I can't get it!" Danny yells.

"What is going on over here?" Glory runs over, stopping just before they reach the splash zone.

"We don't know," Amira calls back.

Next thing I know she's climbing up on the counter. I rush over, directly back into the spray, and grab her hand, holding her steady as she gets up. At this point, half the kids who were milling around waiting for their drinks have backed away so far, they're halfway out the door, while the others stay rooted in their spots, watching the madness unfold. One of them has their phone out, and I just know I'll see this on TikTok later.

Amira holds on to me for balance and reaches out with her other hand to try to grab the tube while Danny does the same below. It's Danny who gets it first, but by then it's too late. Everything that was in the tube has spluttered out, leaving a mess everywhere, and the tube, which looks slightly bent in the middle, finally lies limp in Danny's hands.

I help Amira back down, and we all take stock of the damage. Danny, Amira, and I got hit with the worst of it, though some of our customers are also wiping themselves off. Amira goes over to offer them napkins, and thankfully they appear to be the type of kids who don't care about being a little sticky.

Derek and Eric, on the other hand, look quite distressed as they reach us with Gracie, still resting peacefully in her stroller. To be honest, I can't blame them.

There's brown sticky liquid all over the counter and the floor, both behind and in front of the counter.

"What happened?" Derek asks.

Amira and I turn to Danny, but he looks just as confused as we do.

"I don't know," he says. "Rochelle said the soda machine wasn't working, so I checked it out. The other nozzles seemed fine, but when I pressed on the Coke, there was nothing. I thought maybe the tube was stuck somehow, so I opened it up and I found this closing off the tube."

He holds up what looks like one of those clips my mom uses to keep her bags of potato chips closed so they don't go stale. Amira takes it from him.

"Someone did this on purpose," Amira says.

Although she addresses all of us, her eyes lock with mine, and I can already tell what she's thinking. Up until now we wanted to believe that someone wasn't actually messing things up intentionally, but now there's no denying it. That clip didn't get there on its own.

"Why would someone do that?" Eric asks, looking genuinely bewildered.

"I have no idea," Glory says. "But we're going to get to the bottom of this, I swear."

They look between both of their uncles, but it's Derek's tight face that makes me tense up.

"We'll need to have this carpet cleaned," he says, finally. "And make sure it's fully dry so we don't get mold. We'll need to call a cleaner. We're not equipped for this."

Eric's face falls. "And how much will that cost?"

"No idea, but I guess we'll have to make some calls."

He says nothing else before moving away from the mess and into the office. Eric looks between all of us with a sympathetic smile.

"Don't worry, you all did nothing wrong here," Eric says. "Money has been a bit tight lately, and this is just an added expense we don't need. Everything will be fine."

I look between Amira, Danny, and Glory. Clearly none of us believe that, and Eric can see it on our faces.

"Really, do not freak out, this is a minor mishap," he adds. "It'll be okay."

Gracie chooses that moment to start wailing, and Eric

bianches, moving around to the front of the stroller so he can look at his daughter and start fussing with her.

"I'm just going to take her outside and give her a bottle," Eric says to us. "If Derek comes looking for me, will you let him know?"

Glory nods. "Of course."

Eric smiles and places a reassuring hand on their shoulder before heading outside with Gracie. As soon as he's gone, Glory throws up their hands in defeat.

"Well, this was an absolute disaster," they say.

"Glory, it'll be okay," Amira says gently. "You heard what Eric said. It's fine."

"He's just lying to make us feel better," Glory says. "To make *me* feel better. But this is the last thing they need. Horizon needs to be bringing in money, not costing them more money they don't have. It's over."

"Um, hi, sorry, can we still get our food, please?"

We all spin to find one of the boys, presumably the leader of the pack, staring at us.

"Crap," Amira murmurs under her breath, before turning to me. "Rochelle, can you help them, please? Danny, you said the other streams are working?"

Danny winces. "I mean, yeah, they were, but do we really want to risk it?"

"Fair point," Amira says.

"Definitely not," Glory says at the same time.

"We'll get you your food right now, and refund you for the drinks," Amira says to the kid. "One sec."

"We don't need refunds," he says. "Just our food, please. The movie's about to start."

"And I like the previews," one of his friends behind him says.

"Right, of course, sorry," Amira says. "Rochelle, I'll help you with this."

"I should see if Uncle Derek already got a quote for this mess," Glory says with a sigh. "Maybe it won't be all that bad."

"If it is, it probably can't get worse," Danny says.

We all look at him, incredulous, but Danny just shrugs. I guess he's reached his cap for words spoken aloud today.

"I'll be back soon," Glory says, ending the silence. "Let's make sure everything runs smoothly from here on out—and no more drinks out of the soda machine until we're positive it hasn't been tampered with in any other way."

"Got it," we all say in unison.

Glory walks away, and the three of us get the kids their orders and into their movie just in time for previews. Once they're gone, Shawn and Brigit run over.

"What just happened?" Brigit asks.

Amira runs them through the whole story, and they both look as worried as Glory and Amira did.

"So, what happens now?" Brigit asks.

Just then Derek comes out of the office with Glory quick on his heels, and by the look on his face, things do not look good.

Amira sighs as we watch them head outside.

"I have no idea, but the more important question is who would do this to us and why?"

"Didn't we already have this conversation?" Danny asks.

Apparently, he has a few words left.

"I think it's time we revisit the question," Amira says. She turns to me and asks, "Did Kerry come in today?"

I shake my head. "No, she had rehearsal, so she's not here, unfortunately."

Amira seems to hesitate a second before she turns her attention back on Danny.

"And what about Pete? Was he here today?"

Danny narrows his eyes. I add this image to the "Danny's Expressions" Rolodex card I keep in my head. I think I'm up to three.

"He didn't do this, Amira," he says.

"How can you be so sure?" Amira asks.

"I just am. Just because you all didn't like Pete, that doesn't mean he's a bad guy. And he wouldn't do something like this. So, drop it."

This is the most serious I've ever seen Danny, and it's quite unnerving. Based on the way everyone freezes, I'm not the only one who's uncomfortable.

"Okay," Brigit says, moving over to him. She reaches over the counter and takes his hand in hers. "Okay. We'll drop it."

Danny mumbles a quick "Thank you," before turning away to keep wiping down the counter.

I exchange a glance with Amira, unsure of where to go from here. We need to figure out what's going on. While I don't know this Pete guy like everyone else here does, I know Danny. At least a little bit. And the fact that he's so defensive about this is suspicious, but things feel too tense to bring that up now.

I chew my lip, trying to think of what I *can* say. Thankfully, Shawn claps his hands together, drawing all of our attention to him.

"I think we can all agree today sucked, yeah?"

We all share a few looks with each other before nodding in unison.

"So, you all know what we need, right?"

"A detective," I suggest.

"A rich relative," Amira says.

"Security cameras," Brigit puts in.

Danny, of course, says nothing.

Shawn hangs his head in disappointment.

"Wow, I've really taught you all nothing." He presses his hands together like a prayer and closes his eyes, taking a deep, dramatic breath before letting it all go.

"We, my friends, need . . ." He pauses to make eye contact with all of us, and says, "A pool party."

Amira blinks and looks up at him. "Really? A pool party? How is that going to fix anything?"

"It won't," he agrees. "But for one night, we can push all our problems to the side and just have fun. Come on! It's summer, and we haven't thrown a single party yet. That's not like us at all!"

"Didn't you throw a beach party like a month ago?" I ask.

Shawn waves a hand. "That was a beach party. This would be a *pool* party."

"That is true," Amira says. "There's a difference."

She looks to me, her eyes finding mine.

"What do you think?"

Everyone turns to me and I freeze. I don't do parties. Amira *knows* I don't do parties. So, why on earth is she asking me?

"Um, I think if you want to, you should," I say.

"Will *you* come?"

She tosses the question to me like it's a challenge, and everyone turns to me again like they're watching a tennis match. There's only one correct answer here, obviously, and yet I am loath to give it. I, Rochelle Marie Coleman, do not go to parties. It's like my thing. Amira knows it's my thing. I let her get away with the sleepover because that was chill, but this? A pool party? With all those people? And music? And drinks? And swimsuits? And water that someone might pee in?

It sounds like my worst nightmare.

And yet, I did tell Taylor and Kerry that I would go to a party this summer. And Ma would be thrilled, probably. Though, are you supposed to tell your parents you're going to a party? I feel like people usually sneak out for these kinds of things. For now, I try to turn my frown upside down and say, "Sure, why not?"

TWENTY-SEVEN

THE PARTY'S PLANNED FOR THURSDAY, since that's when Amira, Shawn, and I are all off.

Jennie, Lisa, Danny, and Brigit will all head over after their closing shift. I haven't been able to stop thinking about Danny and Pete, and the possibility that they're the ones ruining things at Horizon, but I attempt to put it out of my mind at least for one night. I can't believe this party is expected to last long enough for people to arrive after closing shift.

That already has me tired.

Add in the fact that this party has grown from being something just us kids are doing, as Ma put it, to being a full-on barbecue at the Rodriguez home, and I'm low-key stressed.

Amira and I have told no one that we've gone from friends to more, but I think I'm ready to, and tonight may be the perfect time. We can tell everyone all in one swoop.

All I need to do is run the plan by Amira, but I'm sure she'll be down with it. Our moms will be annoying about the whole thing, but I think it'll be better to just have everything out in the open.

Still, the nerves about tonight have me second-guessing everything, especially what I'm going to wear. It's taking me way too long to get dressed and Ma notices.

"You're *still* not ready?" she asks from the doorway of my room. "We're running the risk of being actually late, instead of fashionably late."

Ma knows like I do that the Rodriguez family never starts a function on time. So, while Amira and Mrs. Rodriguez said to arrive at 8 p.m., we both know they don't expect people to start trickling in until 9. Despite that, my mother, being who she is, cannot fathom actually getting there an hour late, so the compromise is 8:30 p.m. Except now it's 8:25 p.m., and I am still not dressed.

"Everything I own is bad," I say, before face-planting onto my bed. I groan into the mound of clothes I've created.

"Since when do you care about what kind of clothes you wear?" Ma asks as she steps into my room. She starts pulling at various articles of clothing from underneath me, making my comfy clothes mountain deflate.

"I don't *care*," I say.

And I don't. I just want to look good for Amira, because she always looks good. If I'm going to spend most of the party with her, I don't want everyone looking at us and wondering why she's spending time with me. Even though they'll probably be thinking that no matter what I wear.

"Okay, so just wear whatever makes you comfortable," Ma

says, nudging my shoulder. "It's a pool party anyway. All you need is a bathing suit and shorts."

I push up from the clothes and turn to face her. I realize now that she's wearing a bathing suit with a sheer blue cover-up dress. She, of course, looks stunning as always. Her hair is straight, which means she has no intention of actually getting in the pool, and it's pulled back in a sleek side bun. She's wearing a little bit of makeup and is holding a pair of white wedge sandals in one hand and a white wristlet in the other.

My mother is hotter than I am. How embarrassing.

"I don't have a bathing suit that fits me," I say with a groan. "I need to go shopping."

"Well, we can do that tomorrow," she says. "For now, just throw on a tank top and here"—she grabs a pair of whitewashed jean shorts from my pile and tosses it to me. "And these. Let your braids down, throw on some gloss, and call it a day."

I pick up the shorts from where they've landed in my lap and hold them out in front of me as if I've never seen them before. A yellow tank top falls into my lap next, and I look up at my mother, who's staring back at me, arms awkwardly crossed with the things in her hands.

"Get dressed," she says. "I'm leaving in five whether you're in the car or not. Don't make me honk for you."

"Yes, ma'am," I grumble, but I can't help the small smile that tugs at my lips. Especially when she opens her wristlet and pulls out a dark brown gloss.

"And use this," she says. "You've been blessed with flaw-less skin, which must come from your father's side because it certainly didn't come from me. But the gloss will look good on you."

I take it from her hand, turning it over. I've never committed to wearing makeup enough to spend my own money on it, so all the makeup I have I've gotten from Kerry, Taylor, and my mother, either as gifts or something they've let me "borrow" indefinitely. So, both me and my mother know she's never getting this back.

"Thanks," I say.

"Five minutes" is her only response as she turns on her heel and heads for the door.

I quickly put on the outfit she threw together and swipe the lip gloss on. I'm halfway out the door when I double back and grab the butterfly necklace that's been sitting on my dresser since I brought it home from Claire's.

I know Amira said I should wear it for me, but I think wearing it for her is a good reason too.

We can hear the music as soon as we get out of the car.

Ma and I follow the sounds down the block to Amira's house, where people are heading around the side to the gate where the pool is. I follow Ma through the front entrance and inhale deeply as I smell plantains frying and a whole bunch of various seasonings.

One thing I've never hated about going to Amira's house was the food. I was only slightly disappointed that we had pizza for her sleepover, but her parents had been out somewhere, so I understood. Now, though, the familiar smells of rice, chicken, shrimp, and who knows what else have my stomach rumbling, even though Ma and I had dinner before we left.

"¡Robin, qué linda!"

Ma and I both look up to see Amira's mom coming down the stairs, arms wide and a smile that looks just like Amira's. She's barefoot but wearing a perfectly pressed dress that looks like something out of the '50s with its puffed-out skirt and cinched waist. The dress is white and covered in lemons, giving summer vibes, and her tight curls are pulled up in an immaculate bun, with her baby hairs laid expertly. All in all, she looks much more dressed up than my mom and I do, but if our attire bothers her, she doesn't show it.

She pulls my mom to her, as if they haven't seen each other in years instead of just a couple of days. Amira's mom steps away so she can inspect my mother's full ensemble.

"I love this! Where did you get it?" she asks, before answering her own question.

"Marshalls," they say in unison, laughing.

I can't help but roll my eyes and scan the room. More people pass through the house, but none of them look like the girl I'm looking for.

"Amira's outside in the back if you want to say hello." Amira's mom answers the question I'm too embarrassed to ask. I turn my attention back to her and give an appreciative nod.

"Thank you." I'm about to jet off and then remember I haven't properly greeted Mrs. Rodriguez. "Also, hi, Mrs. Rodriguez. Thanks for having us."

I step into her arms for a hug, and she pulls me in. Mrs.

Rodriguez has always given the best hugs. She's made of pure softness, no hard edges to be found, and always smells like whatever she's been cooking. Today she either just took a shower with something that smells like cinnamon, or she made her iconic cinnamon swirl cake for dessert. Access to that cake is truly one of the greatest things to ever come out of Ma and Mrs. Rodriguez's friendship.

"You're perfectly welcome, Rochelle," she says, letting me go. "Amira tells me you two are working overtime to help save Horizon."

My mother looks from me to Mrs. Rodriguez. "Save Horizon from what?"

I guess maybe I misunderstood Amira's eye conversation when she was over for dinner the other day. In my mind, the saving Horizon plan is something we're doing on our own and not worrying our parents about. Hence why I never said anything about it to Ma.

Amira, however, clearly doesn't feel the same way, if she's been talking to *her* mom about it. I wonder when Amira mentioned it to her mom. The fact that she somehow hasn't already told Ma about it makes me believe it had to have happened recently.

"Horizon hasn't been doing so well," I confess. "Financially. We're hoping we can figure out a way to help so they don't have to close."

Ma raises her eyebrows. "I didn't realize you cared about the place so much."

My first instinct is to say I don't care at all, but I know that's not true. I don't know why I feel the urge to pretend.

I end up shrugging instead. "It's grown on me, I guess."

"Well, Amira said you've been doing a great job," her mom interjects. "I'm so glad you two are getting along."

My lips twitch, as I try to hold back a smile. What an understatement.

"Me too," I say. I turn to my mother. "I'm gonna head out back."

"All right, go have fun with your new friends," she says, waving me off.

Mrs. Rodriguez takes her arm, leading her into the kitchen, as I make my way through the sliding-glass doors in the back.

I step outside, and the music is even louder than it is inside. Tiki torches light up the backyard, and the pool is lit. I'm able to make out most people, but I'm still struggling to find Amira. Then, as if we're in a movie, the crowd parts and there she is.

Her hair is straight, falling effortlessly over her bare shoulders. She's wearing a sundress just like her mom's, except hers is strapless and the hem is shorter, stopping just above her knees. Someone next to her, who I belatedly realize is Shawn, says something to make her laugh, and she throws her head back. It's like I'm watching her in slo-mo.

"What is happening right now?"

I blink at the sound of Taylor's voice, and suddenly Taylor and Kerry are standing on either side of me, holding Solo cups. Kerry hands one to me.

"Aw, she's mesmerized by her girlfriend," Kerry singsongs in my ear.

I blink, startled. "She's not my . . . why would you say that?"

"Because anyone with eyes can see the way you look at her and the way she looks at you," Kerry says. "So, what's the crush status? Have you told her how you feel yet? You haven't given us any updates, but you two are almost always attached at the hip."

"And you two clearly snuck away to make out at the sleepover," Taylor adds.

Kerry and I both whirl around. "What?"

Now Taylor blinks, confused.

"I'm sorry, was that not public knowledge?" she asks.

I look around the party, but thankfully no one's paying attention to us. I grab Taylor's arm and move her farther away from the pool, Amira, and Shawn. Kerry follows.

"How do you know about that?" I whisper.

"I mean, you two were pretty obvious," Taylor says with a shrug. "You went to the 'bathroom' and then so did she, like, a second later."

"Why do I have no memory of this?" Kerry asks.

"Because Jennie was talking your ear off about *Crash Landing on You*," Taylor explains.

Kerry nods, remembering. "Oh, yes, a great program. Some would even argue it's the blueprint."

"Can we focus, please?" I snap. "Taylor, I thought you were asleep."

"I was simply resting my eyes," Taylor says. "But also, who cares if I know? The real question is why haven't you told us. What's going on with you two? Are you dating now?"

"We're . . ." I let my voice trail off as I try to find the words.

"I don't know what we are. We've kissed and we've hung out and I really like her, but I don't know. I was hoping to talk to her tonight and maybe figure that out."

"Ah, yes, you need to DTR," Kerry says, nodding.

Taylor squints at her. "Respectfully, what do you know about defining the relationship?"

"Excuse me. What part of 'I love romance, I just don't want to be in one' have I not made clear?" Kerry says.

"What are y'all talking about?"

Taylor, Kerry, and I all jump at the sound of Amira's voice. Amira and Shawn have magically appeared beside us, and I desperately want to know how much they heard.

"Nothing," we all say in unison.

"Riiight," Amira says, dragging the word out, before focusing her attention on me. "You came." Her eyes drift down to where the butterfly necklace rests comfortably above the scoop neck of my tank top. "And you're wearing the necklace."

I smile. "Yes, well, I figured it shouldn't stay in my room collecting dust."

Amira smiles knowingly, and I force myself to look away. I can feel Taylor and Kerry watching us.

"Where's your bathing suit?" Shawn asks.

Amira rolls her eyes and Taylor groans.

"He's been asking everyone this question," Taylor says.

"It's a pool party!" Shawn argues. "That implies that people will get into the pool."

"People are in the pool," Amira says with a sigh. She points over to where some kids from school, as well as a few younger ones I vaguely recognize as Amira's cousins, cannonball in.

"Okay, but *we* should be getting in the pool," Shawn says, wrapping an arm around Taylor's shoulders.

Taylor neither leans into the touch nor pulls away, which seems just right for her.

"I told you I would dip my feet in," Taylor says ever so calmly. I look down at her feet, which are in her trademark combat boots, but I decide to mind my business.

"We'll all dip our feet in when Jennie, Lisa, Brigit, and Danny get here," Amira says. "Okay?"

Shawn clearly doesn't believe her but nods anyway.

"Okay, glad that's settled." Amira moves closer to me and drapes her arm around my shoulders so we're mirroring Shawn and Taylor, and it feels like the most natural thing in the world. I can feel myself warming under her touch. I wonder if I should move away, until we can have that conversation we need to have, but I like the feel of her arm around me too much.

"Now, shall we show Rochelle here how to have fun at a party?" Amira says.

Kerry claps her hands and grins. "Oh, we absolutely must."

"Why am I scared?" I ask.

"Because you probably should be," says Taylor.

I release a deep sigh and accept my fate.

TWENTY-EIGHT

MOVIES THAT FEEL LIKE MOVIES

Jennie: We're free!

Brigit: Glory let us off early since the last show is playing and we closed up concessions.

Lisa: *Nicki Minaj voice* TO FREEDOM!

Taylor Brown was added to the conversation.

Taylor: Now who taught her about freedom?

Jennie: Omg Taylor's back?

Kerry: She literally just came back to ask that question lolz. She was reading over our shoulders.

Me: She's nosy by nature.

Taylor: ☝

Lisa: Kerry made me and Jennie listen to Queen radio and we went down a rabbit hole.

Brigit: Anyways, we're taking Danny's car. I'll be driving since he's decided to . We'll be there soon.

Amira: Don't go through the front, come around the back!

Lisa: You got it dude.

Jennie: More like dudette.

Taylor Brown has left the conversation.

🍿

By the time Jennie, Lisa, Brigit, and Danny have arrived, I've been forced to interact with so many of our classmates that I have to hide inside with my mom and Amira's, stuffing my face with delicious food, to decompress.

Amira has to practically drag me back outside, but not before I grab a tamale to take with me. Food in one hand, and Amira's hand in my other, it takes me a second to figure out why everyone's staring at us.

"Are you two holding hands right now?" Jennie asks.

I look down at our interlaced fingers and then up at Amira, unsure but hopeful. Now seems as good a time as any to come clean. Amira squeezes my hand as if to say she agrees and turns to our friends with a bright smile.

"Yes," Amira says, rather proudly. "Yes, we are."

A feeling of warmth spreads through me at her use of "we." Then she takes our interlocked hands and pulls them up into the air like we just won gold at the Olympics or something, and I can't help laughing.

Jennie's and Lisa's mouths actually fall open, and they've never looked more identical. Shawn and Kerry hoot and cheer, Taylor and Brigit exchange a knowing look, and Danny is wearing sunglasses again, so I have no idea what he's thinking.

I stop worrying about it when Amira pulls down our hands and pulls me in so close our noses brush, and a second later so do our lips. Despite the fact that I still have the rest of a tamale in my other hand, and our parents are congregating a mere few feet away inside, all I can think about is Amira and how soft her lips are, sliding against mine.

Amira pulls back before the kiss can really gain any traction, and I have to swallow a whimper.

"All right, all right, we don't need to see you two make out," Shawn says, wagging his fingers at us. "But I'm happy for you. I knew when Amira got you the job at Horizon that it was only a matter of time."

It's like someone just splashed me from the pool, and I'm forced out of the happy daze I was in mere seconds ago. I turn to Shawn.

"I'm sorry, what?"

Amira, who was leaning on me, pulls herself up to standing as Shawn's face falls.

"I thought . . . you knew?" he says, his voice trailing off as he looks between me and Amira.

"We thought *you* got her the job," Taylor tells Shawn, and thank God for her because I feel like I've lost the ability to speak.

Shawn looks even more confused now. "Why would you think that?"

"You said *you* told the 'boss lady' that I'd be perfect for the job," I say, accusingly. And that's when it dawns on me. I turn to Amira. "You were the boss lady, weren't you?"

"Yes?" Amira says, though it comes out as a question.

A laugh that lacks humor bursts out of me then because, of course, Amira got me this job. Not only could I not get a job on my own, but Perfect Amira had to be the one to get it for me. At least with Shawn, I was able to convince myself that he owed me for helping him pass algebra last year, but why would Amira do this for me? She didn't even like me then.

"Why?" I say. "Why would you help me? You hated me."

"I didn't hate you," Amira says, reaching for me, but I pull away from her grasp.

"We should probably go . . . somewhere else," Brigit says.

I forgot she and everyone else were still here. She grabs Danny's arm, tugging him away, and Jennie and Lisa follow, though Jennie looks like she'd like to stay for the drama. Only Shawn, Taylor, and Kerry remain, and while I'm not sure what's about to happen with me and Amira, I'm grateful Taylor and Kerry are here.

"I didn't hate you," Amira says again more softly. She lowers her head, trying to meet my eyes, but I feel confused and irritated and maybe a little mad. I don't want to say the wrong thing, but I don't understand this.

"Then, why didn't you just tell me you got me the job?" I ask.

Now Amira laughs humorlessly. "Because you would've reacted like this! You probably wouldn't have even taken the job, as if me doing you a favor was some kind of cardinal sin."

"That's not true!"

"Yes, it is," Amira says. "You were ready to quit that first day when I got to Horizon. You probably wouldn't have even shown up if you'd known I was working there. That's why—"

Amira cuts herself off, and I stand up straighter, my eyes glued to her now.

"That's why what?" I ask.

My voice sounds harsh and cold, and I don't think I've ever spoken to Amira like this before, not even when she was the bane of my existence. But there's something in the way she's refusing to look at me now that has me on edge. I know, I just know whatever it is she isn't saying could very well break me and end us before we even begin.

Amira puffs out a long sigh, before she finally looks at me.

"That's why I told our moms that it was probably best if you didn't know," she says, finally.

This is, of course, when Kerry, who is nothing if not dramatic, gasps. I barely even register it, though, because it feels like something is shattering inside me.

Ma has been lying to me all summer. I asked her, I *literally* asked her, if she got me this job, and she lied right to my face. She didn't just know Amira would be at Horizon—she knew she got me the job, and she said nothing.

This whole time she's been pushing me about being nicer to Amira and asking me how it's going, and she's been lying to me. And here I thought Amira and I had this special thing between us, just for ourselves. Meanwhile, this whole time she's had her own little secret with my mom, and as always I'm the odd one out.

"I need to get out of here," I say.

"Rochelle, no, let's talk about this."

Amira reaches out, and I don't know if she's trying to take my hand or what, but I don't find out because Taylor's there, blocking her way.

"I think maybe you've done enough talking for right now," Taylor says. She turns to Shawn. "Can you take us home?"

Shawn looks between us and Amira, clearly unsure.

"Never mind," Taylor says, taking the decision out of his

hands. Looking around, she pauses until her eyes land on the rest of our friends by the pool.

"Bridge, we need a ride!" she calls out.

Brigit is up in seconds, and Danny slowly follows her up as well. Jennie and Lisa exchange a look but don't move, probably sensing the last thing I want to do is to engage with even more people right now.

"Rochelle, please," Amira says again, but I can't look at her. Because if I do, I'm not sure I'll be able to walk away from her, and I need some time to think.

"Since you and my mom are so close, I'm sure you'll let her know that I went home" is all I say before I follow Taylor, Kerry, Brigit, and Danny out the side gate and to the car.

TWENTY-NINE

TAYLOR AND KERRY TRY TO get out with me when we reach my house, but I tell them I just want to go to bed. I'll text them in the morning.

They give me a big group hug, and Brigit even hops out to join, which surprises me. She seems perfectly fine, but I still don't really know her all that well. I accept her hug all the same.

Then they all leave, Danny in the front seat totally knocked out and probably unaware of everything that's just happened. I still don't know if I trust him, but right now it's hard to believe he's an evil mastermind out to take down Horizon with his partner in crime.

By the time Ma gets home, I've showered and changed into my comfiest oversize tee and pajama shorts and snuggled down into my bed with my computer, rereading *Lore Olympus*. I just want to feel something other than whatever I'm feeling about Amira's revelation. Amira has texted and called, but I've ignored all of it.

When Ma knocks on my door, I close my laptop and sit up, ready for battle.

Or just a conversation.

Whatever.

"Come in," I say.

Ma opens my door with an unreadable expression. I can't tell if she's mad that I left without telling her, guilty because Amira told me the truth, or maybe a mix of both.

"I thought you might've already gone to bed," she says as she steps into my room.

It's a little after ten, but I feel wide awake and, thankfully, my shift at Horizon tomorrow is in the afternoon so I'll be able to sleep in.

"Technically, I am in bed," I say, unable to help myself.

She only nods as she comes closer and sits down on the edge of my bed. I have the urge to tell her she shouldn't be sitting on my bed in her street clothes, but I really don't care anymore.

"Amira told me what happened," she says.

"Of course, she did," I mutter under my breath. "It seems like you two have a really open line of communication."

Rationally, I know I told Amira to tell my mom, but it still irks me. How many private conversations have the two of them had about me behind my back?

"Rochelle, I'm sorry."

Ma places a hand on my ankle that's peeking out from under my sheet, but I pull my leg up so it's tucked under me, out of her reach. She pulls her hand back, resting it in her lap with a sigh.

"Why did you lie to me?" I ask her, because that's what matters the most. I can understand why Amira did it, even though I don't like it, but why would my mother go along with it?

Ma pulls her legs up so she's facing me with her legs tucked under her, our knees touching, as she meets my gaze head-on.

"Honestly, I convinced myself that it was more of an omission of truth than an outright lie," she says.

Ma holds up her hand before I can respond to this. "I know; that's still a lie. But that's how I spun it in my head. I figured things were going so well for you at Horizon and with Amira that it didn't matter how you got the job, all that mattered was that you were finally putting yourself out there. You were making new friends and having fun. You've barely even brought up Wharton this whole summer!"

I cut in then. "Why are you saying it like talking about Wharton is a bad thing? Isn't it good that I have goals?"

"Of course, it is, Rochelle, but when you talk about Wharton . . ."

Her voice trails off, and I feel like I'm going to pull my hair out. Why are people not finishing their sentences tonight?

"When I talk about Wharton, what?" I ask.

Ma's face hardens for a moment, as if she's going to reprimand me for having an attitude, but her face softens again when she seems to change her mind.

"It's like an obsession for you," Ma says, her voice so low, I find myself leaning in to hear her. "It's like at some point, I don't even really know when, you decided that Wharton was the end-all, be-all for you. I think it's your way of maybe honoring your dad, but—"

"This isn't about Dad," I say, incredulous. "It's about you!"

My words throw a hush over the room, and Ma looks stricken. I immediately recoil, but how can she not understand? She is all I've ever wanted to be. She is who I am. My inspiration, my drive, my ability to succeed. If I don't get into Wharton, what was it all for? Getting married, having me, putting her dreams on hold, and then letting go of them entirely when Dad died. What was it for if I fail?

How can she not understand that?

"Rochelle . . ."

I don't even realize I'm crying until she reaches over and swipes a thumb under my eye, wiping a wayward tear away.

"Baby, what's going on?" she asks me, cupping my cheek, which makes me just cry harder.

I can't even remember the last time I cried like this. I hate crying. My face always feels so dry after, and I'm an ugly crier. I can already feel all the snot on my upper lip like Viola Davis serving yet another award-winning performance.

"What do you mean this is about me?" she asks.

"I mean, I want to be the best *for you*!"

The words burst out of me as if I've been holding them in for so long, they can't wait to be free, and maybe I have, because once I start, I can't stop.

"I *have* to be the best," I say again. "I'm doing everything I can to succeed so everything you've done for me, all the sacrifices you've made, will mean something. And it's like you can't even support me! Instead, you're always telling me I have no social life and I have no fun. Well, I already have friends and we do have fun! I am not a loner just because I don't like to go out all the time. And despite what you and Amira think, I still would've taken the job if you had just been honest with me, because I needed it for Wharton! But you didn't even believe in me enough to let me make that decision myself. It's like you don't understand me at all."

Ma jerks back at my words, but I stay perfectly still, letting all the tears and snot roll down my face. I feel exhausted, and all I want is for her to leave so I can curl up into my bed and cry myself to sleep, something I haven't done in years.

But Ma doesn't move. Instead, she lowers her head and twists the sapphire ring that's always on her right hand. It's the engagement ring my dad gave her, and she never leaves the house without it, even though it's been over a decade now since he passed. Instinctively, I reach up to grab hold of the butterfly pendant I still have around my neck, rubbing it through my fingers. I marvel at how in so many small ways I'm just like her, but when it comes to the big stuff, we couldn't be more different.

"Rochelle, you do not have to do this for me," she says. I can feel her eyes back on me, but I keep my eyes down on my necklace.

Of course, she would say that. She would never come out and say she expects amazing things from me, but I know if I don't go to college or get a good job someday, she'll think she failed me.

Probably sensing my doubt, Ma pushes on.

"Look at me." She hooks a finger under my chin, tilting it up until I either have to shift my gaze elsewhere or meet her eyes.

"Yes, there were things I wanted to do before I met your dad and had you," she says. "But plans change. And I still went to law school, albeit a little later than planned, and I have a good job that I enjoy. Maybe I didn't become the jet-setting lawyer who changed the world, but I still have plenty of time to do that. Right now, my main priority is taking care of you.

"Everything I've ever done was so you could live the life that *you* want to live." Her voice is firm as she says it. "I do not care if you go to my alma mater, community college, or a trade school. I do not care if you decide you want to pursue an acting career like Kerry or be a painter like Taylor. I just care that you are happy and healthy with a roof over your head. That to me is what makes everything I've ever done feel worth it.

"And if Wharton is truly what you want, then I'm sorry I made you feel like I don't support your dream. Because I do support you in all things, always. You hear me?"

She takes my face in both hands and holds me steady as she says it again.

"Always."

My body shakes as my tears turn to ridiculous sobs. Ma doesn't say anything else, instead pulling me into her, wrapping her arms around me as I get snot all over her very nice cover-up dress.

"I'm so sorry I ever made you feel like you don't have my support," she says into my braids. "I'm so, so sorry."

"It's okay," I say between sobs. "It's okay."

I don't know how long we stay like that, but by the time I pull back and start trying to clean off my face with the back of my hands, my legs feel cramped. Ma gets up and grabs the tissue box on my desk, handing it to me, and I blow my nose in the loudest fashion imaginable. Ma lets out a little chuckle at my elephant sounds, and I glare at her and know we'll be okay.

My phone vibrates from where it is on my nightstand, and I don't have to glance over to know it's Amira, but Ma grabs it for me and holds it out.

"I know you're mad and you have every right to be," Ma says. "But you should give her a chance to make it right."

I take my phone from her and put it down on the bed next to me.

"I will," I say, when she's still looking at me expectantly. "But not tonight. It's late."

Ma nods, accepting this for now.

"I'm going to hop into the shower and head to bed," she says. "Some of us have to get up early for work tomorrow and don't get to sleep in."

A small laugh breaks free from my throat, and she smiles as if I've just given her a gift. Maybe I have. Maybe this really is all she wants from me. To be happy. I want to believe her, and the rational part of my brain does, but there's still a little part of me that isn't sure. Maybe that'll just go away with time, or maybe it's time I went back to therapy.

Either way, it's too much to think about tonight, and I feel like I can barely keep my eyes open. But before she leaves, I know there's something I need to be honest about too.

"Wait, Ma," I say as she reaches for my door. She turns back and looks at me, expectantly.

I swallow and then say the words I've been holding in for a while now.

"Amira and I are kind of dating," I tell her, saying it so quickly, it comes out more like one long word instead of a complete sentence.

Ma's lips turn up in a slight smile. "How mad would you be if I told you I knew?"

"Ugh, did Amira tell you that too?"

Ma laughs. "She didn't have to. You are both very bad at hiding your feelings. Anytime you talk about her or get a text from her or something, your face lights up in a way I haven't seen before. It's nice."

I can feel my face doing that thing she's talking about now, and I look anywhere but at her. "Yeah, I guess it is," I finally say.

Ma's face softens a bit, and she comes back to sit on my bed, taking her hands in mine.

"I know that you're committed to Wharton, and I will respect your drive and not push," she says. I sit up straighter, bracing myself for wherever she's going with this. "But I do want more for you than just diplomas and a successful career. Remember that when these things happen, all the things you're working toward, you'll want the people who love you around to celebrate you. I'm happy you and Amira are together, and I hope you can work this out, because you deserve this too, Rochelle."

She pats my cheek gently and goes to stand, but I stop her.

"Ma, was it worth it?"

The question comes out almost like a whisper, and I have to

force myself to glance up and look at her when I ask it. Her face is open but confused.

"Was what worth it, Rochelle?"

"Being with Dad," I say, pushing the words out. "I mean falling in love with him, putting your career on hold, having me. Was it all worth it, even though you lost him?"

"Oh."

Ma inhales sharply and then her fingers go back to the ring, twisting and turning, before she blinks back up at me, unshed tears in her eyes.

"Of course, it was," she says finally. "Losing him hurt like hell, but I'd do it all over again. The time I had with him and the gift of seeing him in you every day are priceless."

THIRTY

THE NEXT MORNING, I FINALLY check my phone.

I scroll past the various notifications from Amira, knowing that what we both need to say is probably best saved for when we see each other in person. Instead, I click into the "Movies That Feel Like Movies" group chat that is currently blowing up with messages in real time. I scroll up until I see the first message from Kerry.

MOVIES THAT FEEL LIKE MOVIES

Kerry: EVERYBODY WAKE UP RIGHT NOW I'M SO SERIOUS

Kerry: I'VE FOUND THE PRANKSTER

Kerry: <PranksOnTheHorizon on Instagram: "The soda thing was a hit! What should we do next? Poll in my stories! 😺">

I tap the link and then sit up in bed as the video starts to play. The paintings on the wall make it obvious it's Horizon. My first thought is that kid I saw with his phone out, but this video looks like this was filmed far away, because the shot is a bit grainy, like it's been zoomed in. The camera shifts a little, and I can see one of the game machines in the corner. Whoever did this must've been hiding behind the machines.

On-screen I watch as Danny's hand goes into the soda machine, and I already know what happens next, but I watch anyway as soda comes firing out, getting everywhere. The video lasts for a little longer, showing Danny, Amira, and I attempting to figure out what to do. Of course, there's an excellent shot of me getting totally drenched before the video cuts out.

Great.

I leave the video and go to the Instagram profile and see it's just filled with a bunch of different videos of all the pranks that've been happening at Horizon this summer. There they are, switching the film reels for the movies my first day, and there's another one of them sneaking more kernels into the popcorn machine when Danny's back is turned.

And yet we never see the person's face. At best we get a glimpse of their hand, white, but nothing identifying.

It's obvious that Danny isn't the one doing the pranks, but he's on shift for almost all of them, and Pete is white so it could very well be him.

I jump back to the group chat where everyone is still firing off messages. It's a mix of outrage that we have concrete evidence someone's been messing with us all summer, but no one's pointing out the obvious about Danny. Amira's also noticeably silent through the whole conversation, as is Shawn.

MOVIES THAT FEEL LIKE MOVIES

Brigit: So, what do we do now? Do we show this to Glory?

Danny: We could, but what good would it do?

Lisa: It'll prove nothing's our fault at least. Or Horizon's. It'll show that once we get this prankster, everything will be fine and there's no reason to shut down.

Kerry: I hate to say it, but isn't the bigger issue money? How does catching this prankster fix that issue?

Brigit: They can pay for the damage they caused for starters. That's costing the uncles a lot of money.

Jennie: True! And we have our paraphernalia table!

Me: The props you mean?

Kerry: Omg she lives!

Me: Anyway . . .

Me: I agree. If we find the prankster, it's a good start at least. And now we at least have an idea of who we're looking for.

Jennie: We do?

Me: Yeah. That hand is palm colored so they're most likely white and so is Pete. If he shows up at the theater, I think we should question him.

Danny: Question him? I already told you guys he didn't do anything.

Me: You don't know that for sure though. Besides, if he is innocent, then he should have no problem answering our questions. I think that's fair.

Kerry: Agreed.

Danny: Fine, whatever.

I wait a bit, wondering if Amira will respond to what I've said, but when five minutes pass and there's still nothing from her, I know she won't. Pushing up out of bed, I start getting ready for work and prepare to face whatever will happen when I get there.

It feels weird going into Horizon without Amira.

Lately, she's been picking me up anytime we've worked a shift together, but I know better than to call her and ask. I don't think having our "talk" in the car on the way to work is the best idea either.

Instead, Taylor offers to give me a ride since Ma is already long gone to work by the time I have to go in. Taylor fills the car with some loud synth goth music that I can't understand, but I'm happy not to talk. After my conversation with Ma last night and the revelation Kerry made this morning, I'm feeling all talked out.

So, when we pull up to Horizon and the words "What the hell?" fall out of my mouth, it makes sense that Taylor looks surprised. But then she sees what I see.

"Whoa."

The marquee is lit up, and rather than the typical show times, it says, "Welcome to Horizon Cinema. Black cinema history exhibit open today!"

Hanging under the marquee are those little flags that are usually hung up at car dealerships.

The front doors are wide open, and big burly dudes are strolling in with boxes while others come out with the game machines.

"What is going on?" Taylor asks.

"I have no idea."

I unbuckle my seat belt and quickly hop out of the car, following the men inside, and discover mayhem.

Glory is in the middle of everything, directing people to go either this way or that, while their uncles stand by concessions watching someone install a new soda machine. Gracie is in Derek's arms, being happily bounced up and down.

I glance around looking for Amira but do not see her in the mayhem. Instead, I see what was once the corner for arcade games has now been cleared out and replaced with rows of metal columns that have glass boxes on top of them, each filled with a different set piece or film reel from the boxes we'd found downstairs.

There are spaces for placards on each one that are currently empty, and I have to jump out of the way as another man passes by to place an additional column in the space.

Taylor, who was clearly in less of a hurry to get answers, comes to stand behind me.

"Well, this is certainly interesting," she says.

All I can do is nod and then leave her to explore the new displays as I make my way to Glory.

"Glory, what is all this?"

They look up from their clipboard and blink back as if they're surprised to see me. Their surprise is confirmed when they say, "Rochelle, what are you doing here?"

"I have work," I say, but for some reason they're still looking at me as if I'm the one who's confused.

"No, you don't," they say, matter-of-factly. "I sent an email letting everyone know they didn't need to come in today."

My brow furrows as I pull out my phone and check my email. There is, of course, no email from Glory. Just as I'm about to tell them so, Amira and Shawn appear from behind the rope leading to the theaters, except neither of them is wearing their Horizon uniforms. Instead, they're both dressed casually in workout shorts and T-shirts.

Amira's even wearing flip-flops.

"I don't think you sent an email," I say to Glory quickly. "It's not in my in-box."

Glory doesn't even glance up from their clipboard.

"I'm positive I did—you probably just missed it."

I thankfully don't have to prove my case any further when the twins arrive, dressed for work, and pull up short when they see all the commotion. I throw a pointed look at Glory, but they don't even notice it, stepping away to go talk to one of the many men moving around here today.

I can practically feel Amira getting closer, and I turn to face her, ready to finally deal with what happened last night. But she apparently isn't, because when she sees me, she pivots hard and runs into the bathroom.

Cool, cool, cool.

Shawn looks from me to the space where Amira was beside him two seconds ago and shrugs.

"I'm going to say hi to Taylor," he says. "Good luck with that!"

I assume by "that" he means Amira. He strolls over to Taylor, who's clearly over the fact he didn't give us a ride home last night. Shawn wraps his arms around her, and she doesn't push him away, which is basically a kiss in their love language.

A pang hits my chest, and I let my eyes stray to the women's restroom. Even though Amira was colluding with my mom, I still want her arms wrapped around me like Shawn's are with Taylor. I want her vanilla scent to overwhelm me, and her curly hair to tickle my nose.

I want *her*.

My feet make a decision before my brain does, and I walk through the door. But Amira's not standing at the sinks where I expect her to be.

"Hello?"

Nothing but silence answers me.

"Amira?" I try again. "I saw you run in here. You can't hide forever."

Just when the fear that I've somehow fallen into a horror movie starts to make my heart race, I hear the lock on one of the stalls unlatch and out pops Amira.

She looks the least put together I've seen her. From a distance I only noticed her athleisure, but up close I can see dark circles under her eyes and her hair is pulled up in a messy ponytail that *actually* looks messy, not messy in that cute styled way she usually does it.

And when she crosses her arms over her chest, I'm pretty sure I notice a hole under one of the arms of her T-shirt.

"Here I am," Amira says. "So, just get it over with."

I can feel my face contort with confusion.

"Get *what* over with?"

"Break up with me," Amira says with a huff. "I know you hate me again, so let's just get this over with."

I cannot believe after all the time we've spent together this summer, she really thinks I could just go back to the way things were.

Amira won't look at me, even as I take a step closer, and then another and another until the toes of my sneakers hit the edge of her flip-flops. Finally, she looks up, and her eyes meet mine.

"For someone who claims they can challenge me for valedictorian, you're really not that smart."

Amira gasps with indignation, but my mouth closes on hers before she can say anything. For a moment nothing happens, and I worry I maybe should've saved the kissing for after we talk. But then Amira's arms wrap around my waist, and she's pulling me even closer. We kiss each other senseless.

When we finally come up for air, she rests her forehead on mine, her eyes searching my face.

"That was unexpected," she says.

"Was it?" I ask. "Everyone seems to have known how we felt about each other before we did."

"I thought when you ignored my texts and calls, you were pushing me away again," Amira says.

I sigh and finally step back from her, though she reaches out for my hand, still holding me close, and I let her.

"I was just mad," I say. "I needed time to think, and my mom and I ended up having a good talk. Even though I don't like that you both lied to me, I understand why you did what you did."

Amira blinks at me. "You do?"

I nod. "Yeah. I know I wasn't exactly your biggest fan before we started working together . . ."

Amira snorts. "Fan? You were my mortal enemy, and for no reason! I don't even care about being valedictorian. I only started caring when you made it seem like I couldn't be. Like I was some weight pulling you down with my stupidity or something."

I think she wants her words to be a joke, but there's no hiding the hurt there. It stings because I know even though I've apologized, Amira hasn't moved past this pain I caused her. Not really.

"Amira, I never thought you were stupid or that you'd bring me down," I say.

"Oh, right, sorry, I was just some goofy distraction," she says, rolling her eyes.

I realize that she really doesn't get it, which is fair. I should've just told her the truth once I realized it.

"You were never just some distraction to me," I say, taking her hands in mine. Amira looks up at me tentatively and I press on. "I said I pushed you away because I thought you'd get in the way of me doing well in school, but that wasn't it. I mean, that was it, but—"

I take a deep breath and squeeze her hands as I try to find the words to say what I realized a while ago now.

"Being around you made *me* feel stupid, Amira," I say, looking up at her. "I felt tongue-tied and like I couldn't pay attention in class, and you were always there. In school, at my house, whenever my mom dragged me along to hang out with your mom. I couldn't study around you. I couldn't do anything around you, because when I was with you, all I could focus on was you, and when you weren't around, all I could think about was you. It was . . . frustrating and terrifying, and I'd never felt anything like it before."

The corners of Amira's mouth twitch.

"I think you're describing what normal people would call a crush," she says.

"Yes, well, Kerry and Taylor said the same thing," I say with a shrug. "I just didn't want to believe it at first."

Now, she's full-on grinning, and I can't stand it, but I can't stop myself from smiling too.

"You like me!" she says, poking me in my side. "You really like me."

"Oh my God."

I move away from her, making my way to the door, but she wraps an arm around my waist and pulls me to her, my back to her front.

"You like me," she whispers in my ear.

"So what?" I say, rolling my eyes, though the smile on my face only grows bigger. "You like me too."

"I don't recall saying that," she says, spinning me around in her arms.

"You didn't have to," I say. I kiss her again and don't stop.

THIRTY-ONE

ONCE AMIRA AND I PULL ourselves together, or rather apart, we go back out to the lobby, where she and Shawn finally explain what's going on.

"All right, so as much as we loved our little display table," Amira begins.

"It wasn't enough," Shawn finishes.

I wonder if they rehearsed this joint presentation.

"At least that's what someone in our Instagram DMs said," Amira adds.

Taylor, who's standing next to me, raises her hand.

"Babe, you don't have to raise your hand," Shawn says. "This isn't school."

"Raising your hand isn't just for school," I say. "It's to give structure to a conversation."

Amira coughs, but it sounds a lot like "Nerd." I glare at her, but she smiles at me all innocent and, God, do I love her smile. Is this what flirting is? Are we doing this right?

It feels right, and I think that's all that matters.

"Thank you, Rochelle," Taylor says, standing up straighter in triumph. "Anyway, why are we listening to someone who slid into your DMs?"

"To be clear, they slid into Horizon's DMs, and we're listening to them because they've donated this. All of it."

Amira gestures with her hand like she's some lady on a game show revealing the grand prize. Stupidly, we all turn. By now, the guys have finished setting up the display cases, and it looks like a little museum in the front. The new soda machine is also put together, and I can't be sure, but it looks like it has more than just three different flavors of soda now.

I turn back to Amira and Shawn, who look ridiculously proud.

"Wait, so some random person just offered to do all of this?" I ask. "Isn't that weird?"

"That's what I said," Shawn jumps in. "So, we brought it to Glory."

I look between the two of them. "When did all of this happen?"

"In the last forty-eight hours or so," Amira says. "Well, actually we got the DM after I posted about the table, but it went into our requests, so I didn't notice it until recently. Also, the person DMing wasn't actually the person offering to help. It was their assistant."

"Someone's *assistant* DMed you?" Taylor asks. "Who is this person?"

"We're not at liberty to say," Amira says, but it's clear she's near bursting with the information. "But she used to live in Long Island and loves Horizon as much as we do and doesn't want to see it fail."

"She also maybe has an Emmy and is on a comedy show about teachers, but I don't know for sure," Shawn adds, wiggling his eyebrows.

Amira elbows him in the side. "Seriously? At this point, why don't you just tell them?"

"No, no, we must keep the secret," Shawn says, before proceeding to hold up a finger to his lips in the universal sign for silence.

Truthfully, I'm not sure I know who they're talking about, but I'll Google it later.

"What are we talking about?"

We all turn to see the twins bounding over, each of them with an ice-cream cone in their hand.

"Where did you get those?" Taylor asks.

"There's a Mister Softee truck circling the parking lot," Jennie says, pointing her thumb behind her.

"And since we apparently don't have work today," Lisa says, her voice laced with more irritation than I've heard from her all summer, "we decided to go get some."

"So, what's up?" Jennie asks. "Why the huddle?"

Amira and Shawn run through their spiel again, and once we're all on the same page, I turn to Amira.

"So, what does this mean exactly?" I ask. "We have this cool display and the new soda machine—"

"And new letters and lights for the marquee," Shawn adds.

"Right," I say. "But is this enough? Enough to make sure Horizon really stays open?"

"I think so," Amira says. "But we'll know more tomorrow."

"What's happening tomorrow?" Jennie asks.

"A community event!" Amira exclaims. "It was Glory's idea."

"What does that mean exactly?" Taylor asks.

"I'm so glad you asked, my lady love," Shawn says, before booping Taylor on the nose.

I look at Taylor aghast, but she simply wrinkles her nose and says nothing.

"We're opening the doors of Horizon to the community," Amira says. "There'll be the usual concessions, but also food from local restaurants and free drinks—all of which is *also* being donated and paid for by our anonymous patron. We'll let people explore our little exhibit, and we'll be showing classic Black films all day for the low, low price of just five dollars a ticket."

"Whoa," I say. "That sounds amazing."

"Right?" Amira says. "Of course, I'll be gathering footage all day for social. Uncle Derek and Eric even said they'd try to get some local news stations here."

"Have you been planning this since the soda explosion?" I ask her.

Amira shakes her head. "Everything kind of came together in the last two days. Glory's been brainstorming since the explosion though and with this gift"—she directs her hand to the new display cases—"they came up with the perfect idea to get more people in here. And Uncle Derek and Uncle Eric aren't ready to give up on Horizon yet. They're hopeful this may turn everything around."

Lisa raises her hand, and Amira rolls her eyes.

"You do not need to raise your hand but, yes, Lisa?"

"What if the prankster comes and ruins it?"

I snort. "You mean what if Pete comes and ruins it."

"We don't know that it's him," Amira says, and a flash of annoyance courses through me, but I don't argue. I didn't know him like Amira, Shawn, and Brigit did. Even if they don't like him like Danny does, it's probably hard for them to believe their former coworker would sabotage them, even if all the signs are there.

"Me and Kerry can keep an eye out," Taylor says. "And we know a couple of other people we can enlist to help too. We'll all just stay vigilant, and who knows? Maybe we'll even catch the person, whoever it is, once and for all."

Lisa chews on her lip, clearly still worried, but her sister knocks her hip into her.

"It'll be fine," Jennie says. "Great, even! Umma and Appa and Brian can come."

"Who's Brian?" Amira asks.

"Our little brother," they say in unison.

Amira's brows rise. "How did we not know you had another sibling?"

"I knew," Shawn says, but Jennie just shrugs. "You never asked."

Amira's mouth opens and then closes again, aghast.

"Well, anyway, we'll have enough eyes around this place to

make sure the prankster doesn't ruin the day," Taylor says. "I think this will be great."

"Me too," I say, surprised by how much I mean it. "It'll be perfect."

We all look around the circle at each other, and I can feel the hopefulness and determination surging through us.

"Feels like we should hug," Shawn says, much to my and Taylor's dismay.

"I don't think that's necessary—" I start to say, but Shawn's already stretching his arms long to tug us all in.

"Ah," he says, sighing. "Me and my girls."

We all groan but it turns into laughter, and it's just like I said. Perfect.

THIRTY-TWO

AT SOME POINT, GLORY REMEMBERS to send the email they claimed they sent before detailing the plans for Saturday.

It'll be all hands on deck for the event, which means for the first time since training, we'll all be at Horizon, which honestly sounds kind of fun.

Plus, with all of us here, that means we'll finally find out if Danny's been telling the truth or if he and his good friend Pete are as guilty as I believe them to be.

Amira's driving me to work again.

We arrive at Horizon early, because even though Amira won't say it, she's obviously anxious. Once we arrive, it's clear she had nothing to worry about.

We see News 12 and NY1, two of our local TV news stations, with their vans parked out front. When we get out, we can see newscasters being filmed. One is talking to Uncle Derek and the other to Uncle Eric, who is holding Gracie.

"Oh my God, this is really happening," Amira says, reaching

for her phone. She starts snapping pics and videos. Unsure what to do with myself, I simply follow, taking her backpack when she hands it to me.

When the interviews appear to be wrapping up, Amira and I make our way to the uncles.

"What did they say?" Amira asks before even saying hello. "Are they going to stay for the event?"

"Yes," Uncle Derek says with a low chuckle. "They want to get some B-roll, so they'll be around with the cameras for at least the start. Hopefully, we'll have a good showing, so it doesn't look bad on TV."

"It'll look great," Uncle Eric says, resting his hand on Uncle Derek's shoulder. "Don't sweat it."

"I will be sweating if we stay out here much longer," he says, taking Gracie from Eric. "Let's get into the AC, shall we?"

We all file in behind him, and then my mouth drops. All the art on the wall that was black-and-white literally yesterday is now filled with color.

"Oh my God," Amira says.

I get the feeling she may be saying this a lot today. After I close my mouth, I hook a finger under her chin and close hers too.

Glory comes out of the office then, covered in paint-splattered overalls.

"Oh, Glory, did you sleep here last night?" Uncle Eric asks, hurrying over to them.

"Only a little," Glory says. "But doesn't it look great?! And don't worry, I didn't do this alone. My friends helped."

"It looks amazing!" Amira says, running over to one of the walls. Tentatively, she touches Whoopi Goldberg. "And it's already dry."

"I'd hope so," Glory says. "We finished around three, I think. And we didn't have to use too much paint. I outlined this all pretty well, and all of the shadowing was already there. I'm glad I finally got to finish it."

I whip my head around to them. "Wait, you *drew* this too? Not just colored it in?"

Glory snorts. "Yeah, who else?"

"But . . . I mean . . . this is incredible!"

Glory squints. "Why do you sound surprised?"

I start and stop, struggling to find the right words as everyone stares at me. The truth was that Glory, who's always running late and never in proper work attire, never gave me the vibes of a gifted painter. Though Taylor is a painter too, and I'm sure plenty of people would be surprised to know that. That's what I get for judging a book by its cover.

"I—I guess I am surprised," I say finally. "Sorry."

I really mean it. But before I can say more, Amira places her hands on my shoulders and pushes me out of the circle. "All right, let's get moving. We need to get concessions ready. When will the food be here?"

"At ten," Glory says. "We'll need to clear the counter space to make sure we have enough room for the Sternos."

"You got it, boss," Amira says. She then pushes me away, toward our task.

Time flies as the rest of the staff arrives, along with the

volunteers donating food. By the time we officially open, I'm already exhausted, but the whole place looks amazing. Glory's art makes the place feel brighter and warmer, and the AC is thankfully on full blast. We've relinquished space at concessions for the caterers, and Amira, Shawn, and I are handling drink and candy purchases, along with accepting donations. We didn't expect them, but people just started handing us money "to save Horizon." We used a cup to collect the extra cash at first, but that quickly proved insufficient, so Glory went into the office, grabbed a large plastic jug, and cut a hole in the white lid so people could slot their money in.

At one point Jennie and Brigit come over and gaze at the jug amazed.

"I can't believe so many people still carry cash," Brigit says in wonder.

"Of course, they do," Jennie says. Then, lowering her voice, she adds, "Old people," and shrugs.

Shawn and Danny take it upon themselves to sweat outside, holding poster signs at the entrance of the parking lot inviting people to come in and watch *Boyz n the Hood*, *Friday*, *The Best Man*, *Love Jones*, and, for the kids, *The Princess and the Frog*.

Our showings throughout the day either sell out or almost do, and it's the busiest we've been all summer.

"I think we should start doing this once a month," Glory says at one point.

Amira and I are finally taking a break, sitting on the cushioned benches in the lobby. Glory has decided to sit with us.

"Maybe not as big as this," they add. "We don't need to have food vendors come in every month."

"That could be cool though," I say.

They both look at me, and I realize they're waiting for me to continue.

"I just mean it'll be a good way to support other local businesses. We could just do one vendor each time, and they could plan a menu with the prices, and we could get an extra register for them to keep their money separate from ours."

Glory grins. "That's really smart, Rochelle."

"Why do you sound so surprised?" I ask, and they laugh at the callback to my earlier flub.

I'm about to say something else when I see Taylor and Kerry walking around, and I remember there's something I still need to do.

"Excuse me for a sec," I say, jumping up to grab Kerry.

"Hello," I say when I reach her. "It's time."

Kerry smiles and exchanges a look with Taylor, who looks equally clueless.

"Time for what?" Kerry asks.

"Your first big break or whatever," I say.

Before she asks me any other questions, I take her hand and lead her through the crowd. We stop in front of Derek and Eric, who are eating hot dogs while my mother, of all people, bounces Gracie up and down on her hip.

"Ma, when did you get here?" I ask.

"A little while ago," she says, not even looking at me. Gracie has her little fist around Ma's thumb, and Ma is letting her think she's moving her hand up and down. "I was going to say hi, but you seemed so busy, and then I found the cutest baby in the whole wide world."

"Oh boy, don't go catching baby fever."

Ma doesn't even dignify that with a response.

I turn to the uncles, pushing Kerry a bit closer. Though she seems to have forgotten how to function. "Uncle Derek. Uncle Eric. This is my friend Kerry, an up-and-coming actress. Kerry, these are the uncles. Say hi."

"Hi," she squeaks out.

"That'll do," I say. "I'll leave you three to it. Bye!"

As I walk away, I can hear Uncle Eric saying, "Hi, Kerry. It's lovely to meet you," and Kerry saying something that sounds like "Likewise," but for once her volume is at a more measured level, and I know she's doing everything she can to remain professional.

I throw her a little thumbs-up as I make my way back to Amira.

THIRTY-THREE

WE'RE ON OUR LAST SHOWING of the day when the power goes out.

Amira and I are in the middle of making an order when it happens. We both freeze in place, and I can barely see.

"Um, guys?" Lisa says from . . . somewhere.

I pull my phone out of my pocket and turn on the flashlight. Amira and Lisa quickly do the same, and pretty soon everyone in the lobby is lighting up the place. At first it was eerily quiet with all the machines stopping, but now everyone's talking at once, trying to figure out what's going on.

"Do you think it's a blackout?" Amira asks. "Or maybe we're using too much power and blew a fuse?"

"Maybe," I say. But there's a sinking feeling in my gut that that isn't it.

"Hold on, Glory's calling me," Amira says, stepping away to take it.

Lisa steps closer to me, and I'm grateful that it's late in the day and the food vendors have already packed up and left. The last thing we need is more people (with hot food) fumbling around in the dark.

"It'll be fine," I say to her quickly. "We'll figure this out."

Lisa nods as we attempt to look out into the crowd with the little bit of light our phones grant us.

Amira ends her call and joins us. "Glory says the power's fine; it's just the theater. They said they already asked the boys to check the breakers since they're still outside."

Before Amira can finish her sentence, the lights flicker back on, and people start clapping.

"Well, that was quick," I say, looking around.

That's when the front doors open, and Shawn staggers in, holding on to someone who has a black ski mask with holes cut out for their eyes. Danny holds the door open so they can get inside.

"What the hell?" Amira says.

She doesn't even bother trying to open the gate and instead hops over the counter. Lisa and I exchange a questioning look before shrugging and doing the same.

We run over to meet Shawn and Danny, who's now helping hold on to the person with the ski mask.

"Who is this?" Amira asks and anticipation thrums through me. I look to Danny, but if he's worried about finally being caught, nothing on his face gives him away. He only looks focused on keeping a solid grip on the person who's wriggling around, not saying anything.

"No idea," Shawn says. "It was hard enough grabbing him before he ran off. We found him next to the fuse box."

A second later Glory and the uncles have rushed over along with Amira's parents and my mother, who still has Gracie in her arms.

"What's going on?" Glory asks.

Surprisingly, it's Danny who speaks.

"We went to check the breakers like you said," he begins. "And before we even turned the corner, this guy starts running at us."

"Almost toppled me over, which is crazy since he's actually not that big," Shawn adds.

The guy grunts, still struggling and failing to get away.

"I held on to mystery boy until Danny flipped the switch back on," Shawn finishes.

Brigit suddenly appears beside Danny, grinning and batting her eyes at him.

"That is *so* heroic."

Amira, Lisa, and I all say "ew," collectively.

Jennie comes up next to Lisa. "What's happening?"

"I think we found the person making all our lives miserable for the past month and a half," Glory says. They step forward and the guy (person?) finally stops squirming, seemingly accepting defeat as Glory reaches for the bottom of the mask, pulls it up, and reveals—

"Pete?" Glory exclaims at the same time Danny says the boy's name with a defeated sigh. As vindicating as it feels to be proven right, the disappointment on Danny's face is obvious. He really didn't know.

Danny lets go of Pete, stepping away as he shakes his head.

Brigit goes to him, lacing her fingers through his as the adults around us take in the situation, clearly more surprised than we all are.

Uncle Derek cocks his head and squints. "You used to work here, didn't you?"

"Yeah, I did," Pete says, vehemently. "I was supposed to be the assistant manager before she—"

"They," we all correct automatically.

"Before *they* fired me," he finishes, pointing at Glory.

Shawn still has a firm grip on him, but with Danny stepping away, Pete now has at least one hand free. I'm not really worried he'll do anything, but it makes me nervous, nonetheless.

Amira steps closer. "I can't believe it. You really did all of this just to get revenge because Glory promoted me instead of you?"

Amid the anger and hurt on Amira's face, I can see guilt there too. This was her worst fear, and now she's blaming herself for this, even though the real culprit is standing in front of us. I want to pull her to me and tell her none of this is her fault, but Pete starts talking before I can interject.

"At first," he says, "I wanted to show everyone that you didn't have what it takes to run Horizon. Not like me. But then I started posting my pranks, and people were really into them." His voice turns excited now. It's like he's completely forgotten we just caught him red-handed messing with the theater.

"I couldn't just stop," he continues. "I had to do something bigger and better each time. For my audience."

Danny blows out a breath that sounds like a laugh, and we all look at him.

"For your audience?" he asks harshly. "That's what you care about. Building an audience? What about us? What about me? I asked you if you were involved. I told you we could fix it, and you lied to me. And I defended you!"

It's the most Danny's said all summer, and the hurt in his voice is so clear. It makes me even madder at Pete. Danny, who typically only says ten words per shift, really believed his friend was innocent, and why wouldn't he? If someone tried to tell me Taylor or Kerry was sabotaging Horizon, I'd say they were crazy too. I wish I'd realized that sooner instead of thinking Danny was also working against us.

"It wasn't personal, man," Pete says, with a shrug that somehow looks apologetic. "But I was going viral, and people were starting to reach out to me about partnerships. I can make money from this, and I need the money now that I don't have a job."

"And it didn't occur to you to just get another job?" I ask, incredulous.

"Do you know how hard it is to get a job around here?" he asks. "Especially once you've been fired. People talk. There was no way I was getting a regular gig after what Glory did to me."

"Glory didn't fire you for no reason," Amira says. "You were never around!"

Glory steps up to Amira, placing a hand on her shoulder and giving it a light squeeze before taking over the conversation.

"Peter, do you have any idea how much money your pranks cost us?" Glory says, scarily calm. "Not to mention our time. Precious time that could've been used on so many other things to make sure Horizon's doors stay open."

Uncle Derek comes up behind Glory, resting his hands on their shoulders. He looks formidable as he locks eyes with Pete, who I'm pretty sure stands up straighter.

"While this may have seemed relatively harmless to you, it wasn't," Uncle Derek says. "Not by a long shot."

Pete looks around at all of us then. And by all of us, I mean *everyone* in the theater who has stopped to watch all of this unfold.

"I'm sorry," Pete says finally. For the first time he actually sounds remorseful. "Truly. I—I didn't think it was that big of a deal. It was just a few pranks."

Glory looks to Shawn. "Bring him to my office. I'm calling his parents."

Pete blinks and looks between Glory and Shawn, fear in his eyes. It's maybe wrong of me, but I'm glad he finally seems to be realizing that he's in trouble.

"What? No, please, you can't do that. They'll kill me," Pete says. "I said I was sorry."

"That's not going to cut it, son," Uncle Derek says. He takes hold of Pete from Shawn, and Pete looks around at all of us.

"Guys, come on, it's not that big of a deal, right?" None of us say anything, so he turns to Danny, but Danny doesn't meet his gaze.

"Danny, come on, you know I would never intentionally hurt anyone," he says. "These were all just jokes. It was funny."

Danny says nothing, quiet again as Uncle Derek leads Pete to the office, with Glory close on his heels.

"I should probably go in as well," Uncle Eric says. "Really make him feel like he's getting the book thrown at him, you know?"

We all nod, though nothing about Uncle Eric gives off "authoritative figure."

Once they're gone, we all look around at each other, and suddenly Amira bursts out laughing and crying simultaneously.

"Oh dear, I think she may be in shock," her mother says, coming over to rub her back.

"I'm not in shock," Amira says, wiping tears from her eyes. "I just can't believe it was really Pete. The guy who didn't want to have to fill the popcorn machine overfilled it just to get back at us. He really hated us that much. That's insane."

Amira's mom pulls her hand away, as Amira continues laughing. Shawn cracks a smile and so does Brigit. Even Danny's lips twitch up slightly, before they even out into a straight line again.

"I still can't believe he did this," he says.

Brigit takes his hand in hers, lacing their fingers together.

"You wanted to trust him," she says. "It's not your fault he betrayed that trust."

Danny nods solemnly, and silence falls among our group as the reality of what just happened sinks in. That silence is swiftly broken when Taylor and Kerry push through the crowd and look around at all of us.

"What did we miss?" Kerry asks. "What happened?"

Jennie jumps in. "The prankster was, in fact, Pete."

"He's now in the back office so Glory can call his parents," Lisa adds.

"Oh wow," Taylor says.

I look around and realize Amira's parents and Ma have slithered away, and I appreciate that they're giving us space to digest this turn of events.

"Well, you're welcome for finding a massive clue that led to you finding the culprit," Kerry says, proudly.

I tilt my head and squint at her. "Really? Did you *really* help us find the culprit?"

"Yes!" Kerry says. "I found his Instagram."

"I think you did a good job, Kerry," Jennie cheers. "We couldn't have done it without you."

"Uh, thanks," Kerry says.

"And I mean that in a completely platonic way," Jennie adds. "Because we are *just friends*."

My eyes widen as I turn to Kerry, who's shaking her head.

"You do not have to say that every time you support me now, Jennie," Kerry says.

"I like it," Lisa says. "Sets clear boundaries."

"Agreed," Amira says, though her eyes are clearly twinkling with laughter.

"Why do I feel like I've missed something?" Taylor asks.

"Ditto," I say, looking between Kerry and Jennie.

While I'm glad it seems Jennie has finally realized her hope for a romance with Kerry was misguided, Jennie seems way too cheerful about it. If Amira told me she just wanted to be friends right now, I'd probably do something drastic like color my hair.

Kerry sighs. "Jennie asked me out, and while I was very

flattered, I explained that I'm not interested in having any romantic attachments."

"Which I totally understood," Jennie says, smiling. "So now we're just friends."

"Technically, we were always just friends," Kerry says. "But yeah, we're cool. We'll also be starting a K-drama club soon if anyone wants to join."

Brigit raises her hand. "Oh, I'm in!"

"Oh, Bridge, yay!" Jennie says. "This will be so much fun."

"All right, all right," Amira says, clapping her hands. Boss mode activated. "Now that everything's been resolved, I think we should do something to celebrate."

"Like what?" Brigit asks.

Amira locks eyes with me. "Pizza at Joe's?"

I smile. "Sure, why not?"

THIRTY-FOUR

IT TAKES A BIT BEFORE we can actually go to Joe's.

There's tons of clean-up to do, hugs and goodbyes that need to be made with our families, and checking in with Glory and the uncles before we finally make our exit. But once we get to Joe's and discover the place is surprisingly empty for a Saturday, it's like we're finally free.

Although Glory and the uncles were still counting all the money we raised that day, including some checks they'd received and online donations, it was looking like there was plenty to keep Horizon's doors open as we continue to grow with our new promotions.

And yes, I mean we. Although summer's quickly coming to an end, all of us will continue to work at Horizon during the school year. I've already told Glory I can only do weekends. I still have to study after all. She was totally cool with it, since Kerry will be joining the staff next month too.

Taylor politely declined the idea of working with us, despite Shawn's best efforts.

"Maybe if Glory hires me to paint something," Taylor says.

We're taking that as a win.

At Joe's we all squeeze into two booths, and Joe doesn't even let us order.

"I have some new specials for you all to try," he says.

Kerry, Taylor, and I exchange looks, but everyone takes it in stride when he comes back out with various pizzas. One has a variety of different vegetables on it, another has ham and pineapple, and there's another with sausage and pepperoni.

"Um, Joe, these look like your regular pizzas," I tell him.

Joe winks at us. "Yes, but they're *special* because I made them for you all!"

"Aw, Joe!" Amira says. We all say a round of thank-yous as he waves us off and goes back behind the counter.

"I would like to make a toast," Shawn says, holding up his cup.

"Oh God," Taylor groans from beside him. "What on earth are you about to say?"

He smiles sweetly at her. "To Horizon," he says.

We all raise our glasses.

"To Horizon," we cheer.

And then we dig in. It's a mix of chatter, and the conversations ebb and flow, as Joe turns up the music. Today he's playing exclusively Bob Marley, and Danny seems to be digging it, though his sunglasses are on again and I imagine he's also high. After the day we've had, I can't blame him.

As I look around our tables, taking it all in, I think about what Ma said. How life isn't just about my accomplishments or wins, but the people I'll get to share those moments with. Today we accomplished something huge by saving Horizon and discovering Pete, and I can't imagine not having all my friends, old and new, here with me for that.

I'm so wrapped up in the three different conversations going on that it takes me a moment to realize Amira's trying to get my attention.

"Come outside with me," she whispers. Her eyes are twinkling with mischief, and I grin.

We slide out of the booth, ignoring our friends as they ask us where we're going. Amira laces her fingers through mine, tugging me down the street of the little shopping mall area until we're far enough away that we can't be seen through the large windows of Joe's.

Amira turns to me, stepping me back until I'm against the cement wall of one of the shops.

"So, quick question," she says, wrapping a finger around one of my braids.

"You brought me out here to ask me a question?" I ask.

"Yes," Amira says, smiling. "Why, did you think I wanted to make out with you or something?"

"Yes," I say, because, duh, obviously.

"We can do that later," she says. "First, question."

"Okay, what is it?"

"Are you still planning to go to Wharton?"

The question throws me, and it takes me a second to answer.

"Yes, I—I think so," I say. "But I'm open to other schools, I guess. It doesn't have to be Wharton."

"Okay, good," she says. "Because my top choice is Columbia, which is only a two-and-a-half-hour drive from Wharton."

I raise a brow. "You looked it up?"

Amira shrugs. "Maybe. I was just curious, in case we decide to make this girlfriends thing a long-term situation."

Now both of my brows are raised.

"What?" she asks.

"You just said girlfriends," I say. "Is that what we're saying now?"

"That's what I'm saying," she says. "You can disagree if you want."

"I absolutely do not disagree."

"Good, because you're stuck with me, Rochelle Marie Coleman, even if you do beat me for valedictorian."

"Oh, I definitely will," I say with a laugh.

And this time Amira doesn't argue. Instead, she cuts my laugh off with a kiss. And I know it'll probably sound cliché, but it feels just like a movie.

ACKNOWLEDGMENTS

I'M A LEO, SO OBVIOUSLY I have to start by thanking me. Throughout almost every stage of creating this book I was grieving, and it was difficult to celebrate some of my biggest professional wins alongside some of my greatest personal losses. At my lowest of lows, it felt like nothing mattered, especially not my writing, and I have to thank my therapist for seeing me through every part of this journey. I would not be here without her support. And all of my love to Grandma (Cubana Loca), Grandpa, Claire, and Biscuit. I miss you more than I have space here to say.

Publishing a book can be scary, especially as a debut, and so I'm incredibly grateful to have had the Cake/Electric Postcard and New Leaf Literary teams with me every single step of the way. Thank you to everyone, past and present, at Cake/Electric Postcard: Dhonielle, Shelly, Clay, Haneen, Carlyn, Eve, and Kristen. And thank you to everyone at New Leaf Literary: Suzie, Jo, and Sophia. *If We Were a Movie* literally wouldn't exist without all of you.

Thank you so much to Aly and Karina for taking my book on when it was just a proposal and helping me make it so much better! Thank you to Steffi and Laura Mock for creating an amazing cover. And thank you to Sammy Brown and to every person at HarperTeen who had a hand in shaping this book and getting it out into the world.

I've been so lucky to have an incredible family who's always supported my dream to be an author and never once doubted that I could make that dream come true. Ma, you already got the dedication, but thank you for everything. And thank you to Tiff, Auntie Cathy, Tonei, Rha, Paul, Nayla, Sincere, and all of my cousins, whether blood related or not. And also, Sammy, because dogs are family too. I love you all.

And thank you to my chosen family, also known as my friends. Chell and Uzo, my day ones since our own high school days on Long Island. While this book isn't our story and these characters aren't us, the love that Rochelle has for Kerry and Taylor is very much the same love I feel for you two.

Danielle, Joy, Sam, Ediana, Jordan, Mae, Megan, Nat, Angelica, Gertie, Sierra, Sabrina, Sydney, Steph, and Mackenzie. Thank you for your friendship, your support, the laughs, and all the stories. I couldn't have made it across the finish line without all of you.

And last, but certainly not least, to my Unfriendly BIPOC Hotties: Lois, Christian, Bezi, Jess, Kait, James, and Maya. Can you believe this all started because of *Among Us*? What a time! Thank you for every CNC call, subgroup chat, words of encouragement, listening ears, shoulders to cry on, laughs when I needed it, 100+ unread messages, birthday brunches, lunches, dinners, and so much more. I know if our texts ever get subpoenaed we'll all be canceled, but I think it was worth it. I love you all! P.S. xoxo go piss girl.